THORN

ROSEWOOD HIGH #1

TRACY LORRAINE

Editing by My Brother's Editor

Proofread by Paige Sayer Proofreading

Cover by Dandelion Cover Designs

Andy & Amelia

A NOTE

Amalie is British so therefore her points of view in this book are written in British English. This may appear incorrect to some readers when compared to US English books.

1

AMALIE

"I think you'll really enjoy your time here," Principal Hartmann says. He tries to sound cheerful about it, but he's got sympathy oozing from his wrinkled, tired eyes.

This shouldn't have been part of my life. I should be in London starting university, yet here I am at the beginning of what is apparently my junior year at an American high school I have no idea about aside from its name and the fact my mum attended many years ago. A lump climbs up my throat as thoughts of my parents hit me without warning.

"I know things are going to be different and you might feel that you're going backward, but I can assure you it's the right thing to do. It will give you the time you need to... adjust and to put some serious thought into what you want to do once you graduate."

Time to adjust. I'm not sure any amount of time will be enough to learn to live without my parents and being shipped across the Pacific to start a new life in America.

"I'm sure it'll be great." Plastering a fake smile on my face, I take the timetable from the principal's hand and stare down at it. The butterflies that were already fluttering around in my stomach erupt to the point I might just throw up over his chipped Formica desk.

Math, English lit, biology, gym, my hands tremble until I see something that instantly relaxes me, *art and film studies.* At least I got my own way with something.

"I've arranged for someone to show you around. Chelsea is the captain of the cheer squad, what she doesn't know about the school isn't worth knowing. If you need anything, Amalie, my door is always open."

Nodding at him, I rise from my chair just as a soft knock sounds out and a cheery brunette bounces into the room. My knowledge of American high schools comes courtesy of the hours of films I used to spend my evenings watching, and she fits the stereotype of captain to a tee.

"You wanted something, Mr. Hartmann?" she sings so sweetly it makes even my teeth shiver.

"Chelsea, this is Amalie. It's her first day starting junior year. I trust you'll be able to show her around. Here's a copy of her schedule."

"Consider it done, sir."

"I assured Amalie that she's in safe hands."

I want to say it's my imagination but when she turns her big chocolate eyes on me, the light in them diminishes a little.

"Lead the way." My voice is lacking any kind of

enthusiasm and from the narrowing of her eyes, I don't think she misses it.

I follow her out of the room with a little less bounce in my step. Once we're in the hallway, she turns her eyes on me. She's really quite pretty with thick brown hair, large eyes, and full lips. She's shorter than me, but then at five foot eight, you'll be hard pushed to find many other teenage girls who can look me in the eye.

Tilting her head so she can look at me, I fight my smile. "Let's make this quick. It's my first day of senior year and I've got shit to be doing."

Spinning on her heels, she takes off and I rush to catch up with her. "Cafeteria, library." She points then looks down at her copy of my timetable. "Looks like your locker is down there." She waves her hand down a hallway full of students who are all staring our way, before gesturing in the general direction of my different subjects.

"Okay, that should do it. Have a great day." Her smile is faker than mine's been all morning, which really is saying something. She goes to walk away, but at the last minute turns back to me. "Oh, I forgot. That over there." I follow her finger as she points to a large group of people outside the open double doors sitting around a bunch of tables. "That's *my* group. I should probably warn you now that you won't fit in there."

I hear her warning loud and clear, but it didn't really need saying. I've no intention of befriending the cheerleaders, that kind of thing's not really my scene. I'm much happier hiding behind my camera and slinking into the background.

Chelsea flounces off and I can't help my eyes from following her out toward *her* group. I can see from here that it consists of her squad and the football team. I can also see the longing in other student's eyes as they walk past them. They either want to be them or want to be part of their stupid little gang.

Jesus, this place is even more stereotypical than I was expecting.

Unfortunately, my first class of the day is in the direction Chelsea just went. I pull my bag up higher on my shoulder and hold the couple of books I have tighter to my chest as I walk out of the doors.

I've not taken two steps out of the building when my skin tingles with awareness. I tell myself to keep my head down. I've no interest in being their entertainment but my eyes defy me, and I find myself looking up as Chelsea points at me and laughs. I knew my sudden arrival in the town wasn't a secret. My mum's legacy is still strong, so when they heard the news, I'm sure it was hot gossip.

Heat spreads from my cheeks and down my neck. I go to look away when a pair of blue eyes catch my attention. While everyone else's look intrigued, like they've got a new pet to play with, his are haunted and angry. Our stare holds, his eyes narrow as if he's trying to warn me of something before he menacingly shakes his head.

Confused by his actions, I manage to rip my eyes from his and turn toward where I think I should be going.

I only manage three steps at the most before I crash into something—or somebody.

"Shit, I'm sorry. Are you okay?" a deep voice asks. When I look into the kind green eyes of the guy in front of me, I almost sigh with relief. I was starting to wonder if I'd find anyone who wasn't just going to glare at me. I know I'm the new girl but shit. They must experience new kids on a weekly basis, I can't be that unusual.

"I'm fine, thank you."

"You're the new British girl. Emily, right?"

"It's Amalie, and yeah... that's me."

"I'm so sorry about your parents. Mom said she was friends with yours." Tears burn my eyes. Today is hard enough without the constant reminder of everything I've lost. "Shit, I'm sorry. I shouldn't have—"

"It's fine," I lie.

"What's your first class?"

Handing over my timetable, he quickly runs his eyes over it. "English lit, I'm heading that way. Can I walk you?"

"Yes." His smile grows at my eagerness and for the first time today my returning one is almost sincere.

"I'm Shane, by the way." I look over and smile at him, thankfully the hallway is too noisy for us to continue any kind of conversation.

He seems like a sweet guy but my head's spinning and just the thought of trying to hold a serious conversation right now is exhausting.

Student's stares follow my every move. My skin prickles as more and more notice me as I walk beside Shane. Some give me smiles but most just nod in my direction, pointing me out to their friends. Some are just downright rude and physically point at me like I'm some fucking zoo animal awoken from its slumber.

In reality, I'm just an eighteen-year-old girl who's starting somewhere new, and desperate to blend into the crowd. I know that with who I am—or more who my parents were—that it's not going to be all that easy, but I'd at least like a chance to try to be normal. Although I fear I might have lost that the day I lost my parents.

"This is you." Shane's voice breaks through my thoughts and when I drag my head up from avoiding everyone else around me, I see he's holding the door open.

Thankfully the classroom's only half full, but still, every single set of eyes turn to me.

Ignoring their attention, I keep my head down and find an empty desk toward the back of the room.

Once I'm settled, I risk looking up. My breath catches when I find Shane still standing in the doorway, forcing the students entering to squeeze past him. He nods his head. I know it's his way of asking if I'm okay. Forcing a smile onto my lips, I nod in return and after a few seconds, he turns to leave.

2

JAKE

"I don't see what the big deal is," Chelsea whines to her friends. "She's not even really that pretty. Look." I can't help but follow her finger as she points across the quad. My eyes find the tall blonde girl immediately. My lips press into a thin line and my blood boils. Feelings that I've fought for years to keep locked down threaten to bubble up.

Ripping my eyes away, I stare down at the bench below me. My heart races and my vision blurs. Suddenly, I'm a six-year-old boy again watching my world fall apart.

The girls continue bitching but I zone them out, too lost in my own turmoil to care about their pathetic opinions on the looks of the new girl. She won't fit in here. I'm going to make damn sure of it.

"I have no idea what they're chatting about. She is fine with a capital F," Mason, my best friend says, his stare still focused on the blonde everyone seems so fascinated with.

"She ain't all that."

"What the fuck is wrong with you? It's the first day of senior year, it doesn't get any better than this."

"If you say so. I'm outta here."

"Jake, hold up."

I ignore him and jump from the bench. I must only make it two steps when a gasp makes me look up. When I do, I watch as New Girl collides with Shane, one of our players. His hands grip onto her upper arms to steady her. The sight of him touching her, protecting her has fire erupting inside of me. Just looking at her makes me feel vulnerable, and that's not something I ever want to experience again.

"What's going on?" Mason and Ethan flank my sides and stare at the same car crash that I am.

"You calling her?" Ethan asks, following my stare.

Not having a fucking care in the world has resulted in one thing at least. My reputation. I do what the fuck I like, when I like and everyone around here knows it's best to just let me do my thing. That means not turning up to class, getting off my ass drunk, and most importantly, I get first pick of the girls. The others can have her once I'm done if they like, I don't care about passing them down once I'm done. But I never get sloppy seconds. Ever.

"She's off limits."

"I fucking knew you wanted her," Ethan mocks before I turn and fist his shirt. The blood drains from his face as he prepares for the hit he's expecting.

"I don't fucking want her. I'm saying she's off fucking limits. You got that?"

"Yeah-yeah. Off limits, got it."

"And make sure everyone fucking knows it. That bitch don't belong here and we're about to show her."

"Are we done here?" Mason asks. He's always been the slightly cooler headed one out of the three of us. He pulls my arm away from Ethan and steps between us, but not before a confused look passes between the two of them.

Staking claim on a girl isn't unusual, but what I just did. That shit isn't normal and without intending to, I just showed both of them a side of me that I don't want anyone to ever witness. Weakness.

"Are you sure everything's all right?" Mason asks once again when we fall into step in the direction of our first class.

"Yeah. Just feeling the pressure, I guess."

"This year's gonna be great."

Raising an eyebrow at him, I wait for him to explain how that's going to happen. Rosewood High's football team has never been all that. We have all the passion and dedication we need, but historically, it doesn't help all that much. Every year Coach gives the speech that this year is going to be the year but as of yet, we've never progressed more than a few games into the state playoffs. I can admit that our team is performing better than ever, but I don't want to set my hopes on anything epic.

For me, football's a release. A way to work out the tension and to forget about my bullshit life. I might give it my all, but I'm under no illusion that it's my life. Some of the guys have high hopes of getting scouted for college and I'm sure for a few of them it'll happen but I doubt we'll ever see their names on the NFL team sheets.

"Don't give me that look, Thorn. You know as well as I do that this is our year. With you in charge, there's no way we won't make it to the end."

I can't criticize his enthusiasm, that's for sure. It's just a shame I don't feel it. And *her* arrival sure isn't going to help matters.

3

AMALIE

A side from the constant stares from the other students and crashing into Shane, my morning is pretty uneventful. Classes are... fine, and much to my relief, I get set homework in every single one. That should help keep my mind active once I get home. The last thing I want to do is dwell on what my life has become so the more I have to do the better.

I was desperate to start here as a senior and do just one year, but Principal Hartmann point blank refused and explained to my gran that I would have missed too much and it would make getting into college harder than it should be, so in the end I didn't have much choice. I'm stuck here for two years.

Other than graduating, my main goal is just to put my head down, get good grades and focus on the future. A future in which I get to call the shots, not social services, investigating police officers or financial advisors.

I follow the main flow of students as I step out into

the hallway before lunch in the hope it'll lead me toward the cafeteria. It pays off and in only a few moments I'm standing in line waiting to see what delights I might get.

When it's my turn, the lady serving looks at me with raised eyebrows.

Glancing down at the food, nothing looks appealing. Nothing has since the moment I found the police standing at the other side of our front door, but I promised my gran I'd eat, so here I am.

"Whatever's meant to be the best," I mutter, my voice is hollow in a way I'm becoming all too used to.

"Sure thing, sweetheart. My burger and fries will turn your day right around." Her smile lights up her face and I do my best to reciprocate but it falls flat. I get the impression she wants to say more, but when she looks up to hand my food over and notices the waiting students behind me, she just smiles and calls, "Next."

Grabbing my tray, I turn and a shiver runs through me. Lifting my eyes, I find that I'm once again under the watchful eye of the group of guys from earlier, who I'm assuming are the football team and front and center is the guy with the piercing, blue, angry eyes.

My stomach knots as he once again narrows his eyes at me.

"Will you get out of the way," someone snaps behind me before my shoulder is shoved and a group of girls storm past me. I barely catch my tray before it slips from my hands and stand to the side.

When I look back toward the entrance where they were stood, I find it empty. But the tingling of my skin tells me that I'm still very much the focus of his hate-filled stare.

Looking around the cafeteria, I find all the groups of students I expect to find. The artistic ones still wearing shirts covered in paint, the nerdy ones, the shy girls sitting quietly in the corner, and then the group I think I need to be as far away from as possible. The 'it' crowd. The football players and the cheer squad who are crowded around a couple of benches like they own the place. Well, let's be honest, they pretty much do. I might not be able to see the crowns sitting atop their heads, but they are very much Rosewood royalty.

Spotting an empty table between the nerds and the shy girls, I head over, drop my tray down and fall onto the bench.

I'm not really sure what I expected to happen today. But this isn't really it. I've barely spoken to anyone aside from Shane all day and I already have a bunch of haters, one in particular, it seems.

I understand that they probably don't want a new girl coming in. Hell, I don't really want to be here as much as they don't want me to be, but I've got little choice. My life was ripped from under me and this is where I ended up.

"There you are. I'm soooo sorry about not finding you this morning, my car wouldn't start and my parents had already left. Nightmare. Anyway... how's it been?" Camila says, dropping down beside me and pulling a sandwich from her bag. Camila is the one and only person aside from Shane who's really given me the time of day since I arrived. She's one of Gran's friend's granddaughters that I was introduced to. She's great, a real sweetheart and I feel awful that I've been kind of forced on her. She must have friends that she'd rather be spending time with right now.

"It's been... fine." I poke a chip into some sauce on my plate, but I make no effort to eat any of it. I already feel a little sick, I'm not sure adding food will really help.

"Wow. That good."

"Cam. What are you... oh hey, Amalie," Shane says, coming to a stop at the edge of our table.

"You two have already met?" Camila asks, looking between the two of us.

"Yeah, we crashed into each other earlier."

"I'm really sorry about that." Embarrassment colours my cheeks.

"No need. I could think of worse people to crash into. It was my pleasure." The way his eyes assess me as he says this makes my heart drop. I really didn't think I gave him any kind of idea that I might have been interested, but I can see hope and excitement in his eyes. I know we only spoke briefly earlier, but I kinda thought we could be friends. I'm not interested in anything else.

"Are you coming to join the others?" he asks after I look back down at my plate.

"Maybe in a bit. I think today's already been a little overwhelming, right?"

"Something like that," I mutter. "You can go. I don't want to keep you from your friends."

"It's fine. I promised you I'd show you the ropes and

I've already failed. Although, it sounds like you were in capable hands."

"Damn right," Shane says, falling down onto the seat opposite me. His stare burns into me but I keep my eyes down, not wanting to lead him on.

"So, what classes do you have this afternoon?"

4

JAKE

All morning the only thing I've been able to see is *her*. It doesn't matter how many times I tell myself that she's someone else entirely, it doesn't matter. The devastation and betrayal I remember all too well burns within me. I'm powerless to do anything but let it rage. By the time lunch rolls around, I'm just about ready to smash someone's face in.

"What the fuck's eating you?" Ethan asks the moment he falls into step beside me.

"Fuck you."

"I'd rather not."

My fists clench as I try to talk myself down from shoving him up against the wall and letting out some of my frustration.

I knew going to the cafeteria was a bad idea. I should have walked out of school and fucked off. But I didn't. Instead, I continue walking beside Ethan, the majority of the rest of the team joining us at some point until the scent of the crappy food filters down and the vast room opens before us.

My steps falter the moment I see her just about to turn away from the counter. I may only be able to see her back, but I know from the thick blonde hair hanging down her back that it's her. It's like a fucking red flashing beacon to me.

"Shit, sorry," someone mutters behind me, they're not looking where they're going and crash into my back.

My feet refuse to move. It's torture just looking at her but it's like my body is quite happy to send me to Hell and back and insists I wait for her to turn around so I can get another good look at her face. It's not like I need to, they look so similar and I'm never likely to forget the face of the woman who abandoned me without so much as a backward glance.

"Thorn?" someone asks behind me, clearly wondering why I've stopped dead in my tracks.

The second she looks up, her eyes find mine. She looks like a deer caught in headlights, the thought has the smallest of smiles twitching my lips. She should be scared. I have every intention of running her out of this place before she gets too settled.

This is my school. My life. I'll be damned if I'm going to spend what should be the best year of my time here being tormented by her.

It's not until someone bumps into her that she's forced to drag her scared eyes away from mine and I'm able to move. Taking a step, I walk toward our usual area as if nothing happened. When I sit and wait for the others to join, I notice that the majority don't realize anything just went down, but Mason and Ethan's stares both burn into me. They both know me better than anyone, better than my pathetic excuse for a family, so they know something's seriously adrift. I don't expect them to understand. Fuck, I don't really understand it but they're not keeping a huge part of themselves hidden away in their bottom drawer like she never existed. They have no real reason to appreciate how much New Girl looks like that ghost I try to hide.

———

Practice is exactly the kind of distraction I need, aside from my desire to plant my fist into Shane's smug fucking little face. I resist the urge, for now. As our team's quarterback and captain, they all look to me for my ability to make quick decisions and lead them to what might hopefully be a successful year. Of course I want that too. I want more than anything to have some kind of reason to celebrate, hell knows I haven't had many reasons to do so throughout my life. But one thing I have learned is that life is generally better if you're realistic, and I'm realistic enough to know that we probably won't be winning the state championships this year either. That doesn't mean I'm not going to fight like hell to try to make it happen.

Standing beside Coach, I feel like I belong, like I'm making a difference and I can't help my chest swelling with pride. This is what I need right now.

Coach has already warned us that he's hitting us

hard this year and this practice session is no exception. Our first game might not be until Friday night, but he's going to make damn sure we're ready for it.

Standing under the spray of the shower once we've left the field, I allow the water to pound against my shoulders in the hope it might relieve some of the tension.

"What the hell is up with you and that new girl, Thorn?"

Panicking at the mention of her, I look up, but the showers are empty apart from Mason, whose eyes are drilling into mine as if he's going to read the answer within them.

"I just don't like her." I shrug, turning off the water and reaching for a towel.

"That's bullshit and you know it."

The sounds of his light footsteps right behind me tells me that this isn't over. I know that if anyone were to understand, it would be Mason, but that doesn't mean I'm willing to talk about it.

"Whatever. I don't have to explain myself to you."

"No, you don't. But as your best friend, I kinda hoped you would."

Guilt twists my stomach. He's had enough of his own shit going on recently and I've made him talk when he least wanted to, I should have seen this coming.

"I just... I don't like the look of her. She doesn't fit here."

"Beautiful and sexy doesn't fit here? Oh knock it off.

You'd normally be all over that. You're going to have to try harder if you want to pull the wool over my eyes."

Ignoring him, I turn and start pulling my clothes on. I don't have time for this. I'd just about managed to forget about her blue eyes and blonde hair while we were out running plays but now they're right fucking there again.

"Come on, I'll buy you a burger. It might soften you up a little."

Flipping him off, I follow him out toward his car so we can head to our usual hangout, a diner on the shorefront.

5

AMALIE

"I was intending on going home and getting a head start on my homework," I say to Camila when she tries convincing me to go with her, Shane, and a couple of their other friends to a diner.

"I'm sorry, but that's not happening. I promised my gran that I'd help you settle in."

"Really, it's okay. I'll make sure she knows that you did as she asked. I don't want you to feel like you need to babysit me."

"Enough," she snaps but her eyes shine with amusement. Threading her arm through mine, she pulls me forward toward the car park. "I'm not taking no for an answer. Plus, one of Bill's milkshakes will make all your worries disappear."

I don't think that could possibly be true, but I'm up for testing it out. I really don't want to spend the next two years being the social outcast I've felt today. But I'm equally as unsure if I'm really up for socialising and pretending that everything is good with my life.

"Wow, this is like a home from home," I say, my voice tinged with sadness as I climb into Camila's Mini.

"She's awesome, right? Well, when she starts. Keep your fingers crossed." She winks before making a show of pushing the key into the ignition and turning the engine over. Breathing a sigh of relief when it rumbles to life, she looks over at me and laughs.

"Aces on the first day of senior year is tradition. Anyone who is anyone will be there."

I groan, not only am I a junior but there's a whole group of kids who really won't want me there.

"I'm really not sure about this."

"Did something happen today? Did anyone say anything about your parents or..." Quickly glancing over at me, her eyes narrow as she tries to figure me out.

"No, no one said anything. I barely spoke to anyone aside from you and Shane." I keep the hateful stares I received that I think might have been worse than someone saying something hurtful to myself. At least if he'd said something it might give me a clue what his problem is.

The car park is packed when we pull off the main road. There are kids loitering all along the seafront and spilling down onto the beach. Camila really wasn't kidding when she said everyone will be here.

"The guys already have a table for us. Noah skipped out on his last class to get it."

"Seriously?"

"Yeah. Being here this afternoon is a big deal. Ready?" She gives me a smile I attempt to match after she's reapplied her lip gloss in the visor mirror and fluffed up her hair a little. She jumps from the car and I rush to follow suit.

Some of the other kids who are loitering around turn toward us, but thanks to Camila's obscenely short skirt, I'm thankfully not the focus of their attention. I do cause a few whispers once the onlookers have had their fill of her legs.

"Oh, there they are."

I follow behind as she heads toward a table full of students I don't recognise. It's immediately obvious why this place is called Aces. It's all black, white, and red with playing card memorabilia everywhere. Shane spots us walking their way and smiles at me like we're long-lost friends.

"Amalie, good to see you." The enthusiasm in his voice is a little too much as he slides from the booth he's sitting in to allow me to join their group of friends. Camila takes the seat opposite me and cuddles up into Noah's side. I can't take my eyes off him as he gazes down at her and drops his lips to her temple. She looks up at him with such adoration and love that it makes my heart ache and a lump to form in my throat.

I'm soon distracted when a boisterous crowd comes stumbling through the entrance. My stomach drops when my eyes find *him*. His obvious hatred of my mere existence radiates from his every pore.

Once again, his steps slow as he stares at me. His lips set in a thin line, his eyes dark and haunted. As he continues staring, I can't help but feel like he's not really staring at me but through me, as if I'm a ghost he can't believe he's seeing. I don't know about him but I sure as shit haven't seen him before. I'm pretty sure I'd have remembered if I had because although his presence sends a tremor of fear through me, I can't deny that he's hot.

His dark hair is short at the sides then longer on the top, his haunting eyes that have studied me from afar today I can now see are royal blue, and his body. Well... let's just say that it's obvious he's part of the football team because he is cut. His white t-shirt is pulled tightly across his wide shoulders showing off his sculpted chest and flat abs. I'd put money on there being one seriously impressive six-pack under there.

Thoughts of a man's body has thoughts popping into my head that I'd rather not think about right now. I already feel vulnerable around all these strangers who already know too much about my life and how I ended up here, I don't need the past and the emotions it comes with making me even weaker. Especially while my skin's still prickling from his stare.

"What the hell?" Shane asks, looking between me and the guy. "Do you know him?"

"Nope. Never seen him before until this morning. He seems to have some kind of issue with me though."

Dragging my attention back to the people surrounding me, I see that everyone is looking between the two of us expectantly.

"You sure you don't know him?" Camila asks. "He seems pretty interested in you."

"I'm very sure. Who is he?"

"Who is he?" Alyssa, another of Camila's friends,

repeats much like I would imagine she would if I'd just asked who Donald Trump was. "That is Jacob Thorn. Captain of the football team. King of Rosewood High and every girl's wet dream."

"Not *every* girl," Camila quickly adds, looking up at Noah like he just hung the moon.

Eventually his friends must get fed up with the hold up and they drag him off and over to the empty table at the other side of the diner. That doesn't mean I lose his attention. I might refuse to look over, but I feel his eyes on me. My skin heats and butterflies flutter in my belly at knowing he'd rather stare at me than have fun with his friends. I know it's because he clearly hates me but my traitorous body doesn't care right now.

"If I can teach you anything about Rosewood High, Amalie, it's to stay as far away as you can from *that* lot. They're nothing but trouble."

"You sound like your gran."

She shrugs, not in the least bit offended. "I'm serious. I have no idea what's going on with you two, but you'd be best to shake him off as soon as you can and forget him and any of the other football players exist."

"Hey," Shane complains. "We're not all bad guys." He nudges my shoulder to make sure I hear his words.

"Good to know." Although, I must admit that I'm more shocked than relieved. I guess he has the body to fit the image, but that doesn't explain why he's sitting here with the 'nobodies' when he could be over there with his team, living the high life.

"I don't know how you can put up with playing for those assholes."

"I don't play for them."

"Whatever," Camila says, waving him off like she's heard the same argument a million times.

Their conversation soon turns to the year ahead, what parties are meant to be happening and the pep rally on Friday before the first game of the season. They all look at me like I've got three heads when I ask them to explain what exactly a pep rally is. They seem to forget that I come from a completely different world.

Camila bounces in her seat as she runs through what I can expect followed by demanding that I'll be there because not attending is a sure-fire way to get myself on the 'bullied list.'

I refrain from explaining how I couldn't really give a crap about all that, but I figure that if I've got to spend two years here, then I might as well not paint a target on my back.

"Anyway, you've got to be there so you can attend what happens after."

"What happens after?" I ask with trepidation. The excitement dancing in her eyes makes me nervous.

"You'll have to wait to find out, but it's epic. The party of all parties. Plus, you'll get to do it twice. Not many people get that chance."

6

JAKE

Mason's words don't leave me the entire ride to Aces. He's right of course. She is beautiful and sexy, no one with a pair of fucking eyes could deny that. She's too beautiful. That's the fucking problem. Anyone with looks like that can only have evil on the inside. I've experienced it and it's not something I have any desire to repeat, which is why she needs to go. We don't need that kind of poison around here. We've already got enough assholes roaming the halls at Rosewood High.

The place is packed but I'm not concerned we won't find seats. The booths at the back are practically reserved for us. We own this place and Bill knows it. If it weren't for us and our reputation, then his place wouldn't be filled with kids day in and day out.

Holding my head high, I walk through the diner entrance with Mason and Ethan close behind. The entire fucking diner turns to look as we enter and for a fleeting moment, the buzz I usually get knowing that I own this fucking place starts to race through my veins. Then my gaze lands on a wide pair of blue eyes, the exact ones that have been haunting me all day, and that previous elation sinks. That bitch sucks every last bit out of me.

"Keep moving," Mason instructs, but I'm powerless. As I stare at her, one event from my past, that changed everything about my future, plays out in my mind like a fucking movie. My chest constricts and my lungs burn as I try to drag in the air I need. No matter how hard I will it to go, the image of her face as she walked away from me is right at the forefront of my mind. My bullshit excuse of a life is her fault, but sadly she's not here to experience the consequences of her actions. But *she* is.

As my vision starts to clear and New Girl comes back into focus, I notice a few subtle differences from the woman who ruined my life. But I can ignore them. What's more important is that I get to rid myself of the anger and desperation I've carried with me since that day.

I'm so lost that my entire body startles when a hand lands on my shoulder. "You're starting to make a scene."

"Let 'em fucking look." I don't give a fuck what everyone thinks right now. All I know is what I need, and I need to see her broken.

By the time I get to our booths, I've managed to pull on the mask I walk around wearing on a daily basis and it ensures that no one will question me. There are only a couple of people on this planet who've ever seen the real me, the pain and ugliness that festers inside me and I'll happily keep it that way.

Mason gives me a concerned smile before turning to the waitress and giving her our usual order. I can only hope he's right and that one of Bill's burgers will sort me out.

She's only been here for one day and already I'm a fucking mess. This situation needs resolving and fast.

The guys around me talk excitedly about our first game while the girls discuss their cheer routines for the pep rally. I couldn't really give a shit about either, I've got more important things to deal with.

"What's wrong, Jake? The stress of being a senior at last getting to you?" Chelsea purrs, her fake tan encrusted hand landing lightly between my pecs and descending over my abs.

Why I ever allowed myself to go there is beyond me. But it seems Chelsea thinks that just because I've fucked her that she has some kind of claim on me.

"I'm good, thanks," I state, gripping her wrist a little too tightly and removing her from my body.

"Ow," she complains, turning her giant eyes on me like seeing the tears in them will suddenly make me give a shit.

"Don't fucking touch me."

"Aw, come on. You weren't saying that—"

"Enough," I bark. Getting up from the booth, all eyes follow my movement. "I'm done here."

Sliding out, everyone's eyes follow me, but I pay them little attention. They might think I'm leaving to get away from Chelsea or what-the-fuck-ever, but in reality, I'm leaving because of a certain blonde. She was escorted out by Camila, but she's just shot back in for something, so now's my chance to introduce myself.

Shoving open the side door with more force than necessary, it slams back against the wall. The bang reverberates through me and pushes me forward. My skin's still prickling from Chelsea's touch and my muscles are still pulled tight from the memories *she* dragged up earlier.

I spot her instantly leaning up against the diner wall with her foot propped up against the brick.

Excitement and anticipation bubble up in my stomach as I watch her for a moment. It's clear she's got a lot on her mind as she stares off into the distance, but I couldn't give two fucks about her worries right now. Mine are the only thing I care about.

My fists clench and a deep line forms between my brows as I take a step toward her. She might not be the woman who ruined my life, but right now, she's the closest thing I've got.

The milkshake is almost as good as Camila promised, although I don't forget about my worries for even a second, not that I really expected to. My life is a clusterfuck right now and no amount of strawberry milk, ice cream or sprinkles is going to rectify that.

"Good, right?" Camila asks when she sees my eyes roll back the moment the sweetness hits my tongue.

"So good."

"I got you the extra special one seeing as today's kinda important."

My stomach drops and my eyes fly to hers thinking that she's going to spill the secret I've been holding in all day. It's not like it's been hard work or anything and it's also not like I have any inclination to celebrate.

She winks before turning back to her friends. They're trying to include me the best they can, but our worlds are so far apart that I think it's going to take more than a trip to a diner for me to start fitting in.

Pulling my phone from my pocket when it starts vibrating, I find my gran's name staring back at me. "Shit."

I thought you'd be home by now. Is everything okay? Do you need me to come and collect you?

She may have insisted she drive me to school this morning, but I was even more insistent that I take the bus home. I'm very aware of how much I've already changed her life in a matter of a few weeks, and something as simple as getting the school bus is an easy way for me to allow her to continue living her life.

I'm good. Home soon x

Thinking it's the perfect excuse to get away from this place and the pair of eyes that are still taunting me from across the diner.

"I'm sorry, but I need to make a move. Gran's waiting for me. Is there a bus I can get from here or should I just ring for a taxi?"

"Don't be silly. I'll take you."

"No, you said it yourself how important it is you're here. I'll be fine."

"I can come back. Just let me take you, it'll make me feel better." She stares at me, her kind eyes telling me that I've not got a choice until I cave, stand and slide from the booth.

I hear her tell the others where we're going before she starts following me out of the diner. I keep my eyes focused on the door, fighting the need to turn around and confirm that the tingles coursing through my body are courtesy of being under his intense stare once again.

"Shit, I'll be right back. Noah's got my damn cell. Wait there."

She rushes back inside leaving me a few minutes alone to try to make sense of everything buzzing around my head.

The sensation that I'm being watched settles over me, and my heart starts to race. Looking around, everyone seems to be busy doing their own thing. I'm just about to blow out the breath I was holding, feeling ridiculous for feeling vulnerable, when a shadow falls over me. I go to squeal, but hot fingers grasp my chin and I'm forced to meet the dark stare of the eyes that have been haunting me all day.

My body temperature picks up and my hands start to tremble. Fear licks at my insides as he stares at me with dark impenetrable eyes, the blue almost black.

I expect him to say something, but the silence seems to drag out for the longest time. Instead, his gaze flits over every inch of my face, almost as if he's committing me to memory.

When his eyes meet mine, once again my breath

catches. I tell myself that nothing's about to happen. We're in a busy public place and Camila is coming back any second.

My chest heaves as his body heat prickles my skin. Lowering his head, his breath tickles across my ear and down my neck. My traitorous body reacts and covers my skin in goosebumps. Something I don't think he misses if his deep, unamused chuckle is anything to go by.

"You don't belong here, New Girl. I'd take this warning very seriously if I were you because I can make your life very, very hard."

I try to swallow but my throat is too dry. Just when I think he's going to add more or do something else, his grip on me releases and he steps back. My body sways in relief but it's only a second later I realise what happened.

"Amalie, are you okay?" Camila asks, walking around the corner with her phone in hand.

"Uh..." I hesitate, my breathing still erratic and my head spinning.

"I was just welcoming her to Rosewood."

She looks between the two of us briefly before pinning her stare on Jacob. I follow her eyes and take him in. His body's mostly relaxed but the hardness of his face tells me that the threat he just made was no joke.

"Whatever you say, Jake."

"Keep your nose out. I know Mason won't take too kindly to you sticking your nose in our business."

Shaking her head, she reaches for me and I allow her to wrap her warm hand around my forearm and pull me away from him.

His stare burns into my back as we walk away. I tell myself not to look back, but my head moves without instruction from my brain and I find myself locked in his stare once again. His lip curls up in an evil smirk and my stomach drops.

I knew starting over here wasn't going to be easy, but I never expected this... *him.*

"Are you sure everything's okay?" Camila asks once we're in the safety of her car. My breathing has almost returned to normal, but his angry eyes are still the only thing I can see and the skin on my chin is still burning where he held me in his tight grip.

"Y-yeah. Everything's fine." Glancing over at me, I can tell she doesn't believe a word of it, but she doesn't push me for more and I'm grateful. "Just promise me you'll stay away from Jake. He's not a good person."

I desperately want to ask more but I fear coming across a little too interested, so I mumble my agreement and keep my lips shut.

The drive is short and we're soon pulling up outside my gran's bungalow in a quiet part of town. I first thought I might be lonely surrounded by Gran and all her neighbour friends but the longer I've been here the more I like being able to hide. I think I'm only going to appreciate it more now that school's started.

"Thank you."

"Anytime. If you need anything, please call, yeah? I

know how hard it is starting your life over, if you need an ear or a shoulder, I'm here. Okay?"

"Yeah, thank you, Camila. I really do appreciate it."

"You're welcome. Have a good night. Oh and... I know you don't want to celebrate but happy birthday."

A lump forms in my throat. I'd mostly been able to put what today represents to the back of my mind. I have no intention of celebrating without my parents, so I made Gran promise not to tell anyone and not to make a fuss. It seems she may have broken that if Camila knows.

I nod at her, unable to respond for fear of bursting into tears.

Standing on the driveway, I watch as she backs out and waves just before she leaves my sight. I think the two of us could be good friends. We seem to have plenty in common, we have similar kinds of personalities, I'm just not sure I have the energy to let anyone in. Especially as I don't really know what my future holds after two years here. At the moment, my heart is still set on returning to London, but I must admit that after being here a few weeks, I do quite like the sun and the sea. It makes everything feel a little more possible without the dirt and grime of the city I'm used to.

Sucking in a deep breath, I turn and take a step toward Gran's front door. I soon realise that my warning to forget about what today is has been totally ignored because the kitchen is full of balloons and banners.

"I know, I know, you don't want a fuss. But it's your eighteenth birthday, sweetheart. You'll regret allowing it to pass you by." Her eyes are full of love and hope, I don't have it in me to argue, so I allow my eyes to take in the sight before me and the giant number eighteen cake in the centre of the table and force my lips to smile. I walk over and wrap my arms around her thin shoulders. She might be getting older now, but she's no less beautiful. It's obvious where both Mum and I got our height and looks from.

"Thank you, Gran." I really hope it sounds sincere because I don't want her thinking that I don't appreciate all the effort she's put in since the day I moved in. I'm not sure being guardian to her teenage granddaughter was what she had planned for her retirement, but here I am.

"I made your favourite. Fish and chips. Go and freshen up and I'll finish it off. I even did the mushy peas like you talk about."

Thoughts of home have tears burning my throat. I swallow them down, give her another smile and turn toward my room.

I hate being upset in front of her. I know it's meant to be her job to look after me now, but I hate the shadows that fill her eyes and the slight tremble of her lips when she thinks about her daughter. The last words they said to each other weren't ideal, but it's now something Gran is going to have to live with.

Dropping my bag and books on the little desk Gran set up in my room, I fall down onto the bed and squeeze my eyes shut as I try to block everything out. It might work with some of the crap in my head but unfortunately it doesn't work for *him*, Jake Thorn.

What the hell is his problem? I'm new, I get that. But his reaction today, his warning was a little over the top. The skin covering my jaw burns as I remember his harsh grip and the anger oozing from his eyes as they bore into mine. Pure unadulterated hatred poured from them.

8

JAKE

Slamming the door on Mason's truck, I storm toward the house, although there's no fucking way I'm actually going in there. I live around the back. Hidden in the shadows so that my aunt and uncle can pretend that I don't exist. That's fine by me. I'd rather be out here knowing they don't care than be inside their house seeing them treat their own kids like royalty. Why the fuck *she* thought this would be the best place for me when she fucked off, God only knows.

Sliding the key into the lock of my trailer, I slip inside and lock the door. I don't really need to worry about anyone coming to bother me. Every single person in that house ignores my existence. Well, everyone aside from Poppy, my eldest cousin. She's tried to make an effort time and time again, but I shoot down every attempt she makes. My aunt and uncle don't want me to have anything to do with their kids, it's in their eyes every time they see me so much as look at one of them. I've got nothing against Poppy, she's a junior at Rosewood and is a great kid, but for her own sake, I stay out of her way. I don't want to cause her trouble with her parents and as they've told me plenty of times, that's all I am, trouble.

Pulling my cigarettes and a lighter from my top drawer, I fall down onto my built-in couch and light one. Taking a drag, I allow it to burn my lungs as I watch the smoke fill the space around me.

I try to clear my mind, to focus on my movements and breaths but it's no fucking good. All I see is her, all I smell is her sweet scent. The moment I was nose to nose with her, her stark differences to the woman she reminds me of were obvious. Her hair was totally natural, not the peroxide I remember, her eyes are a slightly darker blue, and close up have flecks of green in them that only became brighter with her fear. She's got a smattering of freckles covering her round little nose and high cheekbones, and she had this cute little mole just above and to the left of her top lip. The hate that had been festering within me since my eyes landed on her first thing this morning suddenly morphed into something else, something I refuse to acknowledge because I need the anger. I've waited years to expel it and her similarities are enough for me. They're enough to allow me to believe I'm hurting the woman who hurt me more than should be possible.

Dropping the cigarette butt into an empty beer bottle, I immediately light another but I already know it's not going to be enough to clear my head, to make me forget.

When Mason found me fighting to catch my breath

and leaning back against Aces back wall after she left, it only confirmed to him that something was seriously up with me. He'd been digging all day, but he should know me better than to expect me to spill all my problems. We've been friends for almost as long as I can remember, and I've never once told him all my secrets. I have every intention of taking those motherfuckers to the grave. No one needs to know the truth about how impossible I am to love and who my mother really is. A shudder runs through me at just the thought of my friends finding out. That would be the only thing that could possibly make my life worse right now. New Girl's arrival is one thing but the truth coming out.... No, that can't happen, and I'll do anything in my power to stop it.

Stuffing my second cigarette butt into the bottle, I fall back into the couch wishing I had something stronger here.

My cell buzzes in my pocket and when I pull it out, I wonder if Ethan can read my mind.

Parents gone out of town. Get your ass over here.

Dropping my cell to the cushion, I stand and start stripping out of my clothes as I make my way to the bathroom. I turn the shower on as hot as I can and step under the stream of water. Closing my eyes, I let it rain over me, hoping it'll wash everything away but the moment I close my eyes all I see are hers. The fear in them has my heart rate increasing and my cock swelling.

Wrapping my fist around my length, I fall back against the cold tiles and release some of the pressure built up inside of me. It barely takes the edge off of my restlessness, but until I can get my hands on what I'm hoping Ethan will have at his house, it's the best I can do.

As I walk past the main house, I take in the family sitting around the table together laughing and smiling as they eat their evening meal. The sight used to hurt, it used to be like a baseball bat to the chest, but as time went on and I learned to lock everything down, all I feel is pity. Pity that they can so easily cast me aside like I don't exist. They're just as bad as *her*. Just as selfish as *her*.

Just as I'm about to look away, Poppy glances over her shoulder. Her eyes lock on mine and a small, sad smile twitches at her lips.

Ripping my eyes away, I continue to the sidewalk and make my way toward Ethan's.

————

"How many of them do we need to give you before you start talking?" Mason asks, handing me another bottle.

Releasing the hit I was holding, I look over at him. The buzz from the joint Ethan handed me is mixing with the alcohol and giving me the release I was craving.

"When has that ever happened before?" They know me better than that. No amount of weed or alcohol will get me to unleash the ugliness I hold inside.

"It's gotta happen one day, Thorn." He sits back and tips his bottle to his lips, swallowing down the last of his beer.

A knock sounds out around the house and Ethan jumps up excitedly. He's by far the wealthiest of the three of us. Not that it's all that difficult to have more than me, the guy who lives in the hidden trailer and mostly lives on handouts from my friends or ramen noodles. It's not something I'm proud of, but it's my life nonetheless.

He runs from his den, leaving Mason and I slumped on his giant couches. The sound of excited girly chatter filters down from the front door and my stomach drops.

"He didn't say he'd invited them." Mason looks at me like I've just sprouted another head. "What?"

"Nothin'. It's just not like you to turn down any offer of pussy."

"Yeah, well. Maybe today's different."

"Fuck me, man. That girl's got you all tied up, hasn't she?"

"Girl?" I ask, trying to play it cool but when his response is just to roll his eyes, I know I haven't succeeded.

"Maybe Chelsea can distract you, help you chill the fuck out."

Just as he says that, she slides herself onto my lap and helps herself to my beer. "Who needs distracting?"

Her voice is high and squeaky, and it makes my skin crawl.

None too gently, I push her from my lap and she lands on the polished tiled floor with a thud and a squeal. Slamming *my* beer bottle down on the coffee table, she turns to me, pushes her chest out and rests her hands on her hips.

"What the fuck, Jake?"

"You okay, Chelsea? It looks like you've had a little accident," Mason asks, nodding down to the wet patch on her micro skirt.

Her cheeks flame red and her eyes darken before she huffs out a breath and storms away.

"I'm gonna need more of these if she's planning on sticking around."

Mason fixes his stare on me but one look at my narrowed eyes and tense shoulders and he seals his mouth closed.

Looking out over Ethan's garden, I watch as some of the other girls strip down to their bikinis and jump into the pool. Ethan soon follows their lead and in minutes has two backed up into the corner. I shamelessly watch as he thrusts his tongue into one of their mouths quickly followed by the other. Normally I'd be doing the same, or better, dragging one off to one of the guest rooms. But I'm not interested. Tonight I want to sit in a dark corner surrounded by bottles of beer and a handful of joints.

9

AMALIE

By some miracle, I make it to the end of my first week at Rosewood High without too much drama. Jake has kept his distance. I've caught his piercing eyes across the hallway more than once, but he's never come any closer. I'm not sure how I feel about that. A huge part of me wants to think that his warning on Monday was just a joke, his sick way of welcoming the new girl. I was there though, it was my chin prickling under his hard grip, there wasn't anything jokey or light-hearted about the move. He meant every word he said to me outside the diner and although I try to push the concern down, I know he's waiting in the wings, planning his move. If only I could figure out what his issue is, then I might stand half a chance of seeing it coming.

"For this assignment, you're going to pair up. I want detailed research and then some kind of presentation, I don't mind what form that takes, use your creativity. We'll start them next Friday." There's chatter amongst my classmates as they start planning their new history assignment. "I'll be choosing the pairings," the teacher barks causing everyone around me to groan.

He starts rattling off names, I've no idea who they belong too but I sit back and watch either the happy or pissed off expressions appear on their faces as they accept who their partner is.

"Amalie," he says, meeting my eyes. "You're with Poppy."

A girl with dark hair and even darker eyes turns and offers me a soft smile. I relax slightly when at first sight she doesn't appear to be a wannabe cheerleader or football player groupie.

The teacher reels off the rest of the names on his list before instructing us to sit in our pairs and start planning.

"Hey, I'm Poppy," she says, dropping her bag to the floor and falling down into the now vacant seat beside me. "You're in my film studies class, right?"

"Maybe. Sorry, this week's been a little overwhelming."

"S'all good. Lucky for you, you just acquired an excellent partner for this project."

"Is that right?" I say with a laugh, realising that I like her already.

We make a start, but the bell goes before we make much progress.

"So I'll meet you after school Monday and you can come back to mine?"

"Sounds good to me."

"You at the pep rally tonight?"

"Apparently so."

"You sound really excited about it." She laughs and pulls her bag up over her shoulder before we start making our way toward the door.

"It's not really my kind of thing."

"Na, mine either but my cousin's on the team so I go to support him." I smile but the mention of family has my heart sinking into the pit of my stomach. "So I'll see you Monday?"

"Sure thing." I give her a wave as she heads off toward her next class and I turn to do the same.

––––––

"Today is draaaaging," Camila complains when she finds me hiding in the back corner of the library at lunch. "You know," she says, looking around at the dusty shelves, "I always thought unquestionable stuff happened at the back of libraries. You're kind of ruining that for me."

"Sorry to disappoint. I'm definitely not up to anything *unquestionable*." In reality, I'm surrounded by art books trying to come up with an idea for our history project.

"That's a shame. You could use some excitement. I bet Shane would be up for it."

"You've noticed that too, huh?" I drag my eyes from the book I was flicking through and look into Camila's knowing eyes.

"It's hard not to. He's practically followed you

around like a lost puppy since you arrived. It's kind of cute."

"It might be if I were interested."

"He's hot, what's the issue?"

"I'm just not interested in a relationship. My life's a mess right now, I don't need a guy making it worse."

"I'm sure the right guy could make it better. Relieve some of that tension you're carrying around." I scoff at her, close the book and add it to the pile next to me. "Wait... you are single, right? Or have you got the whole long-distance phone sex thing going on with some British hottie?"

"No, no hot phone sex."

She picks up on the sadness in my tone that I was trying to hide. "But there was a guy, right?"

"Yes, no... I don't really know. We were just messing about, I guess. It wasn't anything serious."

"But it could have been?"

"Who knows," I say with a shrug. "Guess I'll never find out now."

"I'm sorry," Camila says, her eyes darkening as my sadness seeps into her. "Any news from the detectives?"

"Not that I know of. They promised to call if they found anything."

I've been trying to put the idea out of my mind that my parents' deaths might not have been an accident, it makes the whole thing worse to think someone on this planet wanted them gone. I blow out a breath, fighting the tears stinging my throat from filling my eyes.

"Fuck, I'm so sorry. Come on, let me buy you a piece of cake to make up for it."

"I'm okay here."

"Amalie, you need to stop hiding. Or if you refuse to stop then you at least need to tell me what's bothering you."

The image of his harsh eyes as he dished out his threat that's been haunting me all week pop into my head again, but I refuse to admit that he's sent me into hiding. I've endured the worst life can throw at me over the last couple of months, I refuse to admit that I'm scared, and the school's bad boy has me cowering like a wimp in the library.

"Nothing's bothering me. This week's just been a bit much is all."

"I can't even imagine how you're feeling and I'm not going to pretend I do. If I push you too hard, you need to tell me, but you only live once, Amalie. I might never have known your parents but I'm pretty sure they wouldn't want you hiding in here when you could be out there living."

My stomach twists and I fight to drag air into my lungs. The sudden wave of grief that hits me threatens to break me. But I'm stronger than that. I spent the first month of my time here locked in my room at Gran's, hiding from the world and drowning in grief. My life was good, it was settled and then what was meant to be just another trip to Milan for my parents ended in tragedy when their helicopter got into trouble and unexpectedly came down over some French countryside.

Squeezing my eyes shut, I focus on my breathing

and will the panic attack I'm on the verge of away. No one needs to see that side of me.

"You're right," I announce once I'm feeling strong enough and jump to my feet. "Let's go and find that cake."

"I should warn you that the cafeteria cake will probably be dry and as hard as a rock."

"How bad can it really be? Cake is cake, right?"

"I'll let you be the judge of that." Camila threads her arm through mine and I somehow manage to walk out of the library with my head held high, with someone who's quickly turning into a very good friend beside me.

As we stand in line, she catches me up on her week so far and the dumb shit Noah's been up to.

With our cake in hand, I'm starting to feel like everything's going to be okay and that it might actually be possible to enjoy my time here, that is until I look up and lock eyes with him. My steps falter and Camila all but crashes into my back.

"Amalie, what's—oh!" I feel her stare flit between the two of us and when I manage to pull away from his tormented eyes and look back to her, her brows are drawn and her lips are pursed in anger. "What the fuck's his problem? Hold this." She shoves her plate at me and storms off in Jake's direction. Every single one of his friends turns to watch her journey, some are amused by the angry brunette marching his way, other's lust-filled eyes trail over her body, but it's one set of eyes in particular that catches my attention. Mason, the guy who seems to be Jake's right-hand man is staring daggers at her.

I'm busy wondering what the hell the story is there when she comes to a stop, places her hands on her hips and rants at Jake. Fair play to her because I can't imagine many students in this school would willingly go up against him.

Eventually, his lips curl up in an unamused smirk and he waves her off. She takes two steps back, her eyes not leaving his before she quickly glances at Mason, turns and storms back to me.

"That cake had better be bloody good."

"What did he say?" I ask, racing after her when she takes off for an empty table at the other end of the canteen.

"Just a load of bullshit. Didn't believe a word of it."

"Bullshit like what?"

She stares at me and chews on her bottom lip. "He really doesn't like you. But seriously, don't sweat it, he'll get over it."

I'm not sure whether her words are meant to be comforting or not, but they don't make me feel better in the slightest.

"Yeah, we'll see. So what about you?"

"What about me?" She keeps her expression blank, but the darkening of her eyes tells me she knows exactly what I'm talking about.

"Oh come off it. Mason looked at you like he wouldn't piss on you if you were on fire. I might not have known you all that long, but it's enough to know you wouldn't hurt a fly. What's his deal?"

"Our moms are best friends. We used to be, we're not now. That's about it?" Lifting an eyebrow, I wait for her to elaborate but she just fixes me with a stare before totally changing the subject. "Are you looking forward to your first game?"

"Um..."

"It'll be awesome, you'll see." She gives me her megawatt smile, but it does little to kickstart any excitement.

10

AMALIE

Turns out that Camila's car is already packed with everything she's going to need tonight so when we pull up outside Gran's house after school, she climbs out and pulls her giant-ass bag from the back.

"Coming in, huh?"

"I'm not letting you out of my sight. You know as well as I do that given the chance you'll bail on tonight and I won't allow that to happen."

"Maybe." Her brow lifts. "Okay fine, probably."

"You need to let your hair down and that's what tonight is about. Just for a few hours you can let go and just be you, the eighteen-year-old high school student. Get drunk, have fun, maybe have a kiss...or two," she says with a cheeky wink.

I can't deny that just the thought of what she's proposing doesn't make it sound a little appealing. The fun and drinking part anyway, I have no intention of kissing anyone. That kind of thing will only lead to making my already messed up life more complicated.

"Come on then. I've no idea what I should be wearing to this thing."

"Sexy, Amalie. Always sexy."

Gran's on the phone as we walk through to the kitchen to grab something to drink. She smiles at me and it's so genuine that it makes tears burn the back of my throat. She's been desperate for me to integrate myself with life here and finally accept that this is my home now. She never said it out loud, but I think she was worried that I was going to jump straight on a plane the second I turned eighteen and could legally look after myself. Of course, I thought about it time and time again. It would be so easy to go back to London, crash at a friend's house. I might even be able to get myself into university, I've got enough money sitting in my account to make it possible. But do I want to go back and be alone? I might have only been here a few weeks really, but even that is enough to know that I need to be here. I tell myself it's for Gran, my presence lifts the dark shadows her daughter's death has clouded her eyes with, but I also know that being away from London and all the places that will remind me of them is helping me too. I've no idea how I'd be able to go back to my old life when they're not there. In reality, they weren't around all that much, the business took up the majority of their time, but they were only ever a phone call away, even if they were off in a different country.

"There are freshly baked cookies in the tin," Gran says, having hung up the phone.

Camila immediately turns toward the tin Gran nodded at, pulls the lid off and stuffs one in her mouth. "You're a legend, Peg."

Gran and I both laugh as she stuffs her face. "So, game night?"

"Apparently so."

"You'll love it. I used to live for game nights as a kid. The excitement, the thrill of the win, the hope of catching one of the player's eyes." She gets this faraway look and I can't help wondering what she was like as a young woman. She's always been in my life, and we visited quite a few times, but it's only now that I'm living under her roof that I'm really getting to know her.

"I do not want to get anywhere near a football player."

"Oh yeah?" Gran's eyebrows rise in interest and sadly Camila can't help herself.

"She's already got two under her spell, Peg." I groan, grab a couple of cookies and leave the room.

"Of course she has, she's her mother's daughter. She'll have them all tripping over themselves."

My stomach muscles clench at the thought of my mum and I race faster toward my room, afraid to hear any more. I know that Camila's only winding me up, but I don't need reminding of everything I'm trying to ignore at school. Shane's interest and more importantly, Jake's anger. I don't need either of them in my life right now and

I'd rather Gran didn't get involved, because if I've learned anything about her it's that she's a hopeless romantic who will jump at the chance of helping to set me up.

"I'm sorry, I didn't mean to—" Camila says a few minutes later having followed me down to my room.

"It's fine. You don't need to apologise."

"Your gran made us hot chocolate. It's not quite the start to the evening I had in mind, but I'm not one to refuse chocolate." We're both silent as we sip from our steaming mugs. "I think he really likes you, you know."

Catching me off guard, I turn to her, my brows pinched together. "Who?"

"Shane," she says with a roll of her eyes, like she could be talking about anyone else.

"Oh, right. He's not really getting the idea that I'm not interested."

"Why not? He's hot. And I have it on good authority that he's pretty talented...if you know what I mean." She wiggles her fingers in the air and I groan.

"Magic fingers or not, I'm not interested."

She gives me a disappointed look. "That better not be because another member of the team—*the captain*—has captured your interest."

Fighting to swallow the chocolate in my mouth, my eyes widen to the point I think they might pop out. "Please tell me you're joking. He hates me, and I must say, the feeling's kinda mutual."

"So something *has* happened?"

Shit. Every time I've seen her after the incident at Aces she's questioned me. It was obvious that something happened in the few minutes she was gone but I still refuse to relay the events of those couple of horrible moments.

"No. Can we please not talk about him? He doesn't deserve our time or attention."

"I couldn't agree more." She puts her mug down and jumps from the bed. "Let's find you something to wear. I've been dying to get in your wardrobe." I watch as she pulls the doors open, and a smile splits her face. "OMG it's even more than I imagined."

"You can borrow anything. If it fits," I add because our body shapes are very different. While I've got my mother's supermodel body, Camila is a super sexy hourglass and a whole head shorter than me.

"You serious?" She turns to me, a smile almost splitting her face in two.

"Sure." I'm not stupid, I know the cost of what she's looking at is beyond most people's imagination but to me, they're just clothes. I was never that fascinated by the designer labels who used to give my mum free clothes just so she could be photographed in them. I always knew we had money, more than most, but it wasn't until I moved here that the differences became more noticeable.

There's plenty of money in this town, mostly on the east side but it's nothing compared to the people Mum and Dad used to spend time with. Money means nothing to me, I'd much rather have my family than anything in the bank, but that decision was taken from me. It's one of the reasons why anger fills my veins every time I see someone look at what I'm wearing with jealousy oozing from their eyes. Clothes and designer labels aren't anything to be jealous of, they come and go and mean nothing, family though, parents...you only get one lot of those and I'd give anything to have mine back.

Movement at the other side of my room drags me from my morose thoughts and I sit back and watch as Camila pulls out item after item from my collection while making all kinds of ohhs and ahhs. That is until she stops, pulls something out and then turns to me.

"You have to wear this tonight."

"We're going to a football game, Cam, not a club."

Her shoulders shrug. "So? You want to look hot, don't you?"

Not really. "I just want to blend into the crowd. Jeans and a t-shirt will be just fine."

She rolls her eyes but instead of arguing like I was expecting, her shoulders drop in disappointment. "I guess it doesn't really matter what you wear, you'll still look stunning." She drops the silver sequined dress she was holding up. It's the one my mum bought me to celebrate finishing sixth form, but I never got to wear it. I probably never will either now, but there's no way I could ever get rid of it. It was the last thing she chose for me on the last day out I ever spent with her.

"What are you talking about? You're stunning, I'd love to have your curves." I push down the emotions that dress dregs up and walk over to my wardrobe. "What about something like this?" I ask, pulling out a playsuit that would really show off her full cleavage and shapely legs. "I guarantee it'll make Noah's eyes pop out of his head."

"You think?"

"I do. Try it on."

"Okay. And you can totally wear whatever you want *but*—" I groan. "I'm doing your makeup."

"Deal."

An hour later and Camila is standing in my playsuit looking like a knockout while I've got on a black pair of jeans, trainers, and my favorite t-shirt. It's white with 'with pleasure' in a bubble font across the front. Camila has done an excellent job of my simple makeup and adding some loose curls into my blonde hair.

"Shane's gonna blow his load when he looks at you."

"Cam, please don't."

"What? I'm just saying that you're rocking that look. You're gonna turn heads tonight."

"I don't want to turn heads. I just want to blend."

"I know you do, but trust me when I say that you'll never blend into a crowd." A sigh passes my lips but I don't say anymore. "Are you packed for tonight?"

"Packed?"

"Yeah, for the midnight dash party."

"If it's just a party, why do I need to pack?"

"Oh, Amalie." She pulls out a Louis Vuitton bag from the top of my wardrobe. "It's not just a party. The Midnight Dash is a long-held tradition, a rite of passage, type thing. It's an all-night party at the end of the beach. It's a night where you can let go, blow off steam and act crazy before the seriousness of senior year really begins. Plus, what happens at the Midnight Dash stays at the Midnight Dash." Her eyebrows wiggle in excitement and my stomach drops.

"I'm not a senior."

"Maybe not, but you're coming as my special guest. We're gonna get drunk, dance and enjoy ourselves. Now hurry because the pep rally is gonna start soon and we don't want to be late."

She stands with her hands on her hips and an impatient look on her face as I stand from the bed.

"What do I need to pack?" I ask on a sigh.

"Normal camping shit."

"What does that entail?"

"You've never been camping?" She looks at me but doesn't give me time to answer. "I don't know why I'm even asking that, of course you haven't been camping!"

"What? I'm not some stuck up rich kid. I can camp."

"We'll find out tonight. Change of clothes, bikini, and a pillow should do it." Turning from her amused face, I start shoving stuff in my bag, "Oh don't forget wet wipes, they are essential. And condoms if you have any."

"What? I do not need—"

"Oh shhh... it's Midnight Dash, anything could happen...and it probably will."

Dread twists my stomach at the excitement in her eyes. "If tonight's going to basically be one big orgy, please tell me now so I can stay home."

"Now you're just being silly. Come on." She zips up my bag for me, threads her fingers through mine and pulls me from the room.

"You two look beautiful. All ready for your big night?"

"I am," Camila answers proudly before turning toward me. "This one's a little more skeptical."

"You'll be fine once you're there. Here, I got you this," Gran says pulling open a cupboard and revealing a bottle of vodka. "Now, I trust you both to be sensible with it, I do not want a phone call from anyone to come and rescue your drunk butts from the beach. But I want you both to have fun, *you*," her eyes find mine. "Deserve it."

I thank her, give her a kiss on the cheek and the two of us make our way to the car. Camila bounces with excitement while I desperately try to drum up some enthusiasm for anything but making a start on the bottle of vodka in my hand.

11

JAKE

The roar of the crowd as they celebrate our win with us vibrates through me. This is it. This moment is what I live for. Being part of something so huge that my bullshit life no longer matters. No one cares where I came from, how I live or about the anger that resonates inside. All anyone cares about in this moment is that I'm their king. I'm the reason they have something to celebrate. Every single football fan wants to be me right now and every single female set of eyes on me wants a piece. I fucking love it.

"You were on fucking fire tonight," Mason says slapping his hand down on my shoulder. He's not wrong. Everything about tonight just fell into place. All our well practiced plays were executed with the exact precision Coach expects and we ran rings around our opponents. For the first time ever, the guy's words about this year being our year start to sound a little more possible. This might only be the first game of the season, but it's a fucking good start.

"I need a motherfucking drink and a nice piece of ass. Who's with me?" Ethan shouts into the locker room and there are calls of agreement and hollers of excitement. We've all been looking forward to tonight since we were old enough to understand what a party was. The senior year dash pretty much sums up how your final year of high school's going to go. Don't attend, or even worse, not allowed to attend and you're basically an outcast. Turn up and kinda participate and you're accepted but turn up and do exactly what's expected of you and you're set for the year. Tonight's about proving yourself, proving you have what it takes to be a senior at Rosewood high. It's tradition and at fucking last, it's our turn.

"Get that junk good and clean, boys. The girls are gonna be fucking lining up for us when we arrive. But choose wisely my friends, choose very wisely." Laughing at Ethan's antics, I head for the shower and do exactly as he just suggested because I don't intend on spending tonight without getting my cock sucked at least once.

As planned, we're the last ones to the beach. The smoke from the bonfire bellows up, pointing us in the right direction, not that we didn't know where we were going. The second I push Mason's passenger door open the music from below fills my ears and my heart picks up pace. I'm so fucking ready for this. My first week of senior year has been... fucked up to say the least. The new girl's arrival stirred an anger within me that I thought I'd managed to rid myself of but it's back with a vengeance, taunting me, pushing me forward. I've stayed out of her way the past few days, but that doesn't mean I'm not watching her. I see her getting closer to Shane and the way he looks at her like she's something fucking special. I see her walking around like she's got all the world's fucking problems on her shoulders. Well guess what, princess? The rest of us have our own shit to deal with and in order to release some of what I'm carrying I'm about to make your life even worse.

"Let's do this shit." Pulling coolers from the trunk, I follow both Mason and Ethan down to the beach.

A cheer starts up the second we appear, and my chest swells with fucking pride. Most of the cheer squad immediately jump up and our teammates who got here first come running at us. Chelsea makes a beeline for me but unlike I have the rest of the week, I welcome her excitement.

Her hand goes straight for my cock, rubbing it through the fabric of my jeans like the desperate slut that she is. "You're getting lucky tonight." Her high-pitched breathy moan does little for me, but I can't deny that her stroking isn't feeling good right now.

Running her other hand up my chest, she sneaks it around the back of my neck and reaches up on her toes, it's like she thinks I'm going to kiss her. She should know better than that by now. I don't kiss. Ever.

Just as her lips move toward mine and I'm about to shove her away, a flash of blonde catches my eyes. She fucking wouldn't. Would she?

At the sight of her, my body freezes, fury erupts in my stomach as my veins fill with fire. Clenching my fists at my side, ready to march over there and demand she leaves. I don't see her movement until it's too late and Chelsea's full lips press against mine.

She must feel my stare because her eyes lift and immediately lock onto mine. They widen in surprise before darkening when they take in the hussy who's pressed up against my body. Chelsea moans as my cock gets harder under her touch, only it's not for her. I'm hard because of the excitement racing through my body, the excitement for the revenge and pain I'm going to cause.

Ethan, the fucker, hollers at me for getting lucky and unfortunately causes a scene that has every set of eyes turning our way. Ripping my eyes from *her,* I grasp Chelsea's upper arms and force her away from me. She pouts, sticking her bottom lip out like I should be sucking it back into my mouth. She looks up at me and her face pales. I know why, the tension that she's seeing has my entire body pulled tight. My need to storm over there and drag New Girl's sorry ass from the beach is all-consuming.

Mason must sense where my head's at because his hand lands on my shoulder, turning me away from the eyes of every other senior on the beach.

"Why the fuck is she here? She's not even a senior," I spit when what I really want to do is punch something or someone.

"No idea. I guess she was invited."

"Fucking Camila. You need to sort that bitch out." His eyes narrow at me, but he wisely keeps his fucking mouth shut. He might be my best friend, but I have no issues turning him into my punching bag right now.

"Let's go set up camp and get a beer... or five."

Handing me the tent and a few bags that he and Ethan must have grabbed from the car while I was lip-locked with Chelsea, I haul them up on my shoulder and march off toward our spot. The best spot on the fucking beach.

Chelsea skips off as if I didn't just kick her to the curb. Her perky ass and overly big tits bounce in her almost pointless bikini as she moves, almost every male set of eyes follow her movements. Breaking my eyes from her, I take in the rest of the girls. Most are showing off as much skin as possible in the hope of bagging their guy of choice tonight. Dash night is a free for all. All bets are off as you go after the one you want. Not only are a lot of relationships made on this night, but a lot are broken too. The guys are mostly sitting back right now, watching their prey, waiting for the right moment to pounce. Excitement begins to erupt in my stomach as I consider my options for tonight. The thing is, the guys down there might think they have the pick of the bunch, but the truth is, the only people to get that privilege are the team, everyone else gets our sloppy seconds. As my gaze falls over the girls and they start to notice, tits are pushed up, asses get stuck out a little more, none of which do it for me. They all know they're hot and they use it to get exactly what they want. No different to Chelsea.

"Fuck me. Them lot are well up for it," Ethan rumbles behind me. "How are we meant to choose?"

As he and Mason start debating their options, my eyes once again fall on one person. Unlike every other girl here, she's dressed in jeans and a fucking t-shirt. As if she's not already enough of an outcast, it seems that whoever invited her also didn't give her the memo about the dress code. A smile twitches at my lips. She may not be the one I'm going to spend the night with, but she's got a target on her head all right. She isn't going to make it until midnight. I'll make fucking sure of that.

It takes us no time to get the tents up and the beers flowing. "Who are you all tagging?" Mason asks. It's a tradition at any party that we announce our targets for the night. There's no reason other than for bragging rights the next day when we tapped our target.

"I propose different rules tonight, seeing as it's Dash and all."

"Go on," I say, tipping my bottle to my lips and downing the contents, waiting for Ethan to explain his plan.

"I propose we name a tag for each other. Then you've got until dawn to do the deed."

The guys' eyes light up at the dare-like suggestion. "Fuck yeah," someone slurs having had one too many beers already.

"Sure. Name 'em."

Ethan lays back on his elbows and gazes at the party going on slightly farther down the beach. The giant bonfire roars, bathing everyone in an orange hue and the music booms from the speakers someone's set up.

He starts rattling off names, the guys either beam in delight or groan at the epic challenge they have ahead of them. Me? I don't have any worries. Most of the girls down there would do just about anything to be able to say they spent the night with me.

"Mason, you can have Chelsea." A laugh erupts when I noticed the disgusted look on his face.

"Fuck off. I don't want his used cast-offs," Mason snaps, flicking his eyes to me.

"You won't be complaining when she's got her lips around your cock later." Chelsea may be many things, but I can't deny that she sucks good cock, and if she thinks I keep her around for any other reason, then she's got another thing coming.

"You're fucking serious, aren't you?"

"Okay I'll give you a choice." The others groan because they weren't given that option. Mason lifts his brow, waiting to hear what Ethan's got to say but by the look of the wicked smile on Ethan's lips, I don't think he's going to like what he's got to say. "Chelsea or..." I swear everyone holds their breath, no more so than Mason as we all wait. "Camila."

"Fuck you, asshole," Mason seethes. "I'll stick with Chelsea."

"Thought you might." Ethan laughs while Mason sulks and slugs him in the shoulder.

"S'all in good fun, bro."

"Don't fucking bro me." Mason drags himself up and storms toward the cooler for another beer.

"He grown a fucking pussy or what?" A few people laugh, but mostly Ethan's comment is ignored. "So that leaves you, cap." I keep my eyes on the crowd below, watching them laughing and dancing, that is until my eyes zero in on one couple dancing and my anger starts to boil over. Right in the damn middle is Shane and he's dancing with *her*. It was obvious he was interested when he first saw her, but the way his hands are currently resting on her hips and the look in his eyes pisses me off. It should be common knowledge by now that she's off fucking limits. If anyone's going to put their hands on her, it's going to be me.

My growl of frustration comes out louder than I was anticipating, and Ethan turns to me before looking back out at the crowd.

"Thorn," he practically sings he's so fucking excited and if I weren't so distracted by the sight in front of me then I might see his next words coming. "Because you're an overachiever, you get two. Shelly," he says, nodding toward where she's downing shots with Chelsea. I turn to him, his eyes dark and mischievous. "Amalie."

I'm just about to ask who the fuck that is when it dawns. My eyes find her in the crowd but this time she's not just dancing with Shane because as her hips move against his, she's staring right at me.

"Game on, asshole. Game. On."

12

AMALIE

As the alcohol starts to take effect, I realise that this probably isn't the worst idea I've ever had. It's been forever since I've had a night where I've been able to truly forget everything and just be me. Camila was right to drag me here.

I smile up at Shane as we dance together, still not all that happy about the lust I find in his green depths. I've no intention of leading him to think anything will happen between us, but my body can't help but roll with his in time with the music.

The panic that consumed me the moment I first locked eyes on Jake when he arrived has almost been replaced with enjoyment, which is a strange feeling after all this time.

The song changes and Shane spins me around so my back is to his front. The moment I look up I find him once again. His group has set up camp slightly up the beach so they can look down on us peasants like they own the place.

His eyes narrow and drop to where Shane's holding my hips and pulling my body so it's flush against him. Fire burns in their depths and my heart starts to pound. I'm not welcome at this party, that much was obvious when he first arrived. I'm surprised I've lasted this long, but looking at the disdain on his face right now, I fear my time might be up.

"I need to get a drink," I say, resting my head back against Shane's shoulder. Disappointment is written all over his face, which just proves that I need to put some space between us. Letting loose and having fun is one thing, but he's a sweet guy and I don't want to make him think this is more than it's ever going to be.

"I need to pee."

"Do you need me to hold your hand or something?" Camila asks with a laugh where she's dry humping Noah, her eyes bright with the alcohol she's consumed.

"No, but where are the toilets?"

"This is the beach. There aren't any."

"So where do we…"

"Just go into the trees and do your thing."

"The trees?" I glance up at where the beach ends and the greenery starts.

"This really is a different world for you, isn't it?"

I don't get a chance to say anything because Noah pulls her attention back to him and shoves his tongue in her mouth.

Shaking my head, I walk past the other kids who are too busy enjoying themselves to look up at me.

The second I step into the trees, darkness surrounds me. Pulling my phone from my back pocket,

I put the torch on and use it to guide my way deeper into the undergrowth. It might be a little extreme but the last thing I need is someone stumbling across me mid-pee.

Once I'm confident I've left all the partygoers behind, I find a spot behind a tree and do my thing.

It's not until I'm fighting my way back toward the beach that a noise, or more a moan, stops me in my tracks.

Knowing that I need to get away from here before I look like a right creep, I continue forward but before I find the beach, I stumble across the owner of the moan.

A loud snap sounds out as I stand on a stick and his eyes snap to me. The anger I'm used to seeing is there, but it's been overtaken by desire. His full lips are slightly parted and his bare chest is heaving. When I lower my eyes more, I find a blonde on her knees with her head bobbing back and forth while his phone is in his hand like he's filming the event.

My stomach twists in panic. I really don't need to be standing here right now. "I'm so sorry," I whisper going to step away but he's clearly not thinking the same thing because as I move, he barks, "Stop."

Without instruction from my brain, my legs freeze but I keep my eyes downcast, not wanting to intrude on what should be a private moment.

The movement I can see out of the corner of my eyes tells me that the girl hasn't stopped. *She must be enjoying herself more than him right now,* I think and I have an internal battle about what to do. I should run, that would be the easiest thing to do but there's something about his commanding voice that forces me to stay stock still and wait to find out what he wants.

"Look at me."

Hesitantly, my eyes lift until I find his tormented stare. He pins me to the spot with his hate-filled eyes, and while my brain screams at me to move, to run, to do something. My body stays exactly where it is, fascinated, as pleasure washes over his face. His eyes narrow and darken further, if that's possible, his chin drops and the most erotic sound I've ever heard falls from his lips.

My teeth sink into my bottom lip as I watch the show. I'm more interested in watching than I should be. The heat coursing through my veins angers me because the guy I'm currently watching like he's the most fascinating thing on the planet hates my guts. But I can't not watch now I've got this far.

With his hand in the girl's hair, he pulls her back until she hits the floor. I wince but she doesn't seem too bothered. By the time he turns to me, he's tucked himself back into his pants and any pleasure that was on his face is long gone. It's hard once again with the muscle in his jaw twitching in anger.

"Enjoy that, did you? Watching me get my cock sucked. Hopefully it gave you some pointers because you're next. Although, I doubt you need any lessons, girls as beautiful as you are always at home being on your knees."

"Fuck you," I spit, taking a step back as he gets in my personal space.

"You'd be so fucking lucky. I don't fuck whores."

My breath catches at the same time my back bumps up against a tree. "Don't talk to me like you know anything about me. You don't."

"I know all too well how women like you operate, what you do to get what you want. It disgusts me and I intend on proving it." His body moves closer still and I press back into the tree. My heart thunders in my chest, fear making my hands tremble but I refuse to back down to this arsehole. He's no idea what the fuck he's talking about. "I intend to show the entire fucking school what an untrustworthy whore you really are."

"What the fuck is your problem? I haven't done anything."

"Not yet, you haven't. But you will. Girls like you always show their true selves eventually."

"I don't—"

Leaning forward, his chest brushes my breasts and my breath catches at the sensation. "See, you're doing it right now." He moves his chest again and my nipples pucker with the friction. "You'd do anything right now to get your way. Your body is craving it."

"Fuck you." My hand comes out to slap him, but he catches it, his hot fingers circling my wrist so tightly I swear it'll leave a mark.

His fingers grip my chin, making my lips pout. His hate-filled eyes bore into mine before they drop to my lips. His tongue sneaks across his bottom one like he's considering his next move. My heart continues to thunder so hard in my chest that my head starts to feel a little fuzzy.

Moving to the side he leans in, his hot breath tickles

around my ear. "No, but I am going to break you. Show you exactly what you are."

The second the final word is out of his mouth, he releases me and steps back into the shadows. I don't waste any time and run in the direction of the beach. My lungs are burning for air and my legs are shaking by the time I step foot onto the sand, but instead of the escape I was hoping for, I run straight into a solid wall.

A large pair of hands land on my waist to steady me but I fight to get away thinking he beat me out of the trees.

"Amalie, it's okay." The voice is unfamiliar yet kind, it has the desired effect because I stop fighting. That is until I look up and find Jake's right-hand man, Mason. Then I pull myself from his hands and take a giant step back. "Are you okay?" It looks like genuine concern on his face but seeing as he's friends with the arsehole I just left behind I highly doubt he actually cares.

"I'm good. Thanks." My voice is hard and cold and his eyes narrow.

"Did something happen in there?"

"No, nothing. I just went to pee."

A smile twitches at his lips. "Why didn't you just use the toilets?"

"The toilets?" I whisper. "But Camila said..." I trail off when his entire face twists as if he's in pain.

"It was a joke," her slightly slurred voice comes from behind him.

"Oh."

"Amalie, please tell me you didn't actually—" Her

words falter when she spots Mason standing next to me. "What have you said to her?" she barks.

"Me? I haven't done anything. I wasn't the one who sent her into the trees to use the bathroom."

"I thought she knew I was joking. We parked next to the restrooms."

"Well, she didn't." Mason steps toward Camila, I could cut the tension between them with a knife as they stare at each other, both refusing to back down.

That is until someone else appears from the trees. We all look over as Jake walks out from the darkness with his usual swagger and general aura of hate surrounding him. Both Camila and Mason look between him and me. I can practically hear their thoughts running at a mile a minute in their heads.

Jake ignores both of them and walks over to me. His eyes run the length of my body before his hand slides into my hair and his rough cheek rubs against mine. "Watch your back, Brit." To our spectators, it might look an intimate move, but the reality of the situation is so very different.

He pulls back almost immediately, winks at me and starts walking backward, not taking his eyes off my body until he's forced to look where he's going. I know the moment his eyes are off me because the tingles that were following his gaze instantly vanish. I tell myself that it's the burning hate coming from him that causes it, but after having his hot and hard body pressed up against mine, I know it might not be the case. Jake Thorn might be a bastard, but he's a bloody beautiful one at that, and all my body sees is his hot one.

"What the hell was that?" Camila asks, Mason is too busy studying my reaction to say anything.

"It was... nothing."

"Nothing? What the hell happened in there?"

"Nothing happened in there. I just went for a pee, that's all. If you'd told me where the toilets were in the first place, then I wouldn't have been in there."

"I'm sorry. I thought you knew I was joking." Camila looks horrified that I actually listened to her and went in there, but really, why wouldn't I believe her? She'd not given me any reason to think it would be a joke.

"I need a drink." Storming through both of them, I march back toward the party and grab two bottles of beer from a cool box.

I've almost downed the first one when I feel her presence behind me. "Amalie, I'm so sorry. I didn't really think you'd... I thought you'd seen the restrooms."

"It's fine, honestly. None of that was your fault."

"What happened?"

"Five minutes!" someone calls from the other side of the group and cheers erupt from the crowd but at no point does Camila take her eyes from mine.

"Are you two ready?" Noah asks. When I look up, I find Shane at his side, his eyes alight with excitement and probably a little too much alcohol.

"Ready for what?"

"You're gonna love it." Camila practically bounces on the balls of her feet. I truly hope it's more enjoyable than her last 'surprise'.

13

JAKE

The second I saw the fear in her eyes when she found us, I almost came down Shelly's throat. Her appearance at that moment couldn't have been more perfect if I'd planned it myself.

My cock twitches in my jeans as I think about the way her eyes dropped down to my chest and ran over my abs. She might hate me after what I've done to her, but fuck if she didn't wish she was Shelly in that moment. And fuck if I didn't want that too. The thought of it being her throat I was punishing makes my cock weep with excitement. I may want to end her, but shit if I don't want to enjoy the ride, and the ride will certainly lead to her being on her knees, I can guaran-fucking-tee that.

The sweet scent of her perfume mixed with the fear in her eyes was exactly what I needed to feed the fury that fills my veins every time I look at her and remember what she represents. Weak, beautiful women who'll use what God gave them to get whatever they want no matter who they trample or abandon in the process.

My fists clench with my need to have her sinful, slender body pressed up against mine again so I can show her that her allure won't get her anywhere around here. *You're falling into her trap*, a little voice inside me shouts but I drown it with another swig of beer. I'm not falling into anything, I'm teaching the bitch a lesson. I'm getting vengeance for what another version of her did to me years ago.

"What the hell?" Mason asks, dropping down beside me.

"What?"

"Don't play fucking dumb with me. What the hell happened with Amalie in the trees?"

"What do you think happened? And for the record, she sucks like a fucking vacuum cleaner."

His eyes narrow and his teeth grind. "You're talking shit, she's not one of them." He waves his hands toward most of the cheer team who drop their panties for a look alone. "There's no way she did that willingly."

"Who said she was willing?"

"What the fuck is wrong with you right now? This isn't you, bro."

"This is me doing what needs to be done."

"We've been friends since we were in diapers, Jake. If you think for one minute that I can't see what's going on here, that I can't see exactly what you see when you look at her, then you're a fucking idiot. Your issues have nothing to do with her, she's not the one you need to punish for how your life turned out. She's going through enough shit of her own right now, the last thing she needs is you on her case. Now back the fuck off."

Standing, needing to do something to shake the tension taking over my body, I stare down at him.

"The fuck, Mase?" My muscles lock up as I fight the need to wipe the warning he's giving me right off his fucking face. Best friend or not, he's no right saying that kind of shit to me. Climbing from the sand, he stares me right in the eyes, taunting me.

"Go on, hit me. Take your anger out on me, better that than her."

"Why the fuck are you standing up for her?"

"Because she's done nothing other than have her own life ripped out from under her. Don't pretend like you don't know exactly what happened to her parents. You really think she needs you on her case just because she unfortunately looks a little like—"

"Don't say it. Don't fucking say it." I'm right in his face, our noses only a breath apart. One punch from me and the pussy would be down like a stone and he knows it, but yet he still stands toe to toe with me defending her.

My chest heaves, my hands clench but somehow I manage to keep them at my sides. "How was Camila?" I ask through gritted teeth remembering them stood together.

"Fuck you."

"Na, you're all right. I might go and find her though, I bet she needs a good pounding because that fucker she's with clearly isn't capable."

I don't see his fist coming but I sure as shit feel it as it slams into my jaw. I knew mentioning Camila would get him just as riled up as me.

"Don't you dare go anywhere fucking near her."

"Or what?"

His fist hits me again, but at no point do I retaliate. I need this. I need the pain.

"What the fuck?" Ethan shouts, pulling Mason off me.

"It's nothin'," I mutter, spitting out the blood that's filling my mouth from the split that's stinging my lip.

"Don't look like fucking nothin'." His stare flits between the two of us, making sure we're not going to get straight back to it the second he steps away.

Mason shrugs before inspecting his knuckles and walking off in favor of finding more beer. I knew mentioning Camila was an asshole move. But what can I say? I'm an asshole.

"How's it going with your girls?" Ethan asks after we both watch Mason walk away.

"Done."

"Both of them?"

"Both of them," I confirm.

"Wow, I thought Amalie was going to be a challenge too big, even for you, hotshot."

"What can I say? The girls just can't resist."

"You're fucking deluded."

"Don't give a fuck. I got some. Did you?"

"I'm still working on it." After he dished out all the names for us, Rich, another guy on the team gave

Ethan an almost impossible challenge with his girl. There's no way he's getting any from her tonight.

"You ready? It's nearly time."

"Always ready."

Ethan chuckles and we both stick our beers in the sand, getting ready to move.

Someone shouts the signal and every single body on the beach starts moving. Clothes are thrown in all directions, some more than others depending on how brave they are and they start moving for the sea.

Dropping my jeans, I keep one hand over my junk as I continue watching the students lower down the beach. My eyes find her almost instantly, not that it's hard with her platinum blonde hair. I can't tear my gaze away as she watches what everyone's doing around her before gripping the bottom of her t-shirt and peeling it up her slim body. Even from here I can tell that her pale skin is as flawless as I expected it to be. Her small, pert breasts are covered in two small black triangles of fabric that tie behind her neck and back. My fingers twitch with how easy it would be to remove it from her body. Flicking the button on her jeans, she pushes them down her legs, bending over slightly to free her feet, the sight of her barely covered ass has my cock threatening to go full mast. Needing a distraction before my need is obvious to those around me, I follow their lead and take off running.

Midnight Dash is a test of bravery and courage. Those who want to prove themselves strip down to nothing and run full pelt into the sea. As expected, most of the guys drop everything whereas it's mostly just Chelsea and her slutty friends who bare all and flaunt everything they've got like shameless hussies.

Sadly, the water's not cold enough to cool off the image of her ass that's still burned into my head.

"Holy fucking shit," someone squeals behind me as water gets splashed and people laugh and mess about.

I stand waist high in water and watch their antics suddenly feeling totally deflated about tonight and the year ahead.

"This is fucking stupid," I mutter to Mason when he comes near.

"Right? Wanna go grab a beer?"

"I've got a better idea."

He eyes me nervously but being the loyal best friend that he is, he nods and follows me from the water, leaving the rest of our class behind to enjoy themselves.

"Where the hell's our tent?" Camila complains once we've made our way back to dry off.

The space next to the boy's tent where we pitched ours is completely empty. "He wouldn't, would he?" I don't mean for the words to be said aloud but I realise they are when Camila, Noah, and Shane all turn to me.

"Who?" Camila asks but by the narrowing of her eyes toward the football team I know she doesn't really need me to answer the question. "I'm gonna fucking kill them." She strides off toward where they're all sitting around drinking, mostly with the cheer team on their laps.

"Babe, wait," Noah says in a rush, grabbing her arm and pulling her back. "You going over there and making a scene is exactly what they want. Don't feed the animals."

"But they have all our stuff, our clothes, our underwear."

Noah's teeth grind but he doesn't release his hold on his girlfriend. Leaning into her, he whispers in her ear quiet enough that I can't make out the words. When he pulls back, she stares at him for a few seconds, a silent argument passing between the two of them but eventually, her shoulders sag and she says, "Fine. But I will make them pay for this."

"Here," Shane says, handing me his towel so I can dry off. I hesitate to take it, aware that I don't want him to think there's more to this but in reality, I've not got many options right now. "You guys can crash in with us. It's a four-berth, they'll be plenty of space." The excitement that shines in Shane's eyes makes my stomach twist with dread. I really don't want to hurt him, he seems like one of the good guys, despite his involvement with the football team.

"I think maybe I should just go home."

"What? No. Noah's right, that would mean they win and I'm not losing to those assholes."

"I get it, Camila, I do. But you don't need to fight this battle with me. I can just go, and you can continue like I was never here bringing this kinda drama into your lives."

"You about finished?" She stands toe to toe with me, her hands on her hips, her head tipped back so she can look into my eyes. "You're not going anywhere. I invited you because I wanted you here, *we* want you here. Fuck them and their childish games. Let's show them you're made of stronger stuff than that. I know you've got it in you because you wouldn't be here right now if you weren't."

She's right, I know she is, but that doesn't stop me wanting to run home and hide under my duvet from the arsehole that's trying to ruin my life more than it already is.

"Come on, have a drink and let's try to enjoy the rest of the night," Noah encourages, handing Camila one of his t-shirts.

When I turn to look at Shane, he's also holding out a shirt for me to wear. I take it from him, grateful I don't have to spend the night in only my bikini, but I question my decision to put it on when I realise it's his football jersey with his number on the back. I may not know all that much about American high schools yet but one thing I do know is that giving a girl your number is a big thing.

"Don't you have anything else?"

"That's my only clean one."

After a few seconds of staring at him and a little encouragement from Camila, I slip it over my head, feeling better about myself almost immediately having some skin covered. My string bikini might be massive in comparison to what some of the other girls are or aren't wearing, but it doesn't mean I'm comfortable having that much of my skin on show. I might have grown up in the fashion industry and around models who are more than happy to pose in next to nothing, but that's not me. I'd much rather be hiding behind the camera with my dad, than front and center of the attention with my mum.

With Shane's giant number ninety-nine on my

back, I settle myself on the sand with the others and accept a bottle of beer when it's handed to me.

I didn't have any expectations for what tonight was going to be like. Hell, I had no idea what was going to happen seeing as Camila kept the details a secret from me in her attempt to build my excitement, but I can honestly say I didn't expect any of it.

As I look around at the students still splashing about in the sea, the ones who have coupled up and are rolling around in the sand, and then the separate party that the football team seems to be having higher up the beach, I wonder how this became my life.

Even though it happened to me, it's still hard to believe that your life can change in the blink of an eye. The friends I thought I had in London that would be my friends for life are mostly now gone. Even Laurence, the guy I thought I might have had a future with hasn't been in touch for weeks. While I'm here starting a new life, they're all embarking on theirs at their chosen universities and moving on...without me. It stings that we've already lost touch but really, I didn't expect it any other way. I can only hope that the guys I'm surrounded by now might be a little more loyal, or at least stick around long enough to help me through the next few months as I settle in and hopefully find my place. If they don't and whatever this thing is with Jake gets too much, then I'm not sure what my future might look like.

I've always been the kind of person to look forward and see the positive in things, but as I sit here wondering, I can't help thinking for the first time in my life that going backward is a serious possibility.

"Hey," Camila says, lightly elbowing me in the arm to drag me from my thoughts. "Everything okay?"

"Sure."

"I really am sorry about earlier. The joke kinda backfired on me."

"It's fine." It already feels like it happened a lifetime ago.

"Here, have a drink and come dance with me, this is meant to be a party."

Taking the plastic cup from her hand, I swallow it down in one and allow her to pull me from the sand. We make our way to the makeshift dancefloor, Noah and Shane hot on our tails.

A shiver runs through me as I turn to start dancing and when I flick a look over my shoulder, I find exactly what I'm expecting. His eyes on me.

Ignoring him, I turn back toward my new friends, plaster a smile on my face and attempt to do exactly what I should be doing, enjoying myself.

15

JAKE

It seemed like a good idea in my head but now that I'm sitting here watching her wearing his fucking number, I realize that I've screwed up.

Something possessive that I don't want to identify sits uncomfortably in my stomach and causes my muscles to bunch. The need to go and rip that fucking bit of fabric from her slender body is all-consuming. My fingers wrap around the bottle in my hands with an almost painful force.

"What the hell is wro—" Mason follows my line of sight. "Oh."

"Yes, fucking oh."

"I told you it was a bad idea."

"I expected them to lose their shit not just continue like they don't care."

"You can never predict girls, bro. You should have learned that by now." My teeth grind, I can usually predict girls like Chelsea and Shelly perfectly, they almost always do what I expect. But the new girl, she's different. Yes, there's fear in her eyes every time I get too close, but she doesn't back down. She's not afraid to go toe to toe with me and fight for what she believes is right.

Maybe she is right, a little voice in my head says. So what she looks just like the bitch who abandoned me, that doesn't mean she's anything like her.

Downing the beer in my hands, I reach for another, needing to drown out stupid ass thoughts like that. The hatred and anger has been festering inside me for years, now isn't the time to start questioning my intentions. The frustration I'm feeling needs to drive me forward, not turn me into a fucking pussy.

"You were right about Chelsea," he says, dropping beside me.

"Oh yeah?"

"Like a fucking vacuum cleaner."

Throwing my head back, I laugh at the shocked look on his face. "I told you it was good."

"I think she might have ruined blow jobs for me. No one else is ever going to compare to that."

"So what you saying? You gonna tie the bitch down?"

"What after she's had half the school's cocks in her mouth? Na, I'm good thanks. I need to figure out a way to find a good girl who can suck like that."

Shaking my head at his noble intentions to find himself a nice little girlfriend, I refrain from pointing out that he'll probably need to stop acting like such a dog before that happens. All the good girls are going to turn their noses up just like he is at Chelsea.

"You didn't really get her on her knees in the trees earlier, did you?" He nods toward where she's still dancing with Shane and my heart squeezes painfully in my chest.

"I'm not one to kiss and tell, Mase."

"Only because you don't kiss 'em but you always get sucked and tell."

Shrugging, I cast my eyes over the others, looking for some girls to watch who don't make me want to murder anyone. "Nothing to tell. She sucked, I came. Dare done."

"Bullshit. She wouldn't touch you with a ten-foot barge pole after the way you've treated her. And to be honest, I don't blame her."

"I don't need your opinion about this. Surely you've got enough of your own issues to be worrying about what I'm doing. After all, your girl's sucking *his* cock tonight instead of yours."

"She's not my fucking girl."

"Exactly, and that's the whole problem, isn't it?" He blows out a calming breath. It should be enough to stop me baiting him, but I'm in full-on asshole mode tonight. "I don't even know what you see in her. She's nothing special."

He turns his murderous eyes to me, they're almost black with his anger. For a second I think he's going to come at me again. But at the last minute, he throws his beer bottle down the beach and climbs to his feet.

"Fuck you, Jake. Fuck. You. When this all blows up in your face don't come crawling to me."

He storms off, going to join some of the other guys

in the team. My eyes narrow on the Rosewood Bears jersey below me, and fury fills my veins. All of this is her fault. My life was...fine before she showed her face. Now I can't escape the anger of my past like I was once able to and my best friend since childhood just turned his back on me.

All. Her. Fault.

And I'm going to make sure she fucking well knows it.

16

AMALIE

The bright dawn sunlight filters through the thin fabric of the tent and when I come to, I realise that I'm hot and seriously uncomfortable. Trying to move, I soon figure out why that is. Shane is wrapped around me like a freaking snake, his arm hanging over my ribs, the weight causing an ache through my chest. The ground we're on, after giving up the air mattress to Camila and Noah is solid and I've got a lump of sand pressing into my hip.

Trying my best to slide from his hold, my arse rubs against his crotch. A low moan rumbles up his throat, his length grows against me and his arm tightens. I panic. There's no way I want him waking up and discovering we're in this position. Every time I look at him, his eyes darken with desire that has my stomach knotting for all the wrong reasons. The last thing I need is for him to think I wanted this.

Once I think he's fallen back asleep, I try moving

again. He had much more to drink than me last night, almost everyone did. I was more concerned with keeping alert in case Jake decided to give me another visit and to really finish off trying to ruin my night. Thankfully, his burning stare from the other side of the beach was all I was subjected to. He needs to be careful, if I were any other girl, I might start to think his constant attention meant something other than hate. I mean, who in their right mind spends all night staring at a girl they supposedly hate so much when they could be having fun with their friends? Jake Thorn, that's who.

A shiver runs down my spine at the thought alone.

Feeling confident, I go to lift Shane's arms off me but I still the moment I hear his hushed voice.

"What are you doing? Go back to sleep." Dropping his arm once again, he pulls me back tighter against him. Every muscle in my body tenses as his morning wood presses harder against my arse then before.

Nothing about this is right, and it only goes to prove that nothing is ever going to happen between us, no matter how much he might seem to want it. Shane and I are only ever destined to be friends.

"I'm sorry, I really need to pee."

"Really? Now?"

"Really." He allows me to lift his arm again and I quickly jump away from his body.

"Be quick."

I don't respond because anything I might say to ensure he stays where he is would be a lie.

I wasn't lying when I said I needed the toilet, but I have no intention of getting back inside that tent.

Pulling the zip shut, I cast my eyes around the beach and my breath catches. The bonfire's still glowing, and it's surrounded with passed-out bodies of varying array of dress and empty beer bottles.

There are going to be some serious hangovers when they all start waking up.

Tugging down the bottom of Shane's shirt, I make my way across the sand and sadly, in the direction of the football team so I can make use of the actual facilities. There's no way in hell I'm going back in those trees, especially when the sun is only just starting to rise.

My steps slow when I approach a familiar sleeping body. I almost laugh to myself when I realise he's still facing toward where I was. Creepy fucker.

Taking a risk, I stand there for a few seconds taking him in. He looks much less vicious in his sleep. The almost constant scowl has gone and his forehead isn't creased in anger. He just looks normal, no... beautiful.

Shaking the crazy thought from my head, I lower my gaze, taking in his sculpted chest and abs before his V lines disappear into his jeans.

His tattooed arm moves and I almost jump a mile. My heart pounds and I immediately back up. The last thing I need while my head's lightly pounding from last night's beer and still a little sleep-fogged is to deal with a hungover Jake.

My legs move of their own accord and I find myself

practically running toward the toilets and away from any danger.

As I expected, the toilets are deserted although the evidence that there's been a party is everywhere. Bottles and shot glasses are all over the countertops as well as discarded makeup and dirty wipes while a perfectly good bin sits beneath it all. There's nothing suggesting it was them, but my mind immediately holds Chelsea and her posse of cheerleaders responsible.

Lowering myself to the toilet, I drop my head into my hands. I have no intention of going back down the beach. I need to find a way to get home and away from the disaster this place is going to be when everyone starts coming back to life. The majority of people here I doubt will even notice I've left.

I wash my hands without looking up, I'm afraid of what I'll see when I do. Over the past couple of months, I've had to stare at my broken reflection and I've just about had enough of the sad, pathetic look in my eyes that I know has returned. *Returned?* I'm not sure it ever actually left. More like morphed into a different kind of misery. One where I've mostly accepted, although not dealt with, the loss of my parents but hate the life I've now been thrown into. I prayed that I could start at Rosewood high, blend into the background, graduate and move on. But it seems that was a little too much to ask. While I might have found myself a couple of friends, I've made one much worse enemy and I can't see him letting up anytime soon. He's intent on ruining my life here and something tells me that he's not going to stop until he gets what he wants. The only thing I can try to do now is to not show that his actions and vile words affect me.

I am better than the bitter person he could turn me into. My gran deserves for me to be strong and not to bring more drama down on her shoulders. My parents would expect no less than for me to laugh in the arsehole's face. I deserve so much more than this.

With my shoulders a little wider, I walk out of the public toilets with a new lease of life. The sun makes me wince and I allow myself a couple of seconds to enjoy the warmth of it on my face. I'm not used to this kind of weather and I hope it's not something I'll take for granted too soon.

Looking down at my bare feet, I suck in a deep breath and prepare for the painful walk home. I know that I should go and wake the others in the hope of a ride, but the thought of having Shane pull me back down to our little bed and wrap his arm around me is enough to keep me moving. I really don't want to lead him on, but it seems that he's intent on seeing something that isn't there.

I'm not one-hundred percent sure on the way home, but I figure as I get farther inland that I'll start recognising stuff and eventually figure it out. If it weren't so early, or if some arseholes hadn't stolen all our stuff, I could have rung Gran for help but that option is out too.

Thankfully, it's early enough that hardly any cars pass me, and only one has beeped at me so far. I understand why, I'm clearly doing some kind of walk of shame wearing only a Rosewood Bear's jersey that exposes almost all of my legs.

An unsettling shiver runs down my spine knowing what a stupid decision this was. This town is pretty quiet, but that doesn't mean there isn't some nutcase out prowling the streets waiting for their next prey to almost fall into their lap. I'm the perfect target right now.

The rumble of an engine slowing behind me vibrates through my body and my heart starts to pound a little faster.

It could be anyone, a rapist, murderer. Images of what could be about to happen to me play out in my mind like all the films I've seen over the years. My palms sweat and my muscles prepare to run as the car gets ever slower behind me.

Eventually, my fear gets too much and I have to look over my shoulder. The moment the passenger of the car becomes clear, a laugh falls from my lips.

"Are you shitting me?" I ask as I continue walking.

"Get in, Brit," Jake barks through the open window.

"Fuck you."

"Get. In. The. Fucking. Car. Now."

"Fuck. You."

His nostrils flare at my defiance and his lips press into a thin line. He's jolted forward as the car accelerates and I breathe a sigh of relief. That is until the car abruptly stops slightly in front of me and the passenger door is thrown open.

Turning on my tender feet, I go to take off running but strong, tattooed arms wrap around my waist. I still on contact and gasp in surprise when the entire length of his body presses against my back.

"I said, get in the fucking car," he growls, his voice is terrifying. My body trembles, there's no way he misses it and I curse myself for allowing him to feel my fear right now.

Before I get to argue, my feet leave the floor and I'm carried toward the car where Ethan holds the back door open to allow Jake to throw me in.

I squeal as I fly toward the leather seat, quickly scrambling so I can make my escape before the car moves, but when I sit up, I find Jake staring down at me. His eyes are dark and angry but there's a smug smirk playing on his lips.

"Let me the fuck out."

"Feisty this morning, aren't you?" His head tips to the side like he's trying to figure me out and fuck if it doesn't make him look even better. Heat unfurls in my belly as I go to force him out of the way. He sees what I'm planning and before I get a chance to do anything, he's leaning into the car, hands on the seat behind me, caging me in.

He doesn't say anything for the longest time. Instead, his eyes bounce between mine before dropping down to my lips. I bite down on my bottom one, my nails digging into the leather beneath me.

"What the fuck is your problem?" I seethe, hoping to get him out of my face and looking at me like he is right now.

An unamused chuckle falls from him. "My problem? I've got a fucking million, *sweetheart*. But right now it's that you're walking along the side of the road looking like a whore who's been kicked out after a good night."

"Sorry, am I bringing the tone of the area down a few notches?" I ask, and by the darkening of his eyes and the grinding of his teeth, I'd say it only fuels his anger. He wants me to argue, he doesn't know how to respond to me basically agreeing with him.

"Your night with Dunn and his small cock so disappointing that you had to run?" All the air leaves my lungs as he leans closer, his lips only millimeters from mine. His scent fills my nose and I can't help wondering how he smells so damn good after a night on the beach. My eyes focus on the darkening bruise on his cheek and the cut on his lip. I wonder who was on the other end of that fist? They should have done a better job. "Did you spend the whole time thinking of me? Thinking about how I'd fill your pussy to the max and bring you more pleasure than you've ever known."

My stomach knots and I try convincing myself it's with disgust but I'm not stupid and I hate myself for my reaction to him.

"Leave me alone." I try to keep my voice strong but neither of us miss the crack toward the end.

"You don't mean that. I see the way your eyes dilated when I got close to you. You want this. You might hate me like I do you, but you can't deny that you want me to fuck you."

"Get the fuck away from me." I try again but I know it's pointless. My words mean nothing to him.

"Me fucking you wouldn't achieve what you want. You want pleasure, but all I've got for you is pain, baby."

"Enough, Thorn," Ethan barks from the front seat and Jake pulls back a little, allowing me to suck in a few much needed breaths.

"Pain, Brit," he whispers menacingly. "Pain is all I've got for you."

I reach for the handle the second he slams the door shut, but it's useless, they've locked me in.

"Where are you taking me?"

"Home," Jake barks.

I want to ask why. If he hates me so damn much like he keeps expressing, then why not just leave me to cut my feet to shreds on the pavement? But I keep my lips sealed shut and with my arms folded over my chest. I sit back and watch the scenery pass as we head toward home.

"How'd you know where I live?" I didn't think to tell him the address when Ethan pulled the car away from the curb, but not long later he's bringing it to a stop outside my gran's house.

"We know everything that happens around here."

"Riiight. Well, thanks for the lift, I guess. I'd like to say it was a pleasure but...it wasn't."

"Should have left you to be fucking abducted," comes from the passenger seat.

"Ignore him," Ethan says. "He's PMSing or some shit."

A smile almost makes it to my lips as I push the door open. I bite back the urge to thank them properly because they really did rescue me when they could have left me to find my own way, but instead I slam the door and storm toward Gran's bungalow.

I really don't want to ring the bell and wake her up, but I don't know any other way to get inside without my keys. I could really do without all the questions that are going to come with me standing at her front door looking like I am.

With a wince, I press my finger down on the button and the ring sounds out through the house. I'm just starting to think it hasn't woken her when movement by the window to my left catches my eye seconds before the door's pulled open.

"Amalie, what on earth…" Her words are cut off by the loud rumble of an engine behind us. Her eyes lift from mine and she smiles as the car pulls away and disappears down the street.

"I'm so sorry to wake you. You can go back to bed."

"I was awake anyway. What's happened? Where's Camila? Why are you wearing a Bear's shirt?"

"I need coffee first," I say, shutting the door behind me and heading toward the kitchen.

17

JAKE

My body knew the moment her eyes were on me. Fire burned in my belly and my blood turned to lava under her intense scrutiny. As much as I wanted to open my eyes and scare the shit out of her, my need to know what the hell she was about to do was bigger. I expected her to hurt me after everything yesterday. I've got no doubt that she knows it was us who stole their tent and all their stuff.

To my surprise, she just stood there staring.

Coldness engulfed me when she eventually walked away and I knew I couldn't fight it any longer, I had to see her.

I regretted it immediately when my eyes ran up her long legs until they found the bottom of his fucking jersey she was still wearing. The fire raged within me knowing that he's spent the night with her. That motherfucker should have been warned she was off limits, yet he still does whatever the fuck he wants. Same as how he spends his time with his dumb ass friends instead of with his team like the rest of us. We all know where our loyalties lie, but Shane Dunn? He needs to be taught a fucking lesson and I've got the perfect ammunition. He's got a weakness for the new girl and I'm about to use it against him.

"Where to now?" Ethan asks after we've watched her walk into her Gran's house. Waking him up and demanding we follow her was probably a dumbass move, but I couldn't ignore the fact I'd seen her leave the bathrooms and head off toward home wearing only that fucking jersey and no damn shoes. I might want to hurt her, but I'll be fucked if I'm letting anything else happen to her.

"Aces."

"You wanna swing back by the beach for Mason?" I think back to our argument last night and I know he wouldn't come. He made his feelings very clear and as much as it might hurt, I'm not fucking bowing down to him right now. He might think he knows what my life's like, what goes on in my head but he doesn't know the half of it. So what, he knows what my issue with her is? That means nothing.

"Na, he's got plans."

"Wanna talk about it?"

Glancing over at him, I lift a brow.

"Fine. Fine. I was just offering."

"Just buy me coffee and we're good."

Dropping into our usual booth, silence descends as we wait for the waitress to come over.

"That game last night was epic."

Jesus, was that only yesterday? Being on the field feels like a million years ago already.

"It was a great start to the season."

"The fuck, Thorn? You're our captain. Our quarterback. You're meant to be even more excited about our first win than any of us."

"I am excited. I just don't want to get ahead of myself. This isn't the first time the Bear's have won the first game and crashed out soon after. I'm just gonna take each one as it comes."

"I get that, but shit, a little celebration wouldn't go amiss."

"Don't sulk, Ethan. It doesn't suit you." He flips me off as the waitress comes back with coffee. "How'd you get on with your girl last night? She cave in the end?"

"No." His point stays firmly in place. "You?" He was either too drunks to remember he asked me this last night or quite rightly didn't believe me.

"Yeah, man. You know I always get the girl."

"You got the new girl on her knees?" The shock in his voice should be enough to make him question me, but he never does.

"Something like that," I mutter, not wanting to outright lie to him.

"Daaaamn. That definitely deserves breakfast." Two plates full of sweet pancakes and salty bacon are dropped in front of us right on cue and my mouth waters.

———

"You didn't come home last night," my aunt hollers across the yard as I head toward my front door.

"And?" I bark back, it's not usually like her to give a shit about what I'm doing, hence the reason I've been banished to a trailer in the backyard.

"Just worried is all." *Yeah, fucking right she is.* She's probably more concerned that the money she gets for putting up with me will stop if I fuck off. As much as I'd love to do just that, I've not got enough money and she damn well knows it.

"I'm in one piece, as you can see." Fury at her pathetic attempt to look like she cares starts to bubble within me. "Did you need anything else?" I ask through clenched teeth.

Some movement behind her catches my eye and Poppy comes to stand in the doorway and looks between the two of us, her brows pinched together.

"Okay, well..." My aunt trails off before disappearing inside, shaking her head.

Giving Poppy a weak smile at best, I turn away and let myself into my trailer. None of this is her fault, it's not like she asked for me to be shoved into the middle of her happy family all those years ago.

Throwing the small bag I dragged from Ethan's truck a few minutes ago on my bed, I pull my shirt over my head, drop my shorts and march toward the bathroom. I need rid of the sand that's coating my body and reminding me of everything that happened over the past few hours.

The dribble of water from the showerhead does little to release the tension locking my shoulders tight.

Standing with my hands on the wall in front of me, I allow the water I do have to run down my back. I squeeze my eyes shut and regret it instantly. The image of her terrified eyes as I leaned over her in the car are right there, taunting me. Since the day she fucking turned up all she's done is fucking taunt me. Everywhere I look, every time I close my eyes, there she is bringing back everything I try to forget, teasing me with her body and reminding me that she's the reason Mason told me to fuck off last night. We've never fallen out. Yeah, we've thrown plenty of punches over the years but never has it ever come to what it did last night.

Her face fills my mind, the darkening of her eyes as I leaned in closer, the way they dropped to my lips like there was even the slightest fucking chance I was going to kiss her. Her floral scent, even after a dip in the sea and a night on the beach filled my nose and fuck if it didn't make my mouth water, making me wonder how bad that kiss might be.

My cock swells and twitches, catching my eye. Dropping one arm, I fist the length with an almost painful grip. Holding my weight against the wall with one arm I pump my cock, reveling in the escape as my mind empties and my body chases mind-numbing pleasure.

My balls draw up and as I come into the shower tray only one face fills my mind. It immediately ruins any high I might have just found.

Punching the wall in front of me so it leaves a decent dent, I growl out my frustration. How is that bitch managing to bury herself so damn deep under my skin when all I want is to get rid of her.

"What the hell are you doing?" I bark the second I find Poppy sitting on my couch. I'm not surprised, I pretty much expected it after she heard the exchange between her mom and me earlier.

"Just checking in and I brought you some supplies." She nods over to the two bags full of stuff on the counter. I don't need her bringing me stuff from the house, I'd actually rather buy my own food, but she insists that it's what her parents should be doing for me, so she makes it happen.

The corner of my lips twitch when I find a bottle of vodka at the bottom of the bag. "How'd you sneak this out?"

She shrugs, her face dropping. "Just took it after they went shopping last. They're so busy arguing that they probably even forgot they bought it."

My heart aches for her and her situation. I might fucking hate living here but I think I've actually got the better end of the deal being out here away from it all.

"You could keep it. Go out and have some fun."

Screwing up her face in disgust, she says, "No, it's okay. You can keep it. I'll stick to beer thanks."

I can't help laughing at her as I twist the top and take a swig, it makes her face twist even more.

"You should probably water it down with something."

"Yeah, I probably should."

I unpack everything else she brought me before falling down beside her. I used to sneak whatever she gave me back into the house but ever since I got caught and they thought I was actually stealing the shit I decided to stop. I don't want Poppy in trouble for doing something nice for me.

"So, how was Dash?" She tucks her legs beneath her and looks at me excitedly.

"It was..." I trail off as I try to decide what last night was. *Frustrating, painful, a total let down...* "It was fun, you'll love it when it's your turn."

"I can't wait. Another step closer to getting out of this shithole."

"You and me both, kid." She frowns and her lips part ready to rip me a new one for using the nickname she hates, but she obviously decides against it.

"You got homework to do?"

"Probably," I admit.

"I'll go get mine, we'll do it together. We need the grades if we're ever going to get out of here."

I want to say no. To send her back up to her house to leave me to wallow in self-pity alone but the sparkle in her eye at the idea of spending the afternoon here with me is too much to refuse and I find myself going in search of some actual fucking homework as she runs to the house. *Well, this will be a fucking novelty.*

18

AMALIE

"Amalie, you've got a visitor," Gran calls.

Closing the lid of my laptop, I place it on the bed beside me and climb off in search of who the hell's come knocking. I assume it's Camila since I ran away from them all this morning, although why Gran wouldn't just send her down to my room is a little weird.

I understand why when I round the corner and my visitor comes into view.

"Mason?" I ask, thinking that I must be seeing things. Why the hell is he at our front door? Then a thought hits and fire rages through me. "If you're here to do his dirty work, then you can think again. Just because you follow him around like he's God it doesn't mean I'll bend at his commands."

Gran blanches beside me but slowly starts to back away and I'm grateful she's going to allow me to fight my own battles.

"What? No, no. He has no idea I'm here."

"Okay. So why are you here?"

"I've got all your stuff in my car. Thought you might need it."

"Why?" I narrow my eyes at him, not trusting one bit that he's just being nice. Jake and his crew don't do nice.

Putting his hands up in defeat, he holds my eye contact. "Just being nice, I swear. Jake's acting like a jumped up asshole. You don't deserve that, so I thought it was time to do the right thing."

"Okay," I say, still not wanting to trust him as far as I could throw him.

"Come give me a hand?"

"Sure." Slipping on a pair of flip-flops I'd left by the front door, I follow him out to his car.

"I've got Camila's stuff too, would you mind taking that?"

"Why don't you take it to her. You know where she lives, right?" I've no clue if this is the case or not, but I'm desperate to know what the story is between the two of them.

"I don't think she'll take too kindly to me turning up unannounced. It'll be better if you take it." His shoulder slumps a little as he says this, only serving to make me even more suspicious of what their deal is with each other.

We both grab armfuls of bags and head back toward Gran's.

"Would you both like a drink? I've made cookies."

"I should really get go—"

"You can stay for a few minutes, can't you?" The

words are out of my mouth before I have time to decide if I mean them or not, but having him here and seemingly willing to help me, I want to make the most of it. Who knows what information I could glean from my enemy's best friend.

"I'll leave you to it," Gran says, grabbing one of her cookies and disappearing into the living room.

The tension's heavy between us as I make two coffees and lead Mason out onto the patio.

"Why are you doing this?"

"Because you don't deserve any of that shit?"

"Yet up until now, you've been a part of it. So what gives?"

"For the record, I never agreed with anything he did."

"So why follow? Just because he's your captain doesn't mean you need to follow him around like a sheep."

"Trust me, I know. He's just been my best friend forever, and it's always been the two of us. Sometimes it's easy to forget maybe those closest to you don't have other's best intentions at heart."

Sipping on my coffee, I allow the words he just said to register.

"So what's this then? Peace offering?"

"I guess."

Silence descends once again as we both look out over Gran's garden.

"What's the deal with you and Camila?"

His body visibly tenses beside me as he blows out a shaky breath. That alone tells me that I'm right and that there's a definite story there. "There is no deal. We were friends, now we're not."

"Hmm..."

I keep my eyes on the flowers ahead of me but that doesn't mean I don't know the second his stare turns on me. "What does that mean?"

"Nothing. She just said the exact same thing."

"That's because it's true."

"Why aren't you friends any longer?"

"I didn't come here to talk about my life." His voice is suddenly colder, telling me that he really doesn't want to talk about this.

"Okay, so tell me why your best friend hates me so much then."

"Not my story to tell. If he wants you to know then he'll have to tell you himself."

"Well... that's helpful."

"Sorry. I might not agree with him, but that doesn't mean I'll be going behind his back."

"Like being here right now? I'm assuming he has no idea you're here or returning our stuff."

"Uh... not exactly."

"So seeing as you know him so well, what's your advice? How do I get him off my case so I can just get on with my life?"

His hand comes up to rub his jaw as he thinks. "You're under his skin more than he'll ever admit and I don't think he realises that it's not for the reason he thinks."

"Wow, that helps," I say with a laugh.

"Just don't let him walk over you. Stand up for

yourself. He'll respect that."

"I don't need his respect," I snap.

"No, but he needs to know you're strong. That you can look after yourself and handle things when needs be."

Narrowing my eyes at him, I try to read between the lines but really, I've got no idea what he's trying to tell me. "That cryptic message is all you're giving me, isn't it?"

"Like I said—"

"It's his story to tell. Got it."

His phone starts ringing in his pocket and he uses it as the excuse he needs to escape my questions.

"Something I should know about?" Gran asks, wiggling her eyebrows suggestively once I've seen Mason out.

"No, really not."

"Aw that's a shame. He's a good-looking boy. If I were forty years younger." I shudder on the inside, but I clearly don't manage to keep my disgust from my face because she starts laughing at me. "I'm kidding, I'm kidding. I think," she shouts as I turn my back on her and start back toward my bedroom with all mine and Camila's stuff. "You're totally allowed to date, by the way," I hear seconds before shutting my door.

Groaning, I drop everything into the corner and fall down onto my bed.

Grabbing my phone, I make the call I've been dreading. She's going to want answers and I'm not sure I'm ready to explain.

"I've got your stuff," I say, interrupting Camila when

she starts demanding to know where I went this morning the second she answers her home phone. I feel bad about making her worry but even after my encounter with Jake, I know I made the right decision in leaving. Last night might have been bearable when there was alcohol coursing through my system, but waking up pretty much sober with Shane wrapped around me was a big enough sign that I didn't belong there.

"What? How?"

"Mason just dropped it all off. So I guess our suspicions were right about it being them who took it all."

"Why did he bring it back? That was *nice* of him." She says the words as if he's not capable of doing something like that and it only makes my curiosity grow more.

"I just need to shower then I'll come around to pick it all up. Fancy a milkshake?"

"I can't, I've got an English lit paper to write."

"Oh come on, you've already bailed on me once today."

The sadness in her voice forces me to agree. "Okay fine but only for an hour because I've got to get this done."

"Fine. See you in a bit."

Camila pulls up outside Gran's house a little over thirty minutes later. After filling her boot with her stuff, we head toward Aces. I try convincing her to go somewhere else, thinking about how half the school seems to hang out there but she won't have any of it.

Thankfully, he's not there. There are a few faces I recognise from the school halls and Camila says hello to a couple but we're able to find a booth in peace.

"Shane thinks you left because of him. Did you?" Camila blurts out after sucking down half of her milkshake.

"Yes and no."

"Why? You two seemed to be getting along really well last night."

"Yeah, we were... as friends. Then I woke this morning with him wrapped around me and his..."

"Cock?" Camila supplies helpfully.

"Yeah, that, pressing into my arse."

"I love the way you say *arse*," she says, mimicking my accent. "Sorry, sorry. Not important right now. So he was hard? What do you expect from a teenage boy when a girl's in touching distance?"

"It's not that. I'm just not interested and I don't want him to start thinking there could be more. There won't be."

"You sound so sure."

"That's because I am."

"You barely know him."

"I know enough to know that he doesn't do it for me."

"Shame. I was totally hoping we could double date. So who does do it for you? Don't tell me you need someone a little more... asshole-y."

My eyes almost pop out of my head at what she's suggesting.

19
————

AMALIE

"Hey," Poppy calls as she heads toward the bench I'm sitting on waiting for her. "You had a good day?"

I think back over the last few hours. It started off pretty well when Camila turned up with fresh donuts, she said they were a peace offering after the 'joke' she played Friday night. It wasn't necessary, but I wasn't going to refuse a sugary treat first thing on a Monday morning. My day soon started to go downhill the second I spotted Jake across the car park the moment she pulled into a space. One look into his eyes and I may as well have been back in Ethan's car on Saturday morning. My stomach knotted, my fists clenched and my temperature soared. Camila noticed where my attention was and immediately dragged me off in the other direction as she instructed me to ignore him. If only it was that easy.

"Yeah, it was fine." Pushing images of him aside. "Yours?"

"I had a surprise pop quiz in Math. I thought surprises were meant to be good things," she says with a roll of her eyes. "Plus a massive lab report to write up for biology. Nothing like easing into the new year gently. Come on, my car's this way."

I follow behind while Poppy continues chatting away about her day and before long we're pulling out of school and heading toward wherever she lives.

Her house sits on the boundary between the east and west parts of town. The building itself looks like it should belong on the wealthier east side with its colossal size, but the area most definitely looks like the west side.

"Wow, your house is stunning."

"We're pretty lucky to have this much space. I'm sure it's nothing compared to what you had in England." The reminder of home is like a punch to the chest. She's right, my parent's house in Chelsea was opulent and massive but it was just a house.

"I guess," I mutter sadly. "It's different here though. We could never make use of the outdoor space like you can."

The second she pushes the front door open we're met by a loud shout and the vibrations from a slamming door somewhere upstairs.

"Shit."

Footsteps pound down the stairs before a very pregnant and very stressed woman reveals herself.

"Mom, is everything okay?"

"Of course, sweetheart. Hi, I'm Tammi, Poppy's

mom," she says turning to me with a wide, fake smile on her face.

"Hi, nice to meet you."

"Amalie's just come over to work on a project with me."

"That's fantastic. Why don't you both go and work outside. I'll bring you out some snacks in a few minutes."

"Thanks, Mom." Poppy turns to me. "Do you want to go and find a seat. I just need to run up to my room quick and grab my stuff."

"Sure."

"It's just this way, sweetie," her mum calls as she walks off, so I follow. Making my way through the house it's obvious that although it's huge, they don't really have the money to keep up with maintaining it. "Soda okay?"

"Perfect, thank you."

"Just grab a seat anywhere, I'm sure Poppy won't be long."

As I step out into their back garden, the late summer sun makes me squint and I pull my sunglasses down from the top of my head. Glancing around, I take in the few flowers that are dotted around but the most eye-catching thing is the pool. The blue water glitters in the sun and my body practically begs me to strip down and dive in.

Not being able to resist the temptation, I slip off my shoes and go to sit on the edge. The water is so warm after the summer of sun and I sigh in delight as it laps at my calves.

Resting on my palms, I tip my head back and close my eyes. The sound of birds and the rustling of the trees in the distance is so relaxing, it makes me wish Gran had this. I could lose a lot of time doing just this.

Just when I think I'm as relaxed as I possibly could be without lying on a float in the middle of the pool, a voice sounds out around me.

"What the fuck?"

My spine goes ramrod straight. I don't need to turn to know exactly who it is but what the hell is he doing here? Has his obsession with ruining my life now extended to stalking me?

I don't do anything, just pray that he'll leave as quickly as he arrived, but I'm not so lucky because in seconds his woodsy scent fills my nose and his body burns my hyperaware skin.

His eyes run down the side of my body and down my legs to where they're dangling in the water.

"Why?"

His vague question is enough to have me turning to look at him. I take in his creased forehead as he frowns at me like I can't possibly be here, his pursed lips and tired eyes.

When I don't respond, he continues. "Why? Why are you always fucking here?" He taps at the side of his head making me think that it's not my actual presence that's irritating him so much. "Everywhere I fucking turn, there you are, reminding me of everything, fucking me up like no years have passed."

My eyes narrow as I try to piece together what he's saying, but he might as well be talking gibberish.

His chest heaves as he stares at me, his eyes flitting around my face almost like he's committing my features to memory, but that really can't be the case as he's so fed up of me.

He reaches out and I gasp in shock as his hand lands on my lower back and pushes just enough to have my butt sliding across the tile beneath me and toward the water's edge.

"Jake," I squeal, my fingernails digging into the edge in an attempt to keep me out of the pool.

"Give me one good reason why I shouldn't."

"Because," I squeak, scrambling to come up with a reason. "Your cousin's about to come back." My brain suddenly puts two and two together after what Poppy said about supporting her cousin at the football game Friday night.

The pressure at my back reduces and the long breath he blows out tickles down my neck, making my nipples pebble beneath my vest.

"You need to stay out of my fucking way."

"Trust me, I'm not trying to get in your way."

His fingers grasp my chin and I'm forced to turn to look at him once again. He leans in so our noses are almost touching. "Then why are you always fucking here?"

I open my mouth to respond but another voice fills my ears.

"Jake, what the hell?"

At the sound of Poppy's voice, he gives my chin one final squeeze and stands, leaving me to drag some much-needed air into my lungs.

"Just saying hello to your new *friend*. You want to watch who you spend time with, Pop. People aren't always what they seem."

"What the hell is that meant to mean?"

"Just watch your back, yeah?"

No more words are said and after a second he turns on his heels and storms down the garden.

The air's heavy until he's vanished from sight and a bang sounds out.

"Are you okay?" Poppy asks, placing her books down on the table and walking over.

"Yeah, I'm fine."

"Is there something I should know about?"

I glance over at her kind face and I wonder how much I should tell her. Jake's a part of her family, I've no clue how close they are other than the fact she supports him on game nights.

"I don't think he likes me very much."

"Yeah, I got that vibe. Why?"

"I was hoping you could tell me that."

20

JAKE

Slamming the trailer door, I roar out my frustration into the empty space. I've managed to avoid her all fucking day. Every time I saw the flash of her platinum hair across the hallway, my fists clenched with my need to go over to her. I'm not sure exactly what I would have done if I did, I had no intention of finding out. But fuck if she doesn't call to me in a way no one else has before.

Then here she is, in my fucking garden.

My heart thunders in my chest with my need to go back out there and finish what I started. The image of her with her clothes soaking wet, her white vest see-through enough to give me a clue as to what she's hiding beneath makes my temperature soar.

"Fuck," I shout, the word echoing around me.

I make quick work of changing and grabbing my headphones before heading back out and to my make-shift gym. The trailer is right at the bottom of the garden and tucked into the mass of trees that separates this property from the bungalows behind. That's where my homemade gym lives. It's also my quiet place when I need to escape when things just get too much.

Climbing through the undergrowth, I stomp down some brambles that have grown since I was last in here until the small clearing opens up.

This place might not be anything like the gym we've got at school and it's a mile away from the one I sometimes go to with Ethan, but it does the same job. I've even now got an exercise bike that I took from someone's skip down the street over the summer.

Jumping, my hands wrap around the rough branch and I fight to pull my chin up. My muscles burn, reminding me that I haven't warmed up at all, but I don't give a fuck right now. I need to feel the burn, the pain that only I can cause. No one can tell me what to do here. I make the rules and push my own boundaries and limits.

I continue until my arms are trembling and begging for reprieve. Releasing my grip, I allow my feet to hit the floor once again, the ground crunching as I land on old sticks and fallen leaves.

Throwing my leg over the old bike, I turn up the tension.

Sweat pours from my skin as I push harder and harder. My head's filled with images of my past. I push my legs as fast as I can go as I try to escape. I picture her face the day she said goodbye and walked away from me. The way her lips were in an almost permanent smile because of the filler she'd had shoved in them, the ridiculous lashes that were stuck to her eyelids and her damn near yellow peroxide blonde hair. She was about as fake as she could probably get and I'm sure it's only got worse as the years have gone on.

I've done my best to steer clear of ever seeing her face again, but with the job she does, sometimes that isn't possible. I've always steered clear of opening any kind of magazines and walking away when any of the girls at school pull one out. If I have to ever see her face again, then it needs to not be when I have company. Thankfully the day I discovered her most recent career of choice I was alone in the safety of my trailer. No one was around to witness the fallout of that clusterfuck.

The music booms in my ears but I don't hear a word of it. I'm too focused on escaping the memories, the pain, the desperation I still remember all too well.

Almost every single one of my muscles tremble with exhaustion by the time I've finished. Pulling my sweat-soaked t-shirt from my body, I wipe my face and throw it over my shoulder as I head off in search of water.

Soft female voices drift down to me as I step toward my trailer and at the last minute, I change my mind and head toward the main house. I don't really have any desire to go inside but the temptation to torment her is too much.

When they come into view, they've both got their heads down, a pile of books, pens and notepads in front of them as they do their homework like good little girls. A little nagging voice in the back of my head shouts that it's probably something I should also be doing instead of filling my need for vengeance using the innocent new girl but that's all I seem to be able to think about these days.

"I hope you realize that nerds have no fun," I comment once I'm close enough for them to hear me clearly.

"And those who skip class end up flipping burgers. Problem?" Poppy says, her eyes coming up to meet mine, full of amusement. It might not be the first time she's mentioned my destiny being in a fast food joint.

A quiet whimper beside her drags my attention away, and I'm so fucking glad I do because New Girl is playing right into my hands. Her chin's dropped as her eyes roam over my naked skin. If it's possible, my body heats even more under her stare but I don't allow her to see any reaction from her.

"You about finished?" I bark, making Poppy blanch at my outburst.

Her cheeks flame red and I don't miss that it creeps down onto her chest and even as low as the swell of her breasts and she sheepishly looks back down at the book in front of her like nothing ever happened.

Falling down in the seat in front of her, I keep my attention on Poppy. "Any chance you could get me a bottle of water, Pops."

"I...uh..." she stutters, looking between the two of us. I understand her hesitation, I probably wouldn't leave her with me either.

"Please." I smile sweetly and lean forward, placing my elbows on my knees.

Moving my eyes away from Poppy as she hesitantly

gets up and leaves us alone, I stare at the bowed head in front of me.

"What? You shy all of a sudden? I didn't think whores got embarrassed."

"Fuck you," she spits, standing up so fast that the plastic chair she was sitting on goes crashing backward.

I stand, her breasts brushing against my chest where we're so close. Her breath catches at the same time some weird spark shoots through my veins.

"We've been through this. I don't fuck whores."

"Yeah, so you keep saying, but here you are. Again."

Fury bubbles within me at her referring to herself that way. It's irrational because I started it but still, I fucking hate it.

Standing only a few inches shorter than me, she stays stock still, her blue eyes boring into mine. The hate I've been putting on to her suddenly feels insignificant as other urges start to take over. It's easy to imagine that she's someone else at a distance. It's easy to picture another face and fake blonde hair, but up close she's just a girl who's just about as lost as I am.

My eyes drop from hers in favor of her lips and I start to imagine how sweet she actually might taste, how soft her lips might feel pressed against mine.

"Back off, Jake." The harsh sound of Poppy's voice is enough for me to break my stare.

Looking up, I find her in the doorway with the bottle I requested poised like she's about to throw it at me.

The mortified look on her face is enough to distract me, so much so that I miss the movement of arms in front of me and by the time her palms slam down on my chest it's too late.

I take a step back to try to steady myself but there's nothing there. My stomach jumps into my throat as I start falling. I just hear the sound of her evil chuckle before I hit the water and go under.

Fucking bitch.

By the time I resurface, she's kneeling down at the edge waiting for me with a shit-eating grin on her face. Pride swells in my chest. I think I may have underestimated this one. She's not as weak as I first thought her to be and it's only going to make this thing between us more fun.

"Oh, Brit. You just seriously fucked up."

"Is that right? Because as far as I see it, you're the one losing right no-ah!"

The sound of her scream before the splash might be the most satisfying thing I've ever heard.

She fumbles around, arms and legs flailing in her panic. I eventually take pity on her and reach out.

Her waist is so damn small that my fingers almost meet at her spine. I pull her up and she sucks in a lungful of air while simultaneously fighting to get away. That is until I pull her flush against me. The temptation of feeling her curves against my hard planes is too much.

Her hands come up to brush away the wet hair that's sticking to her face and the second our eyes connect she stops fighting.

My fingers tighten around her in my need to show her just how much she's fucked up my life. Close up like this, she's nothing like the woman who caused me the real pain, so I focus on the present. This girl's the reason my life's gone to shit this past week. She's the reason why Mason is still avoiding me and why my nights are filled with dreams of times in my childhood that I'd rather forget.

Leaning in, my rough cheek brushes against hers and her entire body shudders against me. "You want to fight dirty, Brit? I can guarantee that you're going to lose. You have too many weaknesses that I can exploit whereas nothing can touch me." My tongue runs around the shell of her ear and she gasps in shock, every muscle in her body locking up tight.

To outsiders, like my cousin who's stare I can feel burning into my skin, it might look intimate, like I'm whispering sweet nothings into her ear. Well... I guess I am whispering promises as such.

Her chest swells as she sucks in some strength to respond. "I'm not the weak, pathetic girl you think I am. I'm not going to bend over and take it."

"Maybe you should, it'll all be over quicker."

"I didn't think you fucked whores."

Her words make my breathing falter.

Wrapping the length of her sodden hair around my fist, I pull her head back so I can ensure her eyes stay on mine and I lift and press her into the pool wall. I'm confident that she has no idea her legs automatically come up to wrap around my waist, but the moment her heat lines up with my semi-hard cock I'm not going to point it out.

I press harder into her, ignoring the fact that she'll

know she's making me hard right now. I allow myself a few seconds to take her in. The darkness of her blue eyes giving away her anger and desire, the droplets of water that are littering her face and blending in with her freckles, her wet hair, pushed back from her flawless face. She's soaked yet there's no makeup running down her face, it only proves that she really is naturally this flawlessly beautiful.

"Don't," I warn, my voice deep and haunting, my mouth running away with me. "Don't ever call yourself that."

"But it's okay for you to?" Her voice is no more than a breathy whisper. My heart thunders and my cock threatens to go full mast knowing I'm affecting her as she is me.

"I do what I want, Brit. I thought you'd realized that by now."

My eyes drop to her lips because if that statement were actually true, they'd be pressed up against mine right now.

That realization is enough to make me let go and step back. I don't kiss girls. I use them for what I want and cast them aside. This right now, it confuses the fuck out of me and that only leads to more frustration.

"Amalie, are you okay?" Poppy calls. I spot her running toward the corner of the pool where I just was as sounds of water splashing fills my ears.

Jumping from the pool, I keep my back to both of them and begin to walk away to the sounds of their panicked voices.

"Hey, Brit," I shout over my shoulder just before I

know I'm out of sight. I don't wait for a response, the silence is enough to tell me that they're listening. "Remember, I never lose." And with those final words, I get the hell out of there and away from the girl messing with my head.

21

AMALIE

"Let's go and find you some dry clothes and then I think it's probably best we get out of here."

I couldn't agree more as I follow Poppy into the house and up to her bedroom.

My head spins with everything that happened in the last few minutes. I thought I was being smart pushing him when he was distracted but I should have known it would come and bite me in the arse, and if his warning as he walked away was serious then I think I may have just upped the ante where he's concerned.

A long sigh falls from my lips as we walk into Poppy's bedroom. "Bathroom's there if you want to go and dry off. I'll just find you something to change into."

"Thank you," I mumble, heading in the direction she pointed. She's not asked me any questions yet but one glance in her eyes and I know they're on the tip of her tongue.

I make quick work of stripping out of my sodden

clothes and drop them into the basin to wring out. Goosebumps cover my chilled skin but it does little to reduce the heat within my body. I should have hated the feeling of his palms burning into my skin, the pressure of his body being pressed tightly against mine. My head was screaming at me but my body had other ideas. There's something about that arsehole that calls to my body while in my head, I'm imagining a million ways to end him. It was confusing before he pressed the length of his body against mine and manipulated me into wrapping myself around him.

"Wanker," I mutter to myself, resting my palms on the basin and looking up into my darker than usual eyes. I hate him. I fucking hate him. Yet why do I have this constant need to try to dig just a little beneath the surface and find out what's really going on inside his head, what it was that really got his back up about me on my first day that he can't let go of.

"Here you go." Poppy's hand pushes inside the door and I take the clothes she offers. "I hope they fit."

"They're perfect, thank you."

Thankfully, Poppy and I aren't all that different body-wise although she is a few inches shorter than me. If this happened while I was with Camila, then I might have had issues.

I unfold a loose-fitting vest and a denim skirt before quickly sliding them on and wringing out my own clothes. Finding a hairbrush on the shelf above the basin, I make quick work of brushing through my wet, matted hair before piling it all on top of my head out of the way.

With my damp clothes in hand, I pull the door open, expecting to find Poppy waiting for me, only the room is empty.

Not really wanting to snoop around her house, I hesitate at the door but hearing sounds from downstairs, I make my way down.

I find Poppy gathering up our books from the table.

"I'm so sorry for ruining everything."

Turning to me, her eyes narrow in confusion. "You didn't ruin anything. He's the one with the issues. He's always been a little screwed, but that was... shit, I don't even know. You wanna get out of here?"

"Yes." The relief in my voice makes her laugh and once we both have our bags in hand, we head toward her car.

"Do you want to go home or..." She trails off.

"We've still got loads of work to do and I'm not sure I'm ready for all the questions yet," I say, knowing Gran will take one look at me in someone else's clothes and not let up until I give her answers.

"And you don't think I have any?" She chuckles making me groan. "Where do you want to go?"

"Anywhere but Aces."

"You got it."

I stare out the window as the car travels toward the seafront but luckily Poppy parks at the opposite end to Aces and once we've collected our stuff, she directs me to a small cafe that sits a little back from the sea.

"This place is cute." My eyes flit around the place thinking that I could easily step out of here and be back in London.

A long sigh leaves my lips. Poppy turns to me, her face full of sympathy like she knows exactly what I'm thinking.

"I thought you might like it."

We find ourselves a table and grab the menus, my stomach rumbling right on cue.

Once we've ordered, Poppy almost immediately pulls all the books out that she shoved into her bag before we left her house so we can continue where we left off. Or at least that's what I expect her to do so my stomach knots when she places her elbows on the top of everything and her eyes find mine.

"Go on then?" she prompts.

"What?"

"Don't give me what," she laughs. "You're sitting there in my clothes because my idiot of a cousin dragged you into our pool after you pushed him in. You can't tell me nothing's going on there. It was like the ultimate school ground flirting I've ever seen."

I scoff. "I can assure you that that was not flirting." My mind flicks back to the moment he stared down at my lips like he was going to kiss me, my temperature spikes at the memory but I push it down. I read that all wrong, surely.

"I'm pretty sure the tension between you was definitely sexual."

Someone at the next table glances over, my cheeks heat with embarrassment. "Shush. That was not what it was. He hates me. I've no idea why. Can we just forget all about it and get on with this?" I ask hopefully.

She's silent for a moment as I start to think that

maybe she'll allow the subject to drop. Sadly, I'm not that lucky.

"My cousin's a little..."

"Fucked up," I offer when she pauses.

"I was going to say cut off or distant, but that works. He hasn't had the best childhood. I know that's not an excuse," she adds quickly when I open my mouth to argue. "I think his perception of how to act normal at times is a little skewed. He acts out so he doesn't have to deal with his emotions or feelings, well I think that's what he does. I've never managed to make him talk about it."

"What happened to him?" The words fall from my lips before I have a chance to stop them.

"His mother's a total fuck up. I don't really know the whole story, I was too young to understand, and no one talks about her ever. Enough about him, we've still got a ton of work to do."

Relieved that she steers the conversation away from him, I grab one of the books she's been leaning on and we get to work.

Thankfully by the time Poppy drops me home, Gran's already gone out. Monday night is bingo night with her friends and I couldn't be more grateful that I get to have a few hours to myself as I attempt to dissect every moment of my afternoon. My head's a mess after those short few minutes with Jake in Poppy's pool. He was his usual arsehole self but there was something else. The seriousness behind his warning about me calling myself a whore, the way he stared down at my lips like he wanted to suck them into his mouth.

Stripping out of Poppy's clothes, I step under the shower and allow the warm water to wash away the scent of chlorine that still covers my skin from my unexpected dip and pray that it's enough to wash him out of my mind too, although I think that could be wishful thinking.

His final words as he walked away repeat in my head over and over as I lie in bed attempting to get some sleep. *"Remember, I never lose."* I don't doubt for a second that those words were true. He wouldn't hold the position he does at school if he dishes out empty threats. Every other student seems to have him on some kind of untouchable pedestal. The girls quite clearly want to shag him and the guys want to be him. Fuck knows why, he's a wanker. A shiver runs up my spine reminding me that although that might be true, he's a beautiful one. The image of him hot, sweaty and dripping in water is etched on the inside of my eyelids and when sleep eventually claims me, it's still right there, inspiring my dreams.

———

When I wake the next morning, it's with dread sitting heavy in my stomach. I've no idea why, it's like a premonition or something. But something about his final words still haunt me and I just know he's going to keep that promise.

Camila pulls up right on cue and once again there are fresh doughnuts sitting on the passenger seat.

"I accepted your apology, you know that, right?"

"Yeah, but they were so good yesterday that I couldn't help myself. Plus, Noah complained I didn't get one for him so..."

Picking up the box, I climb into the seat and rest them on my lap. "I'm not complaining," I say, grabbing one up and biting into it. The sugar immediately makes my mouth water, it's exactly what I need.

"How'd you get along with Poppy last night?"

"Fine."

"That good?" she says with a laugh.

Blowing out a sigh, I remember last night's events once more. "Did you know Jake's her cousin?"

"Yeah."

"And you didn't think to warn me?"

"I didn't think I'd need to. Why, what happened?"

Much to Camila's amusement, I recall the events of the previous night.

"You ended up in the pool?" she laughs.

"Yeah, I should have seen it coming, really. Pushing him was a stupid thing to do."

"So how'd it end?"

"With him warning me that he never loses. I think I've managed to up the stakes. Fuck knows what I've got heading my way."

"I'm sure it'll be fine. What exactly can he do?" By the slight wobble of her voice, it's obvious that even she doesn't believe the words that just fell from her mouth. She slows at a set of traffic lights and turns to look at me. "Don't be so worried. It's not like he's got any dirt on you. It'll just be pathetic schoolyard gossip whatever it is."

I mumble my agreement, but her words do little to ease the dread twisting my stomach the closer we get to school.

Everything's fine until about ten minutes before lunch. I'm in English lit, hiding at the back and getting on with the assignment we've been set when someone's phone goes off. The teacher barks at whoever it was but I ignore them and go back to what I was doing. That is until I feel eyes burning into me.

Looking up, I find three sets of eyes staring right at me, amused smirks playing on all their lips. Narrowing my eyes, I try to figure out what the hell's going on but before I get a chance to do anything, more eyes turn my way. My cheeks burn with everyone's attention on me.

"Class," the teacher snaps. "Pay attention. I'll be taking these in and grading them once the bell rings."

The majority of students turn back around and continue writing but a couple of the guys apparently find me much more interesting and their eyes stay on me. My skin prickles uncomfortably as their eyes run over me, checking me out.

The second the bell goes, I grab my paper, slam it down on the teacher's desk and attempt to get the hell out of there. Sadly, someone calls my name right before I make my escape. Turning to look over my shoulder, I find the amused eyes of one of the guys who was just staring at me. "You free this lunchtime? I could really do with a little release."

Students surrounding him splutter with laughter and a couple of his mates slap him on the shoulder, jostling him forward.

My brows draw together but the moment his eyes drop to take in my body once again, I run from the room. This is the exact kind of attention I was hoping to avoid.

Seeing as I'd promised Camila last week that I wouldn't spend my spare time hiding in the library, I head toward the cafeteria to meet her.

The second I step foot inside, silence descends as almost every head in the room turns to look at me.

What the fuck is going on?

"There she is," I hear a familiar voice say from behind me and when I turn, I find Camila running toward me. "Are you okay?" Her eyes are wide and she looks manic.

"Yeah... why? What's going on?"

"Have you checked your phone in the last ten minutes?"

"No, why?"

"Hey, Brit. How much do you charge for thirty minutes?" a male voice calls.

"Fuck. We need to get out of here."

"What the hell is going on?" I ask again. Camila looks up at me, her face tight with anger.

"Not here. Come on."

Her fingers thread through mine and she pulls until I fall into step behind her. Stares follow our every move and catcalls and random questions about my prices fill the hallway.

When she tugs me through the entrance to the library, I know things must be bad. She refused to allow me to hide in here anymore, yet here she is dragging me toward the back of the room to do exactly that.

"You need to start talking."

"Okay, so..." she hesitates, bouncing from foot to foot and worrying her hands in front of her.

"Camila, just spit it out." I want to say that I've probably already lived through worse this year, but I push any thoughts of my parents from my head.

"There's this photo that's basically been sent to every student in the school."

"Right?" Wishing she'd just get to the fucking point, I gesture for her to continue.

"It looks like it's you." She pulls her phone from her pocket and holds it up for me to see.

"What the..." My words trail off as I snatch it from her hand and stare down at the girl's head in the photo.

I know exactly when it was taken, I guess I could say I was there at the time but the top of the head I can see is most definitely not me.

"It's from Dash," I whisper.

"You're telling me that is you?" Camila's eyes widen to the point they might pop out of her head.

"No, that is not me with Jake's cock in my mouth."

"I didn't think so. Hang on, how do you know that's Jake in the photo?"

Letting my back hit the wall, I lower myself down until my arse touches the floor. Camila follows my move and is soon staring at me waiting for answers.

"I went into the trees for a pee."

She winces, realising that this is all a result of her 'joke.'

"I did my thing and on the way back I stumbled across Jake and some cheer hussy on her knees. That's her in the picture."

"Her hair's darker."

"It's not hard to edit that on Photoshop, Cam."

"Shit."

"Show it to me again." Reluctantly, she hands her phone over and I stare down at it. "You remember what I was wearing that night?"

"Of course, jeans and a t-shirt."

"You can see the skin of her shoulder under her hair. I was wearing a white t-shirt."

"Doesn't mean you couldn't have taken it off in a moment of passion."

"Wait, you're accusing me now?"

"What? No. I was just pointing out what everyone else will say. I knew this wasn't you the moment I saw it. I didn't know it was Jake, but even still, I didn't think you'd got that close to anyone since you arrived."

"Damn right I haven't and I intend on it staying that way, and I'm certainly not selling it like this suggests." I read the text again. *Brit sucks your crown jewels for a bargain price,* and then my fucking phone number.

I daren't pull it out of my bag and find out just how many horny guys think they're going to get lucky.

"This is a fucking nightmare. Why would he do this?" Camila asks, taking her phone back so I don't have to keep looking at it.

"Because he never loses."

Dropping my head into my hands, I focus on my breathing. How the hell am I meant to go out there and hold my head up high. Every student in the building thinks I'm a slut who drops to her knees for money and no amount of denying it is going to work. It's my word against his, their king. I stand no fucking chance.

"What classes do you have this afternoon?"

My head spins just thinking about what's going to happen when I step foot out of the safety of the library. "I've no idea but I'm pretty sure that whatever they are, that I'm not going to be in them."

"You're gonna skip?"

"What do you suggest I do?"

She shrugs. "You'll look guilty if you run from this."

"Let's be honest here, they'll all think I'm guilty no matter what. I could climb up on the school roof and plead my innocence and no one would hear a word. Jake Thorn rules this school and if he says I'm a whore, then that's what I'm going to be."

"You're going to let him win, just like that?"

"For now, yeah. Not sure what else I can do."

"This is bullshit."

"You're telling me." A laugh falls from my lips but there's no amusement in it.

22

JAKE

My need for revenge as I walked away from the pool dripping fucking wet was all-consuming. I managed to ignore the fact my cock was rock fucking hard after being pressed against her soft but toned body under the water and focused on my need to ruin her. She doesn't get to call the shots around here, that's my job and if she thinks she can humiliate me, even if it's only in front of Poppy, then she's got another thing coming.

Swinging the door open on my trailer, I stormed inside, my muscles still screaming after my workout and I head straight for the shower, my mind running a mile a minute trying to come up with how I'm going to end her.

In the end, I gave up brainstorming and pulled out what was left in the bottle of vodka Poppy gave me the other day and a fresh joint I stole from Ethan and lit it up.

The alcohol and weed running through my system helped to relax me, but the images of her wet body were still front and center of my mind.

Needing someone else to be the reason for my constant hard-on, I pulled out my phone and flicked through some of the photos I'd taken over the previous months. Some totally innocent, others not so much and it was those I needed. Faceless girls, soft curves and hot little mouths. That's what I need right now.

If I hit call on the right number, I've no doubt I could meet one in only minutes and get exactly what she's left my body craving.

I'm scrolling through the photos when one catches my eyes. It takes me a moment to remember when it's from. The head full of blonde hair as she quite obviously sucks on me is all I can see of her. My breath catches as the wrong blonde girl pops into my mind. My veins fill with lava just thinking about her and the effect she has on me.

Opening up my messages, I forward it to someone I know can help.

Can you Photoshop this chick's hair so it's a much lighter blonde.

The three little dots appear immediately.

Give me five.

Taking another swig straight from the bottle, I place my phone on my thigh and wait. It lights up in half the time he said and the result staring back at me is perfect. My cock weeps at the thought of it being the Brit on her knees choking on my cock.

I save the image and wait until the perfect time. I want to be around to witness the fallout and that won't be possible while I'm hiding out in this shithole that I call home.

Knowing the image is sitting on my cell is fucking torture. I almost hit send a million times before school the next morning, but I know it'll be pointless. I want to see her face when everyone thinks it's her. The thought of seeing her pain and embarrassment has my mouth watering and my muscles twitching. It's exactly what I need to settle the angry beast that's festering inside me.

———

"Mr. Thorn, where do you think you're going?"

"I've got shit to do," I shout over my shoulder as I head for the classroom door, leaving the rest of my classmates completing their task like good little children.

"You can't just walk off —"

The door slams behind me, cutting off whatever it was that she was going to say.

Walking into the deserted lunchroom, a couple of the ladies laying out lunch look up at me, but no one questions me. Sitting on top of our usual table, I pull my phone from my pocket along with the new SIM I picked up on the way here this morning. I spent most of first period loading it with all the numbers I'd need, thanks to Ethan handing over his own phone at my demand. He has the number of everyone worth knowing so I know this will hit as I intend. Plus, gossip goes around this place like wildfire on the best of days so I've no doubt that those whose numbers we don't have will have it forwarded to them. No one likes missing out on the latest Rosewood drama.

I quickly slip my usual one out and replace it with the new one. I'm fairly certain that everyone is going to know this has come from me, but I thought it probably best not to be totally blatant about it.

Opening up my messages, I find the image and select send to all. My thumb hovers over the send button. A moment of doubt hitting me, making me reconsider what I'm about to do to her but I picture the reason for all this. The woman who ruined me, Brit might not be her, not by a million years, but she stands for the same thing. She's from the same world and that's enough for me.

With anger beginning to fill my veins once again as I think about the poor little boy she abandoned, I tap the button. A shiver runs down my spine as realization of what I've just done hits me. If she didn't hate me already, then she will after this. Hopefully then she'll stay as far away from me as fucking possible and I can attempt to continue with my bullshit life.

Even though everyone's still in class, I start getting replies almost immediately and it's when I get my first inkling that this might have been a massive mistake.

She can suck on me anytime she likes.

Shit, I'm hard just looking, man.

Come to daddy.

My stomach knots at the thought of her touching someone else. Of someone else's fingers gripping her hair tightly as they fuck her mouth. I know the photo isn't actually of her, she'll know the truth too, but my guy did such a good job that everyone else will believe it's her. I know for a fact that the guys won't be looking that closely at the photo to spot any obvious issues.

Jesus. I'm so fucked.

My hands tremble slightly as I pull the new SIM from the back of my phone and shove it deep in my pocket, hoping that I'll be able to shove the memories of those replies down with it. It's only a few minutes later that the ruckus of students leaving classrooms and heading this way filters through the mostly silent cafeteria.

No one pays me any attention as they come piling in, they're too busy chatting with their friends or more importantly, staring at their phones and showing it to the people they're with.

My fists clench and my muscles burn knowing exactly what they're looking at and exactly what the guys are feeling as they do. They're picturing her with her full red lips wrapped around their cocks.

My heart pounds in my chest and my teeth grind with my need to walk over to every guy who thinks they're staring at my Brit.

My Brit.

"Fuck this shit." Jumping from the table I'm sitting

on, I storm toward the exit before the rest of the team or cheerleaders appear. The last thing I need is them trying to dig into what's wrong with me. As if I have a fucking clue. I'd like to know why I'm so screwed up just as much as they do.

23

AMALIE

I just about manage to keep the mask on my face until I step through the front door. Thankfully, Gran's out so she's not there to witness my meltdown the second I slam the door behind me.

"Motherfucker," I scream, my voice shaky with emotion that's bubbling up from the stress of the past hour.

How can he manipulate that photo to make everything think that's me? He's the fucking whore out of the two of us, not that anyone would ever look at him badly for his escapades.

My chest heaves as I suck in deep breaths and I desperately try to calm down. He doesn't deserve my tears.

I get myself a glass of water before heading toward my room. One look at the photo of my parents on my nightstand and the tears I'd banished instantly fill my eyes once again.

Perching my arse on the edge of the bed, I reach for the frame and run my finger over my mum's flawless face.

"Oh Mum," I sob. I'm fairly sure that no matter how much time passes, there are always going to be moments like these that all I need is a hug from her. I need the reassuring words that only a mother can give to tell me that everything's going to be okay. That I'm not about to become even more of a social outcast than I was already by being publicly humiliated by the school's bad boy.

What would she tell me to do? I wonder as I continue staring at the photograph. My dad would probably be threatening to go to his house and knock him into next week for treating his baby so badly, while my mum simultaneously calmed him down and supported me. Her reaction would be much less dramatic, telling me not to allow one boy to make me think less of myself when he's the one who should be embarrassed by his actions. She'd tell me that I'm better, stronger than this and to go out there with my head held high and allow people to think what they like because I know the truth.

It all sounds so good in my head but in reality, I want to hide and never show my face in that school again. I know that photo that's currently doing the rounds isn't of me, but everyone thinks it is.

Trying to shake the image of what I've left behind in the canteen from my head, I pull out a bikini top and a pair of shorts and head into the bathroom. If I'm going to spend the rest of the day hiding, then I might as well get a bit of a tan at the same time.

Grabbing my book and water, I leave my phone deep inside my bag, not wanting to even look at the kinds of messages I've probably received.

The only bit of the garden that's still in the sun is right at the bottom, so after dragging one of Gran's comfortable loungers down, I settle myself in the warm rays and try to block out the world.

I'm lost in my book and just as things are about to get interesting, the strangest noise hits my ears. It's almost as if someone's acting out the goings-on in my book with the heavy breathing and grunting that seems to be coming from the trees behind me.

Trying to ignore it, I go back to my book, but I can't block it out and end up re-reading the same sentence three times.

I sit there for a few more minutes but when the sounds continue, my curiosity gets the better of me. Putting my book down, I head toward the trees. This place is a kid's heaven, I can imagine all the dens that have been built down here over the years, it's almost a shame that most of the houses that run along the thick undergrowth are old people's homes.

My heart races as I descend farther into the shadows and I start thinking that this is probably the stupidest thing I've done in a while. I'm either about to stumble across a couple going at it or some ax murderer is going to finish me off. That would sure be a dramatic end to Jake and his stupid photo.

The panting continues and just when I'm convinced that I'm going to find a couple of teenagers stealing a moment of passion, I stumble across the real reason for the noise.

My eyes widen and my body stiffens as I watch a half naked, sweaty Jake pull his chin up to a tree branch above his head.

"Ugh," he grunts as he manages it, before lowering back down and repeating.

It might be dark in here with only a little sunlight filtering through the leaves above but the sweat running down his back glistens before soaking into his waistband that's sitting low on his hips.

My stomach twists and tingles fill my entire body. I want to say it's anger, this boy's got his heart set on ruining my life but I fear what I'm feeling right now is more than that.

I should turn to leave, he'd be none the wiser that I was even here but my body refuses to move.

My eyes stay locked on him as he pulls himself up so his chin hits the branch a few more times before he lets go with a growl and drops to the ground. Sticks snap and leaves rustle where his feet land.

I hold my breath, afraid of what's going to happen when he turns and finds me because it's inevitable.

He places his hands on his knees and sucks in a few breaths but even still, my legs stay put refusing to listen to my head and get the hell out of there.

It's not until he stands and turns that his eyes find me standing beside a tree like a stalker.

"What the fuck?" he barks, his eyes widening in fright and his hand coming up to cover his heart.

It's only now that my feet agree to move and I take a step back just as his eyes narrow in anger.

"What the fuck are you doing here? Shouldn't you be at school?"

My eyebrow quirks up. "Shouldn't *you* be at school drinking in all the praise from your posse after showing me for what I really am?"

"And what's that exactly?"

"A whore who sucks off anyone for the right price."

His chest swells as he sucks in a deep breath before releasing it on a growl. Then he's stepping forward toward me. I should probably be scared but for some reason I know that he's not going to hurt me. Not physically anyway.

"What did I tell you about calling yourself that?"

"It's a little late to be concerned about what people think of me, don't you think? The whole school is probably back there talking about what a slut I am while wanting to congratulate you on being able to get me on my knees mere seconds after meeting you. I hope you achieved whatever it was you were aiming for with that little stunt."

"Nowhere fucking near." His voice is so quiet that I'm not sure I actually hear right.

"What exactly is your problem with me, Jake? I've done nothing to you. All I did was turn up after having my life turned upside down. I don't deserve any of this bullshit from you and you know it."

"My problem. Oh, Brit, I have so many that I don't know where one ends and another begins."

Placing my hand on my hip, I jut it out, waiting because what he just said is nowhere near enough for me to back down.

"You didn't do anything, okay? It's what you stand for, where you've come from that I've got an issue with."

"London?" I ask, lines forming on my forehead in confusion.

"No, not London," he says, mimicking my accent. "Your world full of fake, plastic, privileged assholes who think the world owes them something just because they're beautiful."

"How's that my fault? I was born into that."

"It just is." His voice is so low and menacing that it makes my mouth go dry.

He takes one more step toward me and I've no choice but to step back if I don't want us to collide, only when I do, I crash into a tree.

His eyes drop from mine and take in my barely covered chest. My breasts swell under his intense scrutiny and my nipples pucker against the thin fabric, much to his delight.

"So what are you going to do about it, Brit?" He closes the space between us, and I fight to drag some air into my lungs.

"I have a name, you know." My voice is a breathy whisper and I chastise myself for falling under his spell. He knows he's hot and damn him for using it to his advantage.

"I know. You have a lot of other things too."

"Wha—" My words are cut off as his nose runs along the line of my jaw. I drag in a shaky breath and he chuckles.

"You love how much you hate me." It's not a question, so I don't bother responding, not that I think I'm capable right now.

He continues toward my ear and when his warm breath breezes past the sensitive skin, my entire body shudders.

"I bet you're so fucking wet for me right now. Just like you were in the pool. Shall I find out if I'm right?"

His words are enough for the fog to clear for a few seconds. He must sense the change in me because he pulls back and his dark, dangerous eyes find mine. "You don't touch whores, rem—"

I don't get to finish the sentence before his lips slam down on mine and they get lost. His tongue sweeps into my shocked, open mouth and finds mine. My head screams to pull away from him, to slap him for being so presumptuous but my body, that sags back against the tree, my knees damn near giving way. Thankfully, he pushes his knee between my legs and presses his body tight against mine, keeping me in place.

His hands skim up my sides. The gentleness of his touch causing goosebumps to erupt across my entire body.

A low moan vibrates up his throat and I swear I feel it down to my toes. Lifting my arms I place them over his shoulders, my fingers twisting in the short hair at the nape of his neck and I fall further and further under his spell.

My lungs are burning for air when he eventually pulls away from my lips but he by no means stops. Kissing down my neck, his fingers run down the edge of my bikini top, slipping inside to pinch my pebbled nipple.

A loud gasp fills the air around us, but I don't realise it falls from my lips. "Oh fuck," I moan when his fingers are replaced by his hot mouth and my sensitive peak is sucked deep, his tongue circling and sending a strong bolt of electricity down between my legs.

Knowing exactly what I need, his fingers brush the skin of my stomach and slip inside my shorts when they find the waistband. There's no hesitation in his actions, he knows exactly what he wants and exactly what he's doing.

"Oh fuck, oh fuck," I chant, focusing on what's about to come and forgetting every ounce of reality that I should be focusing on right now.

We're just two young adults, hidden under the darkness of the trees in a moment of unadulterated passion. Just two bodies taking exactly what they need and forgetting the consequences of real life and what could happen when this is all over. Regrets mean nothing as my body races toward finding the release I didn't realise I was desperate for until his hands landed on me.

His fingers push inside my knickers and almost immediately find my clit.

"Jesus, Brit," he moans, finding me totally ready for him. He kisses across my chest, pulling the other side of my bikini away and giving that breast the same treatment as his finger delves deeper to find my entrance.

Dropping my hands, I run them down over the muscles of his stomach reveling in the fact they dance under my fingertips. When I meet the top of his shorts, I slip them inside but slide my hand around to his arse, squeezing tightly and pressing his erection harder into my hip. He moans, his hips thrusting against me to find some friction.

"Fuck, you're tight," he moans, slipping another digit inside me and bringing my release almost within touching distance. "Fuck, yes, Come on my fingers, Brit."

His lips find mine once again, his tongue slipping past my lips to explore everything he can, his thumb presses down on my clit and my muscles tighten down on him. He groans. The sound along with the vibrations is enough to push me over. He swallows down my cries as pleasure races through my body. His hand grips my waist and his body presses me harder into the tree to keep me upright, the pleasure threatening to floor me.

I've just barely come down from my high when he pulls back slightly. His usually dark blue eyes are black with his desire, his face pulled tight, and it's enough to have little aftershocks shooting around my body.

Jake looks down at his hand where he's just pulled it from my shorts, I'm not sure if he's considering cutting it off after touching me or what, but what I'm not expecting is for him to lift it to his lips and suck them deep into his mouth.

I can't help myself. I reach for him, not ready for this truce between us to be over. I run my hands up his chest and wrap one around the back of his neck. Lowering his hand, he stares down at me. His eyes run over every inch of my face, it's almost like he's seeing me for the first time which is crazy.

"Jake, I need—"

My words are cut off by a loud shout from the other side of the trees. "Thorn, you in there, man?"

"Fuck." Releasing his hold on me, he backs away. I hate the disappointment that races through me, but losing his touch causes a coldness to hit me that I wasn't expecting.

"Jake?" His name is merely a plea on my lips, and I hate how desperate I sound for a boy I hate.

"Don't," he snaps, looking toward where the shout came from.

"Thorn?"

"Yeah, I'm coming. Wait in the trailer, yeah?"

"Sure thing, man."

Trailer? What?

Turning his hard eyes on me, I swallow as a little fear creeps up my throat. "This never happened."

"What?"

"Just forget it," he barks, leaving no argument. "Take it as an apology for that fucking picture." Reaching out, he takes my chin in his hand, his grip stings but I'm powerless to pull away. His lips crash against mine for one more knee-weakening kiss before he pushes away with such force that I stumble on something and tumble to the ground.

His eyes flash with concern as I moan in pain, but he does nothing. Without another word, he picks up his shirt that's been discarded on the dirt and disappears from my sight.

"Fuck," I grunt, falling back to the ground. *What the fuck did I just do?*

24

JAKE

My chest heaves and my head spins as I make my way out of the trees and away from her. Confusion runs through my veins. I shouldn't have touched her, I should have just left the moment I found her watching me, but I couldn't fucking resist. The tempting swell of her small but perfect breasts hiding behind those tiny scraps of fabric, the smooth, toned skin of her stomach that had my mouth watering and the pathetic excuse for a pair of shorts. I didn't get a chance to check from behind but I'm pretty sure they did a shit job of covering her ass.

As I emerge into the afternoon sun, I can tell myself as much as I like that I shouldn't have done it, but the reality is that my body is demanding that I turn around and finish the job I started. No, if I'm really honest then I want to go back and make sure she's okay after I pushed her away. The little squeal of pain she let out when she hit the ground rings in my ears. I know she hurt herself and I'm a total asshole for leaving her. *But isn't that what you want her to think?*

Shaking the thought from my head, I focus on what I'm about to walk into. Holding my t-shirt in front of the raging hard-on she caused that's still tenting my sweatpants.

Ethan and Mason's voices rumble through the thin walls of my trailer. I've not spoken to Mason since Dash so I can only assume that he's here to give me another asswhipping for my recent actions.

Pulling the door open, I make sure I'm covering my lingering excitement, although I'm fairly sure it'll vanish the second my eyes land on those two.

Their conversation stops the moment I step inside the trailer and two narrowed pairs of eyes turn to me.

"What the fuck happened to you?"

"Just working out."

"Really? Wanna try telling us that when you haven't got girl all over your face." Panicking, I lift my shirt to rub at my lips. "Fucking hell, Thorn, really?"

"What the fuck ever. I'm going to shower."

"I don't want to hear you sorting that little situation out, man."

Flipping them both off, I head toward the bathroom, turn the shower on and drop my sweats. My cock bobs between my legs, taunting me with memories of how I ended up in this state in the first place. I can still taste her sweetness on my tongue, the softness of her skin, the soft moans and mewls that fell from her lips as I brought her to orgasm.

My cock's hard as fucking steel again but nothing

short of her touch will relieve it and that pisses me off more than anything. Not only can I not get her out of my head but now I need her, and I never want to need anyone in my life, ever. Needing someone means handing a part of you over, a part that can be smashed to pieces without a second thought. I will not allow anyone to have any part of me, no matter how small.

Turning the water to cold, I stand there thinking about anything but her body that might allow my cock to return to normal so I can go out and face whatever those two have come to talk about.

"Who was she?" Mason snaps the second I reappear.

"Oh... uh... Chelsea?" I don't mean for it to come out like a question, but it's the only name I can think of without revealing the truth.

"Fuck off, do you really think we'll believe that?"

Shrugging, I grab a couple of beers and toss them over to my pissed off friends.

"One..." Mason starts. "Chelsea was in my class last period, so I know she wasn't here. And two, you don't kiss, and you certainly don't kiss sluts like Chelsea. So come on, out with it before we start jumping to conclusions."

"It was no one."

"It was her, wasn't it?" Ethan asks.

"Enough," I bark. "Did you two just come here to give me a hard time about who I kiss or was there a point to your visit?"

"We came to knock some sense into you."

Placing my bottle down on the counter, I look

between my two best friends. I take a step forward, hands by my side. "Go on then."

"We didn't mean literally, Jake."

"No? I probably deserve it."

"Fucking right you do. That stunt you pulled today was unforgivable."

She didn't seem to have a problem with it a few moments ago. The words are right on the tip of my tongue, but I somehow manage to keep them in. No one aside from the two of us needs to know what happened in the trees this afternoon.

Shrugging once again, I grab my beer and fall down onto the couch now that I know they're not going to take a swing at me.

"This is fucking ridiculous, Thorn. You're ruining her fucking life. How can you not care? I know you're an asshole, but this is insane."

"I care. I care about her dragging up stuff that I'd rather was left in the past."

Ethan's face twists in confusion, but Mason knows more than most.

"None of that is her fault," he fumes. "Just leave her to get on with her life."

"You want her?" My voice comes out calmer than I'm feeling as the realization hits me as to why he's always trying to defend her.

"What? No, I don't fucking want her."

"You sure? You seem to be on her side a lot of the time."

"Yeah, because you're acting like a prick and I'm ashamed to be your friend right now."

"No one's forcing you." Taking a swig of my beer, I look away from him so he can't see how I really feel about that suggestion.

"Fuck you, Jake. You won't listen to my advice, then carry the fuck on. Ruin that girl's life just to spite yourself. All you're doing is trying to cover up how much you want her, we can all see it. I've no problem allowing you to fuck all this up so badly that she'll never look at you again, let alone touch you."

"I don't fucking want her," I seethe, standing like Mason so I can stare right into his eyes.

The fucker has the audacity to laugh. He full-on chuckles in my face. It makes my blood boil.

"So that wasn't her lipstick smeared all over your face when you walked in then? Don't forget, we also know where she lives."

My hands clench with my need to wipe the smug look off his fucking face as he prepares to continue.

"What if I were to tell you that I did want her? What if I were to tell you that I'd already invited her to Shane's party Saturday night and she'd said yes? What if I told you that I intended to fuck her into next—"

"Argh," I roar, flying at him and slamming my fist into his cheek.

"Enough," Ethan demands from behind me, his hands wrapping around my upper arms to pull me from my best friend.

Turning me, his hands slam down on my chest, forcing me to back up and away from Mason.

"You need to pull your head out of your ass, Jake.

You want her, so stop fucking around before you screw things up so badly that you regret it."

I push forward against Ethan, but his hold is too strong.

"I might not want her, but there are enough guys at school who do. You put her front and center of their thoughts today and all of them want a piece of her, none more so than Shane. You need to make her yours before someone else does."

"I don't fucking want her," I lie, the words falling seamlessly from my lips.

"I give up," Mason says, his hands up in defeat before disappearing from sight, the door slamming and the trailer shaking with his departure.

Ethan lets up his hold, walks back over to the couch and pulls a pre-rolled joint from his pocket. Flicking his lighter, he takes a drag before offering it to me.

I take it from him and take a long hit, my muscles immediately start to relax. "So what have you got to say about all this?" I ask, realizing for the first time that he mostly sat there silently while Mason went off on me.

"I feel like I'm missing a huge part of this picture, but I also agree with Mase. You just need to fuck her and get it out of your system."

"Is she really going to Shane's party Friday night?"

"Fuck knows, man. But if he has anything to say about it, then she'll be there, he's been following her around like a lost fucking puppy since she arrived. And if you ask me—"

"I didn't."

"If you ask me, at the rate you're going, she'd be better off with him."

"You're probably right."

"Really?" he asks, his eyebrows practically hitting his hairline.

"Yeah, I won't allow it though."

A small smile twitches at the corner of his mouth and my stomach drops. I may as well just have admitted how badly I want her.

25

AMALIE

"S hit, what happened?" Camila asks the second I drop down into her car the next morning. I'm not surprised, the huge bandage on my arm is kind of impossible to miss.

When Gran got home and found me trying to patch it up with gauze, she was insistent that she took me to the ER and get it looked at properly. I tried arguing but stood little chance against her, especially when she started going on about how it would be what my parents wanted.

Turns out she was right though because I ended up with a few stitches on the deeper part of the cut. I've no idea how falling on a few fallen branches made such a mess. I guess it was karma for kissing the Devil or something, all I do know is that it hurts like a bitch and kept me awake most of the night. I guess I should just be grateful that I didn't break it.

"I fell."

"You fell?" she asks incredulously. "Where?"

"I went for a wander through the trees at the end of the garden and tripped over branches. It was stupid." My face burns red and I'm grateful that Camila is too focused on where she's going so she misses it.

"You don't say." Thankfully, she accepts my lie and moves on, although it's to another topic that I'm trying my best to avoid. "You sure you're ready for this? Things didn't die down at all after you left yesterday."

Groaning, I slump down in the passenger seat of her Mini hoping that it might swallow me up.

"Can't wait."

At some ungodly hour last night when my arm was throbbing, I made the mistake of dragging my phone from the bottom of my bag. Aside from concerned messages from Camila and Shane, all the rest were guys asking when I was available and to my utter shock there were a few very unimpressive dick pics waiting for me as well. None of that pointed to the fact things had already blown over. I know from living a life surrounded by celebrities that gossip is only gossip until something else happens, I was just hoping something crazy would have happened after I left yesterday and that I'd be old news already. I guess that was wishful thinking. Until something else happens, I'll be seen exactly as Jake intended, a whore. Although, after what happened yesterday in the trees, I can't help feeling like there might be a little truth in it.

I'm ashamed that he affected me so much that I allowed him to put his hands on me. I'm also confused as fuck because what he did to me, how he made me feel in those few moments went against everything he's been trying to make me out to be. He told me he'd never touch a whore yet he didn't bat an eyelid about getting me off at the first opportunity.

I think back to the previous evening in Poppy's pool and I can't help thinking that he'd have done the exact same thing if given half a chance.

My body heats as I replay yesterday's events in my head. I can still feel the rough skin of his hands scratch across my stomach as his fingers dived into my shorts. I can still taste him on my tongue and remember his rough voice as he whispered in my ear.

Fuck.

"Are you okay? You're muttering to yourself."

"Yeah, I'm good. Just remembered that I forgot some homework."

"I'm sure the teacher will let you off. No doubt they know all about what happened yesterday as well."

"Fantastic."

"Shit, I didn't mean it like that."

I feel their eyes burn into my skin the second I step from Camila's car, but I keep my head high and focus on where I'm going.

"Amalie." My name being called by a familiar voice drags my attention from the building in front of me and when I look up, I'm relieved to see it's just Shane and not a guy wanting to book a 'date'. "Hey, how are you doing?" His eyes drop to the bandage on my arm, but he doesn't ask about it when I shake my head and roll my eyes like it's nothing to worry about.

"Great, I love being the school bike."

"Don't," he growls, stepping a little closer to protect me from prying eyes.

"You sure you want to be seen with me? You know everyone will think you're paying for my time." I don't mean for it to come out sounding quite so bitter but catching a glance of Jake's group laughing and joking over Shane's shoulder pisses me off.

"I don't give a fuck what they think. We know the truth, that's all that matters."

"You know that it wasn't me?"

"Of course."

"How?" I ask, my eyes narrowing suspiciously.

"It's not the kind of thing you'd do."

"But you barely know me." His confidence in my morals does make me feel a bit better, making me wish everyone could see the same thing.

"I know enough. Can I walk you to class?"

"Your funeral," I whisper, but it's not quietly enough.

"Amalie," he warns once again. "I can feed you to the wolves if you like but I'm thinking you'd rather stay in the shadows."

Just the mention of shadows is enough to bring Jake back to the forefront of my mind. Why don't I feel like I did with him last night when I'm with Shane. He's a good guy, he treats me right. He'd show me exactly how he felt and never do the kinds of things Jake does.

There's something seriously wrong with me that I can feel nothing but the support of a friend as I walk beside Shane.

The catcalls of Jake's group of friends filter down to

us. Glancing over, I spot Chelsea and a few of her followers but he's nowhere to be seen.

"Just ignore them," Shane says, encouraging me to keep moving with a gentle hand on my back. "Come on."

Plastering on a smile for my friend, I chance a look over at him. He's smiling down at me with a sparkle in his eye that has me swallowing in concern. No matter how platonic I try to keep things between us, seems his imagination keeps getting the better of him. His fingers twitch on the small of my back and I step away slightly. His lips curve into a frown but he doesn't say anything.

"If you're going out of your way, I can walk myself."

"Kinda, but I need to know you get there without being harassed by any of these idiots."

"I really appreciate the support."

"And I really fucking hate the way all these horny fucking guys are looking at you right now. It's like they think you're a piece of meat for them to play with. Jake's gonna fucking pay for what he did yesterday."

"Please, don't do anything stupid," I say with a wince knowing that going up against his captain will never end well.

"I can't promise anything."

"Hey, happy birthday, man," a guy I don't know says, walking up to Shane and slugging him playfully on the shoulder.

"Thanks, man."

"Can't wait for your party Friday night, it's gonna be epic."

"Yeah, it should be a good night." Shane's reply is really lacking any excitement.

"Well," he says awkwardly looking between the two of us, probably wondering what his friend is doing with the school bike. "Hopefully we'll be celebrating a win too."

"We can only hope. I'll see you later, yeah?"

"Sure thing." Nodding his head at both of us, he walks away and disappears into the crowd.

"It's your birthday?" I ask, my steps faltering a little with the realisation.

"Yep, I'm all legal and shit now." I look over just in time to see his eyebrows wiggle and a cheeky smile twitch his lips.

"Well, happy birthday. I had no idea so I... uh... haven't—"

My awkward excuse as to why I haven't bought him a gift is cut off when he grabs my forearm and turns me to face him.

"Have dinner with me."

"Oh... uh..." My heart starts to race with the thought that even though I've been trying really hard not to give him any ideas that he might have just got them anyway. Biting down on my bottom lip, I stare up into his hopeful eyes and my stomach drops. I really don't want to hurt him.

"Not like a date or anything." Although by the way his face drops when he says this, it's obvious that it's exactly the opposite of what he wants. "Just friends. You can pay as my birthday present."

"Just as friends?" I ask, feeling like the shittiest

person on the planet for turning down such a sweet guy. He's going to be an incredible boyfriend for someone one day, just not mine. As much as I might wish that he was the one to set my blood on fire and cause an eruption of butterflies in my belly, he doesn't. I also doubt he ever will. Shane and I are destined to be friends and the sooner he comes to terms with that, the better.

Awareness heats my left side, glancing over I find the students who were in front of us have parted and at the end of the hallway, seething in anger, is Jake. His eyes are dark and murderous as he stares between Shane and me. Trying to swallow down my apprehension, I turn back to Shane as he talks.

"Yeah, just friends. No pressure, Am—"

Pain sears through my shoulder as my back and head slams back against the wall.

"What the fuck is your problem, man?" Shane barks as he stumbles back a few steps.

"How much does she charge for dinner? I doubt she's worth it."

When my eyes focus, I find the two of them nose to nose. Jake is an inch or two taller, usually it would be unnoticeable but right now he looks like a giant compared to Shane. His chest is puffed out in anger, his shoulders wide as he tries to intimidate him but fair play to Shane because he holds his head high and gives back as good as he gets.

"You'd have to care about getting to know a girl to understand."

"I care," Jake growls so quietly I almost miss it.

"Yeah about getting between their legs and leaving as fast as possible."

"Watch it." Jake's hands slam down on Shane's chest and he steps back once again. "You need to remember where your loyalties lie." With one final hard stare and a flick of his eyes over to me, Jake storms off down the hallway. It takes a couple of seconds but the bystanders who watched the whole thing soon continue with their earlier conversations and turn their attention away from us.

"Fuck, are you okay?" Shane asks, rushing over to where I'm still standing, back up against the wall. I blink for what feels like the first time since I saw him standing feet away and it's enough to force a couple of tears out of my eyes. "Fuck, did he hurt you?"

It's only as his words register that I remember my head bouncing off the wall behind me as Jake slammed into me. But it's not the pain from that which is causing the tears, it's the memory of how gentle with me he was last night. Yes, his touches were demanding and confident but at no point was he rough or careless.

Blinking a little faster to force the tears away, I push myself from the wall. "I'm fine. Honestly," I add when he looks at me with a raised brow.

"That guy's an asshole. If I never had to see him again, it would be too soon."

I mumble my agreement, although even as I say it something inside me twists painfully. I should be fully on board after everything he's done to me, but there's a part of me even after what just happened that wants to follow him. To try to find out what his problem is and...

help maybe? Chastising myself for the thought alone, it's clear that Jake Thorn is long past being rescued and that if anyone were capable, then it wouldn't be me doing it.

"Yeah, same." My agreement is weak at best and it causes Shane's eyes to narrow at me with suspicion. "So when are we having this dinner?" I ask, trying to get the heat off me.

"Thursday night? We can't do Friday because of the game and party."

"Party?"

"Yeah, my house after the game. It's kinda tradition, didn't anyone tell you about it?"

I shrug, there's a good chance someone might have but football parties aren't exactly high on my priority list right now.

"You'll be there though, right? At the game and party?" The hope that shines in his eyes is enough to tell me that the right answer would be no. I should say no right now, but when his face drops and a sad puppy dog look appears, I have a really hard time refusing.

"Come on, let's get you to class." The rest of the walk is in silence and I'm afraid I might have hurt him when the only thing I want to do is the opposite.

26

AMALIE

The rest of the day, and the next, is exactly as I expected. Full of stares, pointing, hushed whispers and propositions. By the time I meet Camila at her car Thursday afternoon, I've just about had my fill of bullshit.

"How you holding up?" she asks, glancing over at me as I climb into her car.

Letting out a giant sigh of frustration, a quiet chuckle falls from her lips. "That good?"

"Worse."

"It'll blow over soon. With the game and Shane's party this weekend, someone is bound to do something stupid and take the limelight off you."

"I can only hope," I mutter as she pulls away from school.

"Ready for your big date tonight?"

"It's not a date."

"Riiight."

"I'm serious, Camila. Stop getting any ideas about

doubling with you and Noah out of your head. I'm not interested in Shane like that."

"So you keep saying, but he really likes you. Just give it a chance."

"That's not a good enough reason to lead him on. We're going out tonight as friends and that's all we're ever going to be." Even the thought of tonight has my stomach knotting in uncertainty. As much as I might plead that it's not a date, it's going to look like that to everyone else. As much as I don't want them to get the wrong idea, I also don't want Shane's reputation tarnished by spending time with me, the girl they all think charges by the hour.

"Do you know what you're wearing?" Camila asks, dragging me from my thoughts.

"Uh... jeans and t-shirt."

"Jesus, Amalie. I know it's not a date, but you could put a little effort in at least."

"Fine," I huff. "Want to come in and help?"

"I thought you'd never ask."

"How was school?" Gran asks as we walk into the kitchen to grab a drink.

"Yeah, it was good," I lie, feeling Camila's stare burning into the back of my head as I do. "What?" I mouth, turning to look at her, it's not like I came straight home and spilled every detail of the picture that's circulating that makes it look like me giving head. There are some things a gran and granddaughter never need to discuss, and this is one of them.

"You hear about Amalie's date?"

"It's not a date," I seethe, much to Camila's amusement.

"Aw, it's so exciting. I remember my first date. He was such a sweetheart. He bought me flowers, took me for a meal and we had the most romantic walk on the beach." Gran's eyes glaze over as she walks down memory lane. "And when he kissed me at the end of the night, I thought my life was never going to be the same again."

"There will be zero kissing going on tonight. We're just going out as friends."

"Yeah, yeah. Now let's go and find you something to wear that your *friend* will really enjoy."

"Make sure she wears a dress," Gran calls as we disappear down the hall.

"I am not wearing a bloody dress," I grumble, pushing my door open.

Camila goes straight for my wardrobe and begins pulling out suggestions, every single one I refuse. I'm not dressing up, I refuse to allow Shane to think that I made an effort to impress him. We. Are. Friends.

In the end, I relent on a smart casual summer dress with spaghetti straps and flowers all over. I rationalise that if it's casual enough to wear to school, then it's casual enough to wear out on my non-date.

Camila once again insists on doing my hair and makeup and when I eventually step foot out of my bedroom, I've got light but smokey eyes and loose curls hanging around my shoulders. The bandage that's wrapped around my arm does nothing for the look, but there's not a lot I can do about that, nor the constant reminder of the person who put it there.

"Whoa, you look beautiful. He's not going to know what hit him."

Groaning at Gran's words, I immediately turn around to change but unfortunately for me, Camila stands in my way.

"Uh uh... no way." Just as I go to step toward her, the doorbell rings. "It's too late anyway, he's here." The delight that lights up her face makes me want to stomp on her toe with my wedges.

"You're going to pay for this," I warn on a whisper but all I get in return is a joyful laugh.

"Just try to enjoy yourself, yeah?"

"Gran, no," I call when I spot her heading toward the front door. The last thing I need is her joining in on the 'wouldn't Shane make a great boyfriend' party. "Both of you just... disappear."

"He knows I'm here, he'll have parked by my car."

"Uh, fine. Gran, go hide." She pouts but does as she's told and slips into the living room.

Blowing out a long breath, I prepare to open the door. I'm not quick enough though because the bell rings through the house once again.

"Hey, sorry," I say, pulling the door open and plastering a smile on my face.

"No worries. I was beginning to think you'd stood me up on your own doorstep." His laugh that follows is a nervous one, and it doesn't make me feel any better.

"Whoa, you scrub up well." Instead of the standard jeans and t-shirt he always seems to wear at school,

Shane's dressed in a pair of chinos and a smart-ish button-down. It's clear he's spent a little more time than usual on his unruly hair and he smells pretty damn good. His scent has my mouth watering, but it's still not enough to make me want him.

"You too, you look stunning." My cheeks heat at his compliment and I feel awkward for the first time in his presence since the day I crashed into him.

"Right then, have a good time, kids. Make sure you're back before curfew," Camila sings with delight, pushing past both of us and heading toward her car. With a little wave, she pulls away leaving the two of us alone for the first time.

"Ready?" He holds his arm out for me and I feel like a twat when I refuse but I already feel like this night is getting out of control.

"Where are we going?" I ask as his car speeds toward the seafront.

"For the best burger in town, of course."

"Aces?" I ask hesitantly.

"Of course. Where else? You said you wanted casual, and it doesn't get any better than Aces."

Shit.

I don't need to say anything, he must be able to sense my tension.

"It'll be okay. Plus, I refuse to hide you. I couldn't give a fuck what everyone thinks. I know that wasn't you in that photo and so do you. We also know that I'm not paying you to be with me, so fuck the rest of them and their small minds."

My fingers twist together in my lap as I try to

believe what Shane's saying, but I can't help feeling like this night is only going to get worse.

Thankfully, Aces looks pretty quiet as we walk up to the entrance.

"Over here." Shane reaches out and takes my hand, pulling me over to an empty booth. I keep my head down but I don't miss the silence that descends around the diner. Quiet whispers soon start up but the buzzing in my ears means I don't hear any of it. I do however feel Shane's hand squeeze mine tighter so I can only imagine what gossip is going around right now.

He leads me over to the booth and almost immediately a waitress comes over to take our drink order. I'm relieved that it gives me something to focus on other than the multiple stares I can feel tingling my skin. I've never felt more unwelcome in my life.

"I'm sorry, maybe you were right to be concerned."

"It's fine. They'll get bored eventually." Thankfully my voice sounds much stronger than how I feel about the situation.

Risking a glance up, I find Chelsea and her little gang of bitches at the table they were at the first time I came here. Most of them are staring at me but Chelsea has her head in her phone. I manage to contain my groan, knowing that she's probably summoning the rest of her troops including one I really have no intention of seeing tonight.

Things quieten down for a bit and we manage to eat our burgers without being interrupted, although at no point do I lose the interest of the rest of the customers. Even the ones I'm pretty sure don't attend Rosewood seem interested in me. I guess that photo didn't stay within the school population.

I'm just ordering a sundae for dessert when a shiver runs down my spine. I don't need to see the look on Shane's face as he glances at the door behind me to know who's about to walk in.

I tell myself to keep my eyes down on the menu, giving him any attention will only spur him on but my traitorous body has other ideas because only seconds later I find myself looking over my shoulder.

His piercing stare is directed right at me. The moment he realises that I'm staring right back at him, his eyes widen in surprise before they drop down my body. He can't see much seeing as I'm sitting in a booth but that doesn't stop them darkening.

"Well, well, well, isn't this *cute.*"

"Leave us alone, Thorn."

"Or what?" he taunts, causing Shane to slide over to the edge of the booth toward him. "You gonna make me?"

"Shane, just ignore him," I plead, but it's too late. He's already standing toe to toe with Jake. Standing alongside them, I place my hand on Shane's forearm much to Jake's horror if the widening of his eyes and gritting of his teeth are anything to go by. "Sit back down, please. He's not worth it." I'm not above begging right now so that we don't cause more of a scene than we already are.

Taking a step back, Jake turns his eyes on me. They drop down my now exposed body and slowly take in every inch of my bare legs. Without looking over, I sense Shane's muscles tense as he prepares to physically remove Jake's eyes from my body, but he doesn't get the chance.

"Wasted on him, Brit. Wasted." He slowly steps back, taking his time to run his eyes over me once again before turning and going to join his gang of douchebags, which as usual these days seems to be minus Mason.

27

JAKE

hy the hell am I even here? I was asking that question before I even walked through the door but the second I got Chelsea's message telling me that she was here with *him* I didn't have a choice but to see it with my own eyes.

I thought it would be fun to come and taunt her but one look at her sitting there, dressed up all pretty for him and I knew I'd made a huge fucking mistake. A sharp pain pierced my chest as the image of pressing her up against that tree fills my head. My mouth waters as the memory of how sweet she tasted hits me. My muscles tighten with the need to feel her body against me and her tongue dueling with mine once again. The little summer dress she's wearing is just begging to be ripped away from her lean, sexy body and that's not being done by anyone's hands but my own. Teammate or not, Shane needs to understand who she belongs to.

My eyes widen as she reaches her hand out to stop

him squaring up to me, the sight of a fresh bandage wrapping around her upper arm makes my stomach twist. Please tell me I didn't cause that?

I desperately want to ask her, the words are right on the tip of my tongue but thankfully her words about me not being worth it are the dose of cold water I need to remember what the fuck I'm doing, and admitting that anything happened between us can't happen again. It was a mistake, a mistake I might have been dreaming about repeating since, but a mistake nonetheless.

Sitting down with my friends, I fight to keep my eyes on the table in front of me and not the couple on a date just a few feet away. Why the fuck is he dating her anyway, I thought I made it pretty clear she was off limits.

"Who the fuck does she think she is? Does she think she's something special because she's got a fancy accent and famous, rich parents," Chelsea fumes.

"Dead parents," Victoria chips in.

"That don't give her the right to come storming in here and taking the guys right out from under our feet."

"Why, did you want Shane for yourself?"

"Fuck no. He's too much of a goodie-two-shoes. I bet he's a fucking virgin too."

"So what's the problem?"

"Who she's going to go after next is my issue. She'll soon realize he's a square and move on."

My skin prickles as Chelsea turns her gaze on me. "What?"

"You got plans tonight?" Her eyes flit between my eyes and lips.

"Yeah, and they don't involve you." I push her from my lap.

"Ouch."

"Fuck off."

Chelsea seethes, turns her back on me to give another of my teammates some attention.

The movement of Shane getting up and heading to the restrooms catches my eye. As tempted as I am to follow him and ensure he's unable to return to his table, I ignore him and zero my eyes in on Brit, who's stirring the remnants of her ice cream around the dish like it's the most fascinating thing in the world.

Unable to help myself, I push off the chair I'm sitting in and drop down on the bench opposite her.

"I think we should get—what the fuck are you doing?" she asks in a panic when she lifts her head and finds me staring back at her. "Shane's only gone to the toilet."

"Shame. What did you do?" I nod toward the bandage on her arms and she tries twisting away so I can't see it. "No point hiding." I drop my eyes down to where the juncture of her thighs are beneath the table and delight in seeing the color of her cheeks redden.

"It's nothing. You need to leave."

"Did I do it?"

"Why do you care? You want to hurt me, remember?"

"Not physically. Fuck." Rubbing my hand over my face and rough jaw, I stare into her soft blue eyes. Eyes that not so long ago I never wanted to see again but I'm starting to realize that they're nothing like the ones in my memory and everything like ones I want to look into over and over again. "I'm sorry."

I'm taken aback when her only response is to laugh at my apology.

"What's funny?"

"You apologising. That's a joke, right?"

My mouth opens to respond, although I have no fucking clue what to say when a shadow falls over us.

"Do you mind? You're sitting in my seat."

"I'm pretty sure you're actually taking my place right now."

"How's that exactly? Correct me if I'm wrong, but weren't you the one who just sent a very questionable photo around the entire school just to shame her? So why exactly would you want to be sitting here if you hate her so much?"

Isn't that the fucking million dollar question?

"You're right. She's all yours." Bile burns my throat just saying the words, but like fuck am I letting anyone know how I'm really feeling about this little date I'm witnessing.

"Wanna get out of here?" Shane asks Brit, totally ignoring that I'm still sitting here.

"Yeah. The unwanted company is kinda ruining the mood."

I have no idea if she says it for my benefit or because something really is developing between the two of them. Either way, I'm not fucking happy about it.

Reaching his hand out, I almost lean over and slap

it away but to my horror, Brit reaches out and allows him to pull her from the booth and hand in hand they walk out of the diner. My stomach turns over like I could puke right on Bill's checkered floor, that is until she turns back and looks over her shoulder at me at the very last minute. That one look tells me everything I need to know. She's not with him, not in the slightest because just like me, her head's still in those trees and the body she wants next to her is mine.

"You want to get out of here and get drunk?" Ethan's voice filters through the haze that had descended and when I glance up, I find him staring at me with concern written all over his face.

"Yes."

Jumping into his car, we take off and I feel like I can breathe once again now I'm nowhere near her. But at the same time images float around my head about what she could be doing right now... with him. Is she allowing him to touch her, is she going to let him kiss her?

My teeth grind as the images keep coming. I should be the one fucking kissing her. *She's mine.* The sudden realization of how much truth is behind those two words hit me like a truck. Lifting my hand to try to soothe the pain radiating from my chest, I suck in a deep breath.

"You okay?" Ethan asks, glancing over at where I'm fighting to breathe.

"Yeah, just keep driving. You'd better have some fucking good weed."

"What the fuck's that girl doing to you, man?"

"Fuck if I know."

"You want me to try to track them down so you can claim what's yours?"

"She's not fucking mine," I grunt.

"Riiight, Thorn. Whatever you say." He grins, making me want to wipe it off his face. "I'm starting to understand what Mason's problem is, you really are fucking blind, dude."

"Are you just about finished?"

"Not getting involved, man. Whatever you need, I've got your back."

I appreciate that more than I want to admit seeing as Mason's fucked off. He's been my best friend for as long as I can remember, the calming influence to my hot head. He's followed me around like a fucking dog forever, I didn't think I'd ever piss him off. Seems I got that wrong. I miss him, but not enough to go fucking groveling. I'll have to come up with something else to get him on my side.

"Not going to yours?" I'm disappointed when Ethan takes a turn toward my place instead of his.

"Na, my parents are back for a few days. It's gotta be yours if you wanna light up."

"Great."

I tell myself that being so close to Brit won't be an issue. That at no point tonight am I going to want to go through the trees to find out if he brought her home safe.

Fuck, I need a drink.

————

Relaxing back, I allow the weed to flow through me, chilling me the fuck out while the beer warms my belly.

"You think they're back yet?"

"Who?" Ethan asks sleepily from his side of the couch.

"Shane and Brit." I roll my eyes like it should be fucking obvious.

"How should I know? If things went well, then he probably took her up to Head Point to get busy in the back seat of his car."

My entire body locks up tight at the suggestion. "He wouldn't... would he?"

"If he doesn't, then he must have a pussy because she's—"

"Do not finish that sentence."

"Fucking hell, Thorn, you've really got it bad, don't you?"

"I haven't got anything, I'd just rather not think about what they might or might not be up to." It's a barefaced lie and we both know it. Thankfully, Ethan drops it, he shrugs and goes back to his joint and whoever it is he's messaging.

I'm so lost inside my own head that I don't realize how much time's gone by or that Ethan's passed out next to me, snoring like a motherfucker.

Glancing over, I take in his peaceful sleeping face as he drools on my couch. My mind once again wanders to Brit and I find myself jumping up without putting much thought into my actions. I look back at my sleeping friend when I get to the door to make sure he's still out cold, then I push it open and step out into the night.

The weed and beer means my legs are a little unstable as I head toward the trees, but now I've started, I won't turn back until I find what I need to shut my imagination off.

I maneuver my way to my homemade gym without much consideration, I've made the trip a million times. But I find myself having to pull my cell from my pocket to make use of the flash when I trip over a stick as I try to make my way out the other side.

My cell illuminates the space just enough that I don't end up on my ass and before long I'm walking up an unfamiliar back yard toward a tired looking bungalow.

Walking up to the closest window, I find exactly what I was hoping for, Brit fast asleep in her bed. Glancing to my left, I spot a door that I assume leads directly into her bedroom.

Wrapping my fingers around the handle, I gently push down, my heart pounds as I wait to find out if it'll open. A soft click fills the air around me and my stomach twists in anticipation.

Slipping inside the dark room, I'm as silent as possible as I make my way over to her bed, the room only illuminated by the moonlight streaming in through her open curtains.

Crouching down beside her, I take in her beautiful, sleeping face, her long, light eyelashes rest down onto her cheekbones, her cheeks are a rosy pink, almost as if she knows I'm here, and her full lips are parted just slightly as her soft breaths slip past.

My eyes run over every feature, my cock hardening more with each second that passes. Unable to stop myself, I reach my hand out and tuck a lock of hair that had fallen onto her cheek behind her ear.

The moan she emits when our skin connects makes my balls ache and my veins fill with fire. It would be so easy to take what I need with her like this. I might be an asshole but that really isn't my style, even as much as I want to feel her body pressed up against mine right now.

Brushing my knuckle down her cheek and across her lips, she shifts and moans, and I panic, that is until I hear something that has my body frozen to the spot.

"Jake." Her voice is a breathy whisper, just like it was when I had my fingers inside her, and I almost come on the spot. Is she fucking dreaming about me?

But why? I've been nothing but an asshole to her since the day I first laid eyes on her. It's bad enough that I take up any thoughts in her head during daylight hours, but at night as well? That's fucked up. Just like how she never should have allowed me to get a taste of her the other night. Just that one taste has turned my slight obsession with her into something I'm now struggling to control, hence the reason I'm standing inside her bedroom like a creep while she sleeps.

She stirs again and reaches out. Her light fingertips trail down my t-shirt covered chest and my entire body shudders at the contact. I stay stock still, waiting for her to wake up and freak out at any moment but that doesn't happen. Instead, she drops her arm and drifts back off into a deep sleep.

Knowing I need to get out before I'm caught, I stand and make my way toward the door. Spotting a pad of paper and pen on her desk, I stop at the last minute and leave her a note.

28

AMALIE

Waking the next morning, my entire body is burning and covered in a light sheen of sweat. My nipples brush against the fabric of my tank and my core aches. The lingering images of my dream come back to me and my face heats with embarrassment as the picture of Jake sneaking into my room and taking exactly what he needed slams into me. It was so vivid, so much so that if I didn't know I'd just woken up, I'd be questioning if it really did happen.

I need to do something to get him out of my head. I had a great night with Shane last night, why isn't it him who can be starring in my naughty dreams? Why's it got to be the school's arsehole who's set on ruining my life?

After we thankfully left the diner and Jake's angry eyes behind, Shane took us for a drive around the town before we ended up back at Gran's. Knowing she was out, I invited him in and we sat out in the garden with some of her homemade lemonade and chatted away about school, our friends and other nonsense topics. At no point did he try to bring up my past life or my parents, or even Jake, and I was more than grateful to not have to think about such heartbreaking and painful subjects for an hour or two.

If he thought that me inviting him in was code for something more happening between us, then he didn't give them away and he also didn't look disappointed when the night ended with only a friendly hug between us. Even still, I went to bed with a heavy heart knowing he was feeling more for me than I was for him, but I can't help it, I can't force myself to fall for him.

I fell asleep like I have done every night this week with memories of my time in the trees with Jake playing on my mind. Those memories are to blame for the vivid actions of my dirty mind during my sleep and just another reason why I need to block the whole thing from my memory. Nothing good can come from obsessing over it. It's not like I'm going to allow it to happen again even if the opportunity presented itself.

Swinging my legs from the bed, I stand and walk over to the door that leads to the garden so I can swing it open and allow the cool morning air to fill the room. I love the scent of the end of summer mixing with the faint sea air.

A rush of air surrounds me, causing goosebumps to prick my skin as something fluttering to the floor behind me catches my eyes.

Bending down, I reach out to pick up the paper that

floated to the floor but the second I lay my eyes on it my entire body freezes.

Lock your fucking door.

Looking around, I search for clues that anyone was here, but nothing seems out of place. Then I'm reminded once again of my dream. Of his gentle touch, the warmth of his skin.

"Fuck." Placing my palm on my cheek where I remember his trailing fingertips, I stumble back until I fall down on my bed. *Was it all a dream?*

Camila questions me on my 'date' the whole way to school, thankfully distracting me from my potential late night visitor but the second we arrive and I step out of her car, he's all I can think about. I look around and for the first time since I started here, I actively look for him, hoping to find any kind of evidence for the truth about last night. But sadly, aside from his bunch of idiot friends, I don't see any sign of him.

Pushing thoughts of him avoiding me to the back of my head, I head for my first class. He's Jacob Thorn, king of Rosewood High, why would he feel the need to avoid me? For all I know, he did come into my room last night and he's got more damning evidence of me on camera that he's in the process of shaming me with.

My heart races at the thought. If that's the case, he could have done anything. My stomach twists and my breakfast threatens to make a reappearance.

I'm the first into my art class, I stumble toward my desk and fumble to pull the chair out as I try to convince myself that I'm allowing my imagination to get the better of me. I know he's a dick, but he wouldn't take things that far, would he? I try not to focus on what the answer to that question could be.

"Hey, how are you holding up?"

"What? Why? What's happened?" I practically bark at Poppy when she falls down beside me.

"Uh…" Her hesitation has my heart racing and my head spinning. Her eyes narrow and her head tilts to the side in confusion. "Nothing, I don't think. I just meant after the beginning of the week, plus I heard a rumor you had a date last night."

Blowing out a huge sigh of relief that nothing else has happened, *yet,* I drop my head to my hands. "It wasn't a date. Just two friends getting some dinner."

"Does he know that? Even I've seen the way he looks at you."

"Yes, he was fully aware and nothing untoward happened. Not that your bloody cousin would have allowed it."

"Jake was there?"

"Yeah, always everywhere I turn driving me freaking crazy." My cheeks heat as memories from last night hit me once again but thankfully Poppy either doesn't notice or just ignores it.

"He needs to get a grip. He's acting like a crazy man."

"You're telling me. Did you get your bit of our presentation finished?" I ask, changing the subject.

"Yep, all done. We still meeting at lunch to go through it?"

"Yes. Library?"

"If you want."

By some miracle, I manage to keep my head down and avoid almost everyone all day. I spend my free period in the library along with the entire lunch break with Poppy running through our presentation for later that afternoon.

I hear no gossip that anything else has happened and there's no evidence of any new footage of me, so by the time I walk out of school after my last class to meet Camila, I'm starting to relax a little.

"Ah she lives," she chuckles. "I thought I was going to have to come and drag you out from that damn library."

"I had loads of work to do."

"So you weren't avoiding Shane after last night?"

"No. Why would I?"

She shrugs, but it's not enough to make me forget her comment. "What's happened, Cam?"

"Nothing, nothing. He just seemed even more interested this morning. Couldn't stop talking about you."

"He has no reason to, we had a nice night, like I told you this morning. Nothing happened, and I gave him no idea that it would."

"Well, from what I could tell, he's certainly got that idea."

"Fucking hell. Maybe I shouldn't go tonight."

"No chance. It's his birthday, you have to go."

"No, I really don't. I really don't want to spend a night with the football team and the cheerleaders, and I especially don't need to spend the night watching everything I say or do in case I lead him on."

"It'll be fine. Apparently Jake's not going, so that's one less thing you need to worry about."

Fuck. My. Life. How did things get so damn complicated?

"Come on, let's get out of here. We've got a game and a party to prepare for."

———

"So you're telling me that we have to wear school colours tonight?" I ask Camila when she pulls out multiple items of clothes that are all red and white.

"Yep, tradition."

"Fantastic," I mutter, pulling my wardrobe open and looking at my options.

I'm shoved aside as Camila takes over my wardrobe choices. "Hmmm... what about... this," she says, pulling a short white skirt from a hanger. "And... uh... this." A barely-there red handkerchief top swings from her finger. Both items are things I wouldn't have thought twice about sliding into when I was back in London, but here things are different. I know I'm going to be under the watchful eyes of most of the Rosewood High students tonight and it's something I'd rather avoid as much as possible.

"Or this?" I drag out a pair of white skinny jeans and a red t-shirt.

"Nope, too boring. I allowed you to wear what you wanted to the Dash, and you stood out like a sore thumb. Trust me, you'll look hot."

I refrain from explaining that I want to look the opposite of hot so I don't attract attention, but I know it's pointless, Camila doesn't understand.

Taking the clothes she's still holding out toward me, I turn on my heel and head into the bathroom to change.

My legs look a mile long in this skirt even to my own eyes, it most definitely isn't going to help me blend in and the top, although sexy, is even smaller than I remember.

With a huff, I throw the bathroom door open and storm toward Camila. "Can we compromise? The skirt and a t-shirt or the top and jeans?" I ask, exasperated.

"Whoa, you're not serious?" Her eyes almost pop out of her head when she turns and runs them over me. "I'm not into chicks, but I'd totally do you."

"That's the problem, Cam. I don't want anyone to look at me and want to 'do me.' I just want to hide." My frustration about this is beginning to get the better of me.

"Even Jake?" Her serious eyes hold mine and my stomach twists. *Can she read my mind?*

"No, especially not him."

"Really? Don't think I haven't clocked the change in

the two of you. The air between you crackles even from across the school."

"I don't know what you're talking about. Anyway, you said he wasn't going tonight."

"That's what I've heard."

Narrowing my eyes at her, I suddenly get the feeling that she might be stretching the truth slightly.

"It's what I've heard," she repeats, her hands up in defeat. "Don't shoot the messenger."

———

When we walk into the stadium ready for the game a few hours later, it's with red and white face paint across our cheeks and Rosewood flags in our hands. I felt ridiculous in Camila's car but as we join the rest of the school and I realise it's not just the two of us looking like this, I feel a little better.

She eventually relented and I manage to get away with wearing the white skirt with a simple red t-shirt. I feel a little more comfortable, but I also didn't miss some of the stares in my direction as we walked from the car.

The game is much like last week's. The excitement is through the roof, the chants are so loud that it makes the stands beneath my feet vibrate and the elation when we score first is beyond belief.

I've still no clue about the game so while everyone oohs and ahhs around me, I try my best to join in and learn what it is they're so excited or disappointed about.

As we're beginning to get toward the end of the sixty minutes we're winning, but only just. That's when everything starts to unravel. The crowd goes quiet as the ball flies up in the air toward the other team's end of the field. The sound of Shane's name being screamed fills my ears as he takes off toward it to defend their current winning position, but just as he should grab it, he fumbles. The ball hits the ground right before one of the other team's players picks it up and scores.

Shane's shoulders drop in defeat as a couple of his teammates slap him on the back in support while the other team celebrates. Everything seems fine until Rosewood's quarterback comes storming across the field in Shane's direction. The stadium falls silent, Jake's intentions obvious from his body language. The second he steps in front of Shane his hands come out and he forcefully pushes against his chest. The rest of the Rosewood team turn to find their captain taking out all his frustrations on Shane. It takes a couple of seconds for them to react and when they do, it takes two of our guys to pull Jake away.

It all happens so fast, but one moment he's wrestling with Shane and the next he's been sent off and is disappearing from sight, I presume toward the locker rooms.

"Well that was dramatic," Camila comments beside me as the teams get ready to continue for the final few minutes. Rosewood is now behind and tensions are running very high for them to pull off this win. "Don't look so worried, they'll do it," she says when she glances over at me.

"Oh, I'm not worried."

"You might want to tell yourself that. You look as tense as a virgin at an orgy."

"What!?" I balk, dragging my eyes from where Jake disappeared to look at her.

"Ohhh," she sings like she's just figured something out. "You totally want to go after him, don't you?"

"Huh?" I try to come across confused, but I know exactly what she means and I'm having a hard time not doing exactly what she just suggested. It's crazy, I know, but something is calling for me to follow him. To find out what his problem is and if he's okay.

"Don't play all innocent. You know as well as I do that his issue with Shane is you. You said yourself that he was a pain in the ass at Aces last night during your date—"

"It wasn't a date."

"Ugh, whatever. He wants you, and Shane's standing in his way."

"There's nothing going on with Shane." My voice is exasperated. How many times do I need to repeat this?

"I know this. You know this. But does Jake?"

"Why would he care? He hates me."

"Does he?"

Suddenly a roar erupts around us, Camila's head whips toward the field and I follow to find the team celebrating a very last-minute touchdown which gives Rosewood the win seconds before the end-of-game whistle.

My chest swells with pride as I watch the guys on the field celebrate, but something tugs at my chest when I see Mason pull off his helmet and look around for his absent best friend. He's soon distracted when Ethan pulls him in for a celebratory hug. I've no idea if Camila's right and all of that was basically my fault, but I feel awful nonetheless. I don't want to get between anyone, especially if it's going to affect so many others like a loss here tonight would have.

"Let's get out of here. It's time to party!" Camila sings, grabs my hand and pulls me from the stands along with everyone else who's rushing to get out of here and start celebrating properly.

As we exit the stadium, I can't help looking back toward where I know the locker rooms are. I wonder if he's still in there?

29

JAKE

My entire body is locked tight with frustration. I've spent most of the day with that fucker in all my classes and then out on the field tonight. Every time I look at him, all I can see in his eyes is *I have something you want*. The image of him laughing with Brit last night in Aces is burned into the back of my mind. At least I know she didn't spend the night with him.

My cock twitches once again despite the tension taking over my body as the image of her peacefully sleeping comes into mind. I've regretted walking away since the second I silently closed her door behind me. If I'd have woken her, what would she have done? Would she have made me leave or would I have got another taste of her? The way she moaned my name certainly hinted toward the fact she might have allowed me to take what I needed.

As I storm away from the school with the sound of the entire student body shouting and screaming with what I hope was our win, my muscles ache. I'm screwing everything up, and as much as I want to blame her for everything, I know it's all my own doing.

If I'd ignored my burning need for revenge on another woman the first time I laid eyes on her, then none of this would have happened. If I wasn't so screwed up because of that previously mentioned woman, then I might have been able to deal with all the bullshit in my life. But no, one look at a girl who represents the same thing *she* did, and I lose all fucking sense of what I'm doing. One thing's for fucking sure, I wasn't supposed to want her. I wanted to hurt her, not want to make her fucking mine.

"Argh," I scream out my frustration into the night.

I should have stuck around for the team to come back into the locker room and for my ear bashing from Coach for losing my temper against one of our own, but I couldn't stick looking into his eyes once again. That fucker's got something that belongs to me and I'm not going to roll over and watch it happen.

When the lights of a store come into view in the distance, I decide to try my luck.

I nod at the cashier as I enter and breathe a sigh of relief that it's a young guy who looks like he might just understand my need for an escape tonight.

I grab a bottle of vodka, a couple of bags of chips and a few pre-made pasta dishes to shove in my fridge once I make it home tonight and carry the lot to the register praying that he'll just ring it up and let me be on my way.

The guy scans the food, obviously leaving the bottle

until the end and my stomach knots. Now I've got it in touching distance, I need it more than ever. The relief from my fucked up reality is right there, but he holds all the cards. If he IDs me then I'm fucked. I've got a fake at home for these exact situations, but I didn't think I'd need it tonight.

"Bad night?" the guy asks, his fingers wrapping around the neck of the bottle.

"Like you wouldn't believe."

"I've got girl issues myself, I know how that can be, man." His assumption that my issue must be because of a girl pisses me off but sadly, he's spot on.

"Sucks, huh?"

My mood brightens just a little as the little beep from the register rings through my ears and I watch as the guy drops the bottle into the bag with the rest of my purchases.

"Good luck with your girl," he calls once I've paid and started heading toward the door.

"You too, man."

Things look up a little as I head toward the beach with my new purchases under my arm. I'm about to forget everything and it couldn't be more welcome.

I make sure I'm hidden from any passersby and drop down between a couple of dunes. I pull the bottle from the bag and twist the top.

I wince as the first mouthful burns down my throat, but aside from someone punching me in the face for being a total waste of fucking space it's the exact pain I need.

I swallow another and another until the events of

tonight start to get a little hazy. I'm ashamed of my actions. I'm supposed to be the team captain for fuck's sake. I should have all our guy's backs and be fully focused on the game, but I let that slip and all because my head's too full of her. I thought hurting her would get her out of my head, block the memories she dragged back to the surface, but I was so fucking wrong. She might have dampened down the memories, but she's most definitely still in my fucking head.

I have no idea how long I sit in the dunes taking shot after shot of the vodka while munching my way through the first bag of chips I picked up, but eventually the ringing of my cell gets impossible to ignore.

Pulling it from my pocket, I look up for the first time and see that the sun has long set and the moon is reflecting in the inky black sea beyond.

I've got a stream of missed calls and texts from a range of people, I'm not surprised after my disappearing act but it's Ethan's name that once again lights up my screen.

"What?" I bark, the fact I've even bothered answering pisses me off.

"You coming to celebrate our win?"

"No. No one will want me there, I almost fucked it up."

"Enough with the self-pity, Thorn, no one gives a shit. We won in the end, that's all that matters."

"I'm good thanks," I say, looking down at my party for one surrounding me.

"Oh come on, there's booze and pussy for miles. You

know that Shane's parties are the best bit about having him around. Plus, Amalie's here and she looks fucking smoking."

That final statement has me a little more interested and fire beginning to burn in my belly. "Should I care?" I hope the words come out as uninterested, but I have no idea if I succeed. The vodka's starting to make my head spin to the point I'm losing focus.

"Fuck yeah you should, she's dancing with Shane, and the way he's looking at her, man. It's like he wants to—"

"Enough. That's enough." I hang up to the sound of him laughing down the line. The fucker knew how to get me there. If I were sober, I might care about being played but right now all I care about is making sure her body isn't rubbing up against Shane's.

Dragging myself from the ground, I collect up my shit and start making my way along the beach.

Shane's house parties are pretty legendary, although not by his own doing. He's got older twin brothers who went off to college two years ago who are the ultimate party animals and two parents who always seem to be in another state. Oh and wealthier than I can only dream of. Their house is huge and sits right on the beach. His dad was one of the biggest NFL stars this country has seen, and the oldest Dunn boys lived for the celebrity status they were gifted with. They've both gone off to an Ivy League university with full sports scholarships, not that they needed it. Rumor had it that all the top college teams were begging for them, they wanted a slice of the fame too, understandably. It pissed me off more than I'd ever admit that they get a free ride just because of their dad while I'm here with nothing and with no chance at a college education. Yeah, so everyone knows my mother's name, but her reputation isn't going to get me fucking anywhere in this world.

Walking up the street full of massive, pretentious houses, my stomach knots with how my life could have been. Another shot from the bottle I'm carrying soon helps to drown the thoughts. Cars fill the street outside the Dunn house and the closer I get, the louder the music is. The neighbors must fucking hate these parties.

As I round the house there are kids everywhere, many I recognize from school, some that must be college kids, that's only confirmed when I spot the Dunn twins playing beer pong at the other side of the garden with girls hanging off them. Luca nods at me when he spots me but soon gets distracted by the girl who places her hand on his cheek and turns him to kiss her.

Rolling my eyes at them, I head inside to try to find Ethan. When I do, he's got some brunette I've never seen before pressed up against the kitchen counter with his tongue down her throat.

"Hey," I call out but he's clearly way too distracted by the girl. Lifting my hand, I slap him across the back of the head. "Oi, Savage."

Pulling away from the chick, he turns to look at me at the same time he rubs the spot on his head I just hit. "Hey, asshole. Good to see you."

"Fuck off. It's not like you gave me much choice. Where is she?"

"No idea. I hope you're not too late, she was getting pretty wasted."

Fire burns through my veins. If Shane or any other motherfucker have put their hands on her while she's drunk, I'll fucking kill them.

I go to say something back, but when I turn to Ethan, I see that he's distracted again. "Get a fucking room."

He flips me off over his shoulder before pressing even harder into the girl.

Swiping a beer from the side, I set about trying to find my Brit.

My Brit.

Fucking hell, that vodka's affecting me more than I thought. Why do I keep claiming her as mine?

A few of the guys clap me on the back in greeting as I pass, others try to drag me into conversation about tonight's game, but I'm not interested, not until I find her.

I spot Camila with her pussy of a boyfriend first. Wrapping my hand around her forearm, I pull her off his lips, much to her displeasure. "Where is she?"

"What the fuck?" She looks between me and where I'm still touching her with disgust filling her eyes. There's no love lost between the two of us since all the shit went down with her and Mason a few years ago. I know where my loyalties lie and so does she, it seems.

"Where. Is. She?"

"Fuck you, Jake. You must be fucking crazy if you

think I'll feed her to you. You've already done enough damage." Noah, her fucking puppy dog boyfriend, wraps his arm around her waist, pulling her back against him, clearly not man enough to step out in front of her to deal with me himself.

"Just tell me so I don't have to waste time searching this place," I ask, already fed up with this conversation.

"Not a fucking chance." Luckily for me as she says this, her eyes flick over my shoulder. Following her stare, I find exactly what I wanted, or didn't, seeing as Shane's hands are currently on her body. "Shit."

Turning back to Camila, she swallows nervously.

"You fucking hurt her and—"

"And what? What the fuck are you going to do?"

She visibly pales, yet her boyfriend still does fuck all. "I haven't got time for this shit."

By the time I turn around, Brit and Shane have gone. "Fuck."

Glancing around, I find a door to the kitchen but there are so many bodies in the way that I doubt they made it through that quickly or ahead of me is a set of stairs. My heart pounds as images I don't need fill my head.

30

JAKE

Wasting no time, I run up, my slightly wobbly legs take the stairs two at a time with ease until my feet hit the first-floor landing. Working my way down the long hallway, I throw open door after door revealing a mixture of empty and occupied rooms with couples in varying states of dress. I don't bother saying anything until I get to the last room on this floor and swing the door open.

"Get your fucking hands off her."

Shane stills, his hands holding Brit around the waist as if he's about to run them up her stomach toward her... *Shit.*

My fists clench at my sides as I wait for her to say something about my interruption, but at no point does she lift her head from Shane's shoulder.

Narrowing my eyes at his panicked expression, I take a step forward, trying to figure out what's going on.

"What the fuck are you doing?"

"N-nothing. She's wasted, I was just going to lie her down to sleep it off."

"For your sake, I really fucking hope that's true." My voice is low and menacing. The muscles in his neck ripple as he swallows down his nervousness.

It's not until a soft groan comes from the limp body in his arms that I remember what the fuck I'm doing right now.

Slipping my arm between the two of them, I make quick work of pulling her from him.

"What the hell. Just put her on my bed. She needs to sleep."

"I'm not letting her stay within a mile of you."

Shane's face burns red with anger, a vein pulsing in his forehead. "That's not your decision to make. She fucking hates you."

"She's gonna fucking hate you if I leave her here for you to do whatever it was you were just about to do."

"I wasn't..." His hands fly up in exasperation. "I was just getting her away from the party. I wouldn't hurt her."

"Don't believe you," I bark, swinging her body up into my arms. She immediately wraps hers tightly around my shoulders and snuggles her face into my neck. My chest swells but I know it's not the time to focus on that. I need to get her out of here.

"You can't just walk out with her. How do I know you're not going to hurt her?"

"Because I wouldn't hurt a fucking hair on her head."

"Says the guy who sent a photo around the school making her out to be a whore."

"Have you just about finished sticking your nose into my business?"

"Nowhere fucking near, especially when you've got the girl I want in your arms."

"She's not yours, Dunn. Never was and never will be."

"And you really think she's yours?" he calls, but he's too late, I'm already walking away with my girl in my arms.

"Yeah, yeah I do," I whisper to no one.

Heads turn the second my feet hit the ground, a few chins drop and eyes widen as they take in the two of us.

"He's got to be fucking kidding me," I hear Camila fume, but I don't hang around long enough to hear what else she's got to say.

The sea of people part as I head toward the kitchen and thankfully at the end of it I find Mason nursing a glass of water.

"I need a lift."

"What the fuck are you doing, Thorn?"

"Getting her away from his wandering hands." His brows pinch but he doesn't argue. Instead, he places his glass down and leads the way out of Shane's house.

"Wait, wait," Camila calls after fighting her way through the crowds who obviously didn't move for her. "What the hell's going on? What's wrong with her?"

"Drunk? Drugged? Fuck knows. All I do know is that I found her in his bedroom with his hands on her. Not. Fucking. Happening."

Camila blanches, I assume at my overprotectiveness, but really I don't give a fuck.

"Shit, is she okay?"

"She will be."

Camila looks between the three of us, confusion written all over her face. I can see that she wants to take care of her friend, but she also understands that she's not got a chance in hell right now.

"Can I trust you with her?" I understand her concern, hell if the roles were reversed, I'd do anything I could to stop this from happening right now but Camila's not me, and I'm not one to back down.

"You can. I won't hurt her."

"I'm not sure that's true," she whispers.

"I won't touch her, you have my word."

"It wasn't her body I was worried about."

My mouth opens to respond but no words pass my lips.

"Are we fucking going or not. I didn't intend on spending my night out here with her." Mason's eyes flit to Camila and as always, I can see his conflicted feelings for her. He wants to hate her, I understand that more than most, but he can't really make himself do it.

"Yeah, open the back door."

It takes a bit of maneuvering but eventually I manage to get myself and Brit into the back seat of Mason's car. I lay her across with her head in my lap.

Staring down at her sleeping face, I run my fingers through her soft hair, taking in the array of shades of blonde beneath my fingers.

"I hope you know what you're doing," Mason says from the front seat.

"Not a fucking clue, bro. The only thing I know for certain is that I couldn't leave her there. The way he was touching her." My muscles lock up as I remember it.

"Are you sure you weren't just seeing what you wanted to see? Shane's not like that. He wouldn't touch a fly."

"Even if I was, I'm still not happy about her being in his room."

"Fuck me, Jake. You've really got it bad, huh?"

"What?"

All he does is laugh, telling me he knows just as much as I do how I feel for this girl. He knew before I did, hence why he was calling me out on my bullshit.

"You know she has every right to never forgive you for what you've done, right?"

"Yep, I'm aware."

———

Silence fills the car, the only sounds that can be heard is that of our breathing as Mason navigates away from the coast and into the town.

"Where the hell are you going?" I bark when he takes a wrong turn.

"Taking her home."

"No fucking way. We're going to my place."

"You expect me to leave her with you after everything?"

"Uh, yeah. You've just pointed out how I feel about her. I'm not going to touch her." His eyes hold mine in the mirror but after a few seconds, he's forced to look back to the road. "We can't take her home, her gran will be asleep, and she'll want to know what's wrong with her."

Blowing out a long breath, Mason white knuckles the steering wheel. "I'm not fucking happy about this."

"I don't need you to be. I just need you to take us to my place, and to trust me."

"Fine. But if you fuck this up, I'll knock your fucking teeth out."

"I'd like to see you try."

Mason laughs but the tension in his shoulders remains as he turns the car around and heads toward my trailer. In reality, it's the last place I want to take Brit, she's better than my damp fucking trailer but I don't have much else to offer her.

He brings the car to a stop in front of my aunt and uncle's house but doesn't kill the engine as he gets out and helps me pull a passed out Brit from the backseat.

"You okay from here?" Hesitation about allowing this to happen fills his voice. Part of me hates that he's questioning my motives but a bigger part of me is happy that he cares about her and feels the need to be concerned.

"Yeah, we're good."

"Don't make me regret this."

"Thanks for the lift, man. I really appreciate it after everything."

With a quick nod of his head, he gets back in the

car and speeds off. I'm under no illusion that things between us are not going to go back to how they were before the girl in my arms appeared and threw my life into turmoil, but at least we've made progress.

I take each step toward my trailer carefully, although most of the effects of the vodka vanished the moment I saw her in his arms, I know I'm not sober by any means.

By the time I've dug my key out of my pocket and got her inside, my chest heaves with exertion. Maybe I should have asked Mason for help, I wonder as my breath rushes past my lips.

Walking straight through to my bedroom, I gently lower her down. My breath catches at the sight of her blonde hair fanning my dark pillow and her long, slender body lying across my bed. No girl's been in my bed before, fuck, other than Poppy, no girl's been inside my trailer. I wouldn't want any of the girls at school seeing this shithole. Somehow I already know that Brit's not going to judge. Hell, she's probably going to be too hungover, or angry, to even notice.

Dropping to my knees, I carefully slip her sneakers from her feet and place them on the floor. My eyes run up the smooth, muscular lines of her legs and my balls ache to feel how soft her skin is. But I won't. I won't touch without her permission.

Grabbing a clean pair of boxers, I go to leave the room for a shower. I didn't hang around long enough to have one after I got kicked out of the game and I stink. I'm actually surprised the stench didn't wake her from her drunken slumber.

I have the quickest shower possible, totally ignoring my cock that's happily bobbing between my legs hoping that she'll wake up and pay it some attention, I'm too impatient to be with her. Knowing just how much I need to be laying beside her in my bed freaks me the hell out, but I try not to dwell on it. I tell myself that I'm just concerned she'll wake up and not know where she is or that she'll be sick and choke on her own puke. The thought of that happening in my bed makes me shudder, but I'd deal with it for her if I had to.

31

AMALIE

My head's spinning before I even open my eyes. It takes me a few seconds to realise that the last thing I remember from the party was dancing with Shane and feeling my eyes starting to get heavy.

Bolting upright, I drag my eyes open and look at my unfamiliar surroundings.

Where the fuck am I?

It's certainly not Shane's mammoth house. I didn't have him down for a rich kid, or a kid who had a famous football-playing father, just goes to prove that you can't judge a book by its cover.

I'm still trying to piece together what's happened when some movement in the bed beside me startles me.

"How are you feeling?" The rough, sleepy yet familiar voice breaks through my panic. Looking down, my eyes almost pop out of my head.

Why the utter fuck am I in his bed?

"No, no, no, no," I chant as I shove the covers off me and scramble from the bed. "This can't be happening."

In my haste to get away, my foot gets tangled in his sheets and I fly headfirst toward the floor. Clearly, he's got a much clearer head, because just before my nose makes contact with his dingy carpet, two large hands grab on to my waist and I'm pulled back up.

"Get the hell off me," I snap, starting to fight to get away once again. When I'm released, he's not only saved me but deposited me into his lap.

When I glance to my left, inches upon inches of his tanned skin greets me and I feel a little flutter of something between my legs.

No, no, this is not happening.

"Why the hell am I in your bed?"

"You know," he says, placing his fingers against my cheek and forcing me to look up into his sparkling blue eyes. "You should probably be thanking me, not shouting at me?"

His fingers slip around the back of my neck, allowing his thumb to caress the edge of my jaw.

"O-oh yeah?" I hate that his touch makes my ability to think and speak falter. "And why's that?"

"I was your knight in shining armor, baby." Butterflies erupt in my stomach, but they almost make the sick feeling I've been trying to ignore more apparent. It must be written on my face because his eyes soften a little before he begs, "Please don't puke on me."

"It would be no more than you deserve." When I go to get off him, he allows me. I'm not sure if it's because he didn't really want me there in the first place or if he's afraid I am about to cover him in last night's dinner. I stumble back to the wall and allow it to help hold me up as my head spins and my stomach rolls.

"Fair enough," he mutters, his calm demeanor making my brows draw together in confusion.

"I'm sorry, but am I dreaming or am I really in your trailer with you being nice to me?"

"Don't worry, I'm about as shocked as you are."

"You say that, but you're not the one who woke up here with no memory of the journey."

"That's probably for the best."

"Really? Why? What did you do?"

"Me?" he asks, sitting up against the headboard and allowing the covers to pool low across his waist.

Eyes up, Amalie. Eyes up.

"Yeah, you. Did you manage to get me into some compromising positions so you've got some new images to spread around? I might be clothed right now, but I wouldn't put it past you to—"

"I didn't fucking strip you, Brit. I didn't fucking do anything other than bring you here to make sure you were safe." His voice deepens and I know I've touched a nerve.

"Well that was big of you but what exactly were you rescuing me from?"

"Shane."

"What? That's insane. Why the hell would you need to rescue me from him?"

"How much did you drink last night?"

His sudden topic change gives me whiplash. "Uh... a couple of beers and two or three shots."

"So not enough to be totally out of it?"

"I wouldn't say so, no. Why?"

"Because when I found you, you couldn't even open your eyes and Shane was just about to—" He stops himself saying anymore but I don't miss the clenching of his fists at his sides or the pulsing muscle in his neck.

"He was what?"

"Touching you."

"Shane? Really?"

"I can only tell you what I walked in on."

"You're fucking delusional, do you know that?"

"Maybe, but I couldn't risk it."

I really need to get the hell out of here and away from him, but I can't help myself. "Risk what?"

"Knowing someone else has their hands on what's mine."

"Yours?" An unamused laugh falls from my lips.

There isn't a hint of amusement on Jake's face as he swings his legs from the bed, stands and moves toward me. The way his stare stays locked on me reminds me of how a lion might stalk their prey.

He doesn't stop until he's nose to nose with me. I fight to keep my lips closed as my breathing increases knowing that if my breath smells as bad as it tastes then I'll probably turn him off in an instant, not that that would necessarily be a bad thing.

His hands land on either side of my head and his

own, much fresher breath, brushes over my face as he continues to stare.

When he speaks, it's so quiet and low that I start to think I imagined it. "Yeah. Mine."

His head lowers, his lips closing in on mine and I panic.

"You're fucking delusional, you know that?" I ask once I've slipped under his arms and made it to the door.

His shoulders drop when he realises that our time is over. That is until he pulls on the mask that I'm used to. His features harden and I suck in a breath to prepare for what's going to come next. "You're right. I have no fucking idea what I was thinking. I should have left you there. Let them pass you around like the little fucking whore you are."

Tears immediately burn at the back of my throat and climb up toward my eyes. "I hate you," I scream, my voice cracking with emotion before I run through his trailer to find the door.

The sound of his angry roar and a loud crash behind me makes my steps slow a little, but it's not enough to make me turn around. Nor is the fact I realise the second I hit the grass beneath his trailer that I don't have any fucking shoes on.

I run until I get to the trees, then I have to start taking it a little more carefully as I navigate the twigs and stones underfoot.

I just get to the clearing when a snapping twig behind me catches my attention. I prepare to run despite how much it's going to fucking hurt but I don't get a chance. A strong arm wraps around my waist and I'm pulled back into a hard body.

His increased breaths tickle my ears and send a shiver down my spine. "I'm sorry, okay?"

Sucking in a large breath, I prepare to turn around and face him. "No. No, it's not fuck—"

My words are cut off as his lips slam down on mine. I forget all about the state of my mouth as his tongue teases at the seam of my lips and I allow him entry, too keen to experience all he has to give.

Just like before, he's pent up and angry. One arm stays wrapped around my waist while the other threads into my hair, tilting my head so I'm in the perfect position for him. The length of his body presses against mine, his length pressing into my stomach.

It takes at least a minute or two before reality seeps back in. Lifting my hands, I push against his chest.

"Jake, stop," I mumble against his lips. He steps back putting his hands up in surrender.

My eyes drop from his and I realise he came chasing after me in just his tight pair of boxer briefs, which quite clearly show exactly what he's got beneath, and a pair of trainers. As I stare down at the tented fabric, my tongue darts out to wet my bottom lip, my core flooding with heat.

I look back up just in time for his mouth to open. I expect some smug comment about being impressed by his size to fall from his lips so I'm shocked by what I do hear. "Have breakfast with me?"

"What?" His total three-sixty from his attitude as I ran from his trailer totally throws me for a loop.

"Have breakfast with me. It's still early, your gran won't be up yet, will she?"

"No, but... I need to shower and..."

"I have a shower. Plus I know the best place to get rid of your hangover."

I stare into his eyes, waiting for him to tell me that this is a joke, but he doesn't. He just patiently waits for my answer.

I want to say no. I know it would be the sensible thing to do, but the temptation of food eventually gets the better of me.

"Okay, fine. But the second you turn back into the arsehole you usually are, I'm leaving."

His lips curl up into a smile that hits me right in the chest. Why do I get the feeling this breakfast is more for him than it is for me? But that's crazy, after everything, why would he want to spend time with me in public?

Reaching out, he takes my hand in his. The small amount of contact warms me all the way to my toes.

"We're not going to Aces," I warn as we emerge from the trees.

"I wasn't even going to suggest it."

Everything is wrong about this, yet as I step up into his old trailer hidden at the bottom of the garden, everything feels so right.

"Make yourself comfortable. It's not much and I'm sure nothing like what you're used to but it's all I've got." For the first time since I saw him across the school that very first day, I see a little of his insecurity slip in. By some miracle, I've managed to peel away just a corner of the impenetrable mask he always wears. I'm not sure why, or what I did to deserve it but right this moment, the guy I'm seeing in front of me isn't Thorn, king of Rosewood High, but Jacob, an eighteen-year-old guy who's just as unsure about life as I am. Maybe we're not as different as he thinks.

"It's perfect, thank you."

"I'll go and find you a clean towel so you can shower, I'll be back in a bit." He goes to leave but stops before he's out of the kitchen area. "Here. I suspect you need these." I couldn't be more grateful for the little packet of painkillers that falls into my lap.

I wait for him to disappear and listen to his crashing around for a few minutes before I get up, pull the fridge open and grab a lukewarm bottle of water. Downing half of it, I throw a couple of pills into my mouth and hope they get to work fast on the pounding at my temples.

Falling back onto the inbuilt sofa, I prop one of the cushions under my head and close my eyes, trying like hell to drag up any memories from last night.

I must doze off because the next thing I know, a droplet of water hits my cheek and runs off into my hairline.

"What the—oh." I open my eyes to one fine sight. Jake's standing over me, his hair dripping wet from his shower and only a towel hanging low on his waist.

Biting down on my bottom lip, I try to fight the temptation to reach out and tug it from his body to properly discover what's hiding beneath.

"Go on, do it," he taunts.

"Do what?" I ask innocently, looking up at him through my lashes.

Dropping down to his haunches so his head is almost level with mine. "If you think I can't read your thoughts then you need to think again. How are you feeling?"

I take a second to focus on the throbbing in my head and realise that it is actually starting to subside.

"Better, thank you."

He stares at me for a few more seconds. I start to think he's going to kiss me again, but right before I'm about to move my head toward him, he stands and walks to the kitchen. "The bathroom's all yours. I should warn you that the showers not much more than a dribble and it never really gets that hot, but it kinda does the job. I left a new toothbrush on the side for you."

I cringe knowing that he has firsthand experience of just how disgusting my mouth is right now.

"I won't be long."

"Take your time. I'll make coffee... you like coffee, right?"

"I do."

"Maybe you're not so weird after all," he says as I make my way down to his bedroom.

I didn't pay much attention to the room before I stormed out earlier, but I saw enough to know that he's since tidied up and made his bed.

Looking back over my shoulder, I find his naked back as he reaches up into a cupboard and I can't help trying to figure him out. He clearly makes every effort to hide this part of his life, but why? Why does he live down here alone? Where are his parents?

The million and one questions I have about him swirl around my head as I chase the pathetic spray of water around the cubicle in an attempt to wash the remnants of last night off me.

32

JAKE

My body's practically vibrating with nervous energy as the water running in the bathroom sounds out around the trailer.

I have no idea what the fuck I'm doing. All I do know is that she's currently naked with water running down over her slender curves mere feet away, and I can't forget the pain that twisted my stomach almost in half when I watched her run away from me earlier. I wasn't ready for our time together to be over, even if she had no idea it was happening or why she was here. I try to ignore the fact that I'd basically kidnapped her, she had every right to want to run as far away as possible.

I'm sitting on my couch with my elbows resting on my knees and my head hanging between my shoulders when she steps into the kitchen. Glancing up, I find her hair piled on top of her head, one of my t-shirts covering her tiny frame and tied at her waist. Her long ass legs are still on full display in her short white skirt. My eyes damn near pop out of my head.

"I hope you don't mind, my top smelled of last night."

"N-no of course not. It... uh... looks better on you than it does on me."

She smiles shyly before glancing down at the counter. "This mine?"

"Yeah. Is it okay?"

"Do you have any milk?" I think she realizes her mistake the moment the words fall from her lips. "Actually, it's perfect."

Lifting the mug, I'm fascinated as she delicately blows across the top and then places her lips to the edge. She sips at the black coffee and does her best to look like she enjoys it but she falls a little far from the mark.

"You don't have to pretend to make me feel better," I say, pushing myself from the couch. "Come on, I'll buy you one you actually want to drink."

"Thank you."

It's still early and the only sounds that can be heard as we both step down from my trailer is the birds up in the trees.

Thankfully, there's no movement inside the house as we slip past and head out to the main road. I can sense Brit's stare as we make our way down to the bus stop at the end of the road. If I've got my timing right, then it should be here to take us away from this place any minute.

"Wow, Jake Thorn rides the bus." Her voice is light,

she's clearly only joking but still, my stomach twists and my muscles lock up at her mocking.

"Things aren't always as they seem, Brit."

She opens her mouth but soon decides better of it. When she does eventually speak, she changes the subject, but I can see her desperation to figure me out deep in her blue depths. "I've got a name, you know."

"I'm aware."

I don't give a reason and thankfully she doesn't press me for one because the bus comes around the corner.

Tapping my phone to the pad by the driver, I pay the return fare for both of us and we head toward the back of the bus.

"I can't remember the last time I was on a bus," she muses, watching the houses pass us by out the window.

"Don't tell me, you had a Range Rover or two and couldn't possibly use public transport."

Her eyes are wide and her chin drops at the bitterness in my tone.

"Actually, I didn't have a Range Rover—or two. I had a Mini, but I used to get the tube to college every day. Driving in London was... actually, I'm not defending myself to you. You seem to have me all figured out, so I'll just leave you to it."

Jesus, even when I'm trying to be nice, I end up putting my fucking foot in it. "I'm sorry, I didn't mean it like that."

She shrugs and turns back to look out the window. I feel like a douchebag for snapping at her, but it's not an unusual feeling these days.

The rest of the journey is silent. Tension comes from her in waves and I can only imagine that she's already regretting agreeing to this. She could be at home, sleeping off her hangover instead of sitting here beside me. She only moves when she hears me press the bell, indicating that we're about to get off.

"I'm only following you because I'm hungry. This place better be good," she sulks as she follows along beside me until I come to a stop outside a little backstreet diner I found a few years ago.

"It is good. Best pancakes in the state."

She mumbles something under her breath but I don't say anything. She's got every right to be pissed off with me.

I find us a seat in the back and a waitress with about twenty cans of hairspray coating her dreadful hair do and a little red apron comes running over.

"Good mornin'," she sings way too happily. "What can I get for you both?"

"Two coffees, one black, one with cream, and two chef's special breakfasts."

Brit's eyes drill into me, I ignore them and continue looking up at the waitress who finishes writing our order before looking between the two of us. I'd love to know what's she's thinking right now.

"Okay, coming up."

She turns on her heels and races toward the kitchen.

"I can order my own fucking food, Jake," Brit fumes, her shoulders tense and her lips twitching in anger.

"I know, but trust me. It's the best."

She slumps back against the chair and drops her attention to her nails.

I'm not entirely sure how we went from kissing in the trees to her ignoring my existence, but I do know that it's all my fault.

33

AMALIE

I try to ignore it but his stare burns into the top of my head as I look down at my hands.

Why the hell am I here?

I can only put my stupidity down to whatever it is that still running through my system after last night. I know I didn't have enough to drink to be so out of it that Jake was able to get me back to his place without me even being aware of it. I think it's pretty obvious that someone must have spiked my drink.

But who?

The most obvious suspect would be the guy sitting opposite me, but something tells me that this wasn't his doing. Something deep inside me really wants to believe that he was doing exactly what he said he was, looking after me, protecting me. But again, why? He's made it clear time and time again that he hates me. So why do it, and why chase me this morning and bring me here?

The waitress returns with our coffees and as much

as I want to be frustrated with him ordering for me, I can't be because I'm just grateful to have something drinkable. What he tried giving me back at his trailer was like treacle. I love my coffee, but it has to have milk.

Lifting the mug to my lips, my eyes meet his dark stare and a shudder runs through me. Any signs of the sweet and caring guy who looked after me both last night and this morning have gone. The Jake Thorn I know and... hate, is staring right back at me.

Taking a sip of coffee for courage, I ask the question I've been drying to know the answer to since the first time he looked at me.

"What exactly is your issue with me?"

He's silent for a few seconds and I start to think he's going to ignore that I've even asked a question when his elbows rest on the table and his eyes scan my face.

"It's not you exactly. You just remind me of someone I wouldn't piss on if they were on fire."

Whoa, okay.

Pure hatred fills his eyes and I realise that in reality, he might have let me off easily with the bullshit he's caused. There's something dark living inside him and it's just waiting to explode.

"Who?"

He shakes his head, clearly unwilling to divulge any more details. That's not going to stop me asking though.

"Okay, so how do I remind you of them?"

"At first, from a distance, I thought you looked like her. But... but now, it's just what you represent."

"And what is that exactly?"

"A rich, pretentious, privileged life that's full of fake, plastic, self-absorbed assholes who think anything important is only skin deep." It's not the first time he's said it, but it's the first time I really think about it.

"Wow. And that's the kind of person you think I am?"

"It's the world you came from."

"Maybe so, but I was born into that world. I didn't have a choice about it. But I've always had my own opinions of the industry my parents were a part of."

"Don't try to tell me that you didn't love it. All the attention, free designer clothes, being in front of the camera."

Part of me doesn't want to defend myself when he seems to have decided that he's already figured me out. But at the same time, I hate the judgmental look he's giving me like he knows me, when in reality he doesn't have a fucking clue. "I couldn't give a shit about the designer clothes. They're just clothes. They do the same job whether they cost twenty quid or two-thousand. And not that it's any of your business, but I've never been in front of the camera."

He snorts and I rear back.

"What's that supposed to mean?"

"Come off it, Brit. You've got supermodel written all over you, just like your mother. You're worth too much money not to force you into that world."

Pushing the chair out behind me with a loud screech, I stand and place my palms on the table. My breath races past my lips as I fight to keep control of my anger.

"For your information, my parents were good people. Yes, the industry they were in can be questioned a million ways and trust me when I say that I've done so, many many times. And yes, I might have the right look, but my parents would never, ever push me to do something I didn't want. I have always refused to be a part of that world. No amount of money could get me on that side of a camera doing some of the things those models do."

Jake visibly pales, but I don't want to hang around to find out why. Instead, I dart from the table and toward the exit, only he's quicker. His warm fingers wrap around my wrist and I'm forced to stop.

His body heat burns my back as he steps up to me and his breath tickles my ear. I shudder when his fingers tickle across the sliver of skin his tied up shirt reveals at my waist.

"I'm sorry. I was being an asshole."

"I'm getting used to it," I snap.

"Please come and sit back down. Just to eat and then you can go and never look back."

Something aches inside my chest at the idea of walking away from him for good. It's what I should be doing because he's right, he's an asshole. But for some reason, I'm a little bit addicted to him. A glutton for punishment or some shit because despite knowing better, I just keep coming back for more.

"Fine, but only because I'm hungry."

He releases me. I hate myself for it, but I immediately miss his contact.

When I turn back toward our table, the waitress is

just placing two giant plates down. The sight of the food has my stomach rumbling. The scent of the bacon, eggs, and pancakes hits my nose as I retake my seat and my mouth waters. He might be right about something, this looks amazing.

We eat in silence, but that doesn't mean I don't feel his stare every time he looks up at me. I refuse to meet his eyes in fear he somehow managed to stop being pissed off and looks at me with his vulnerable eyes instead. I knew he was jumping to some kinds of conclusions about me. If I'm honest, I thought it was to do with money. It's no secret that my parents were very successful and wealthy, whereas it's becoming more and more obvious that he doesn't have all that much.

"Why do you live at the bottom of your aunt and uncle's garden?" The words are out before I have a chance to stop them.

"It's where I belong," he says sadly.

"Jake, that's not—"

"It's exactly what it is. You're not the only one who thinks I'm a waste of good oxygen." The honesty in his words is enough to kill any response that was on my tongue. "I'm not what everyone at school thinks I am. But pretending is better than reality. I just need to graduate and then I'm out of here."

"To where?"

"Anywhere. I don't care, I just need a fresh start somewhere no one knows me."

"What about college?"

My brows draw together when he laughs. "You

really think I can afford to go to college? You've seen where I live."

"I know but—"

"No buts. It is what it is. The second I'm done with high school, I'm starting again. I don't give a shit where or what job I work to pay for it."

"Surely you could get a scholarship or something," I muse, not really understanding how it all works yet.

He shrugs. "Doubt it."

"Have you even looked into it?"

"Can you drop it, please?"

The desperation in his eyes means I do as he asks, for now. I don't know him all that well, but I do know he's better than to throw away the idea of college quite so easily.

The rest of our time in the diner is in silence. But it's not uncomfortable like it could be. Jake has slipped back into his softer side, the one I know he doesn't show a lot of people. It makes me wonder why he's dropping his guard with me.

"I should get you home before your gran worries."

"It's okay, she knows I went to a party last night. I can't imagine she was expecting me."

Jake swallows nervously. "About last night."

"What about it?"

"Someone spiked your drink."

"Seems that way. I'm pretty sure it wasn't Shane though. Please don't do anything stupid." I feel like the stupid one the second the words fall from my lips. Why would he do something stupid to protect someone he hates?

"I will find out who it was and they'll fucking pay."

Reaching over the table, I place my hand down on his, the warmth spreading all the way up my arm. "No, Jake. Just leave it, please. I don't need you fighting my battles."

"What if I want to?"

The waitress returns with the bill and Jake pulls out his wallet.

"Fuck," he mutters, obviously finding it emptier than he was expecting.

"It's okay, I've got it."

Handing over some cash, he stiffens at the other side of the table. His lips pressing into a thin line and the muscle in his neck pulsing.

I want to ask about his last comment but I don't get the chance because a shadow falls over us.

"Well, well, well, isn't this cozy."

I know the voice, I don't need to look up to confirm who it is. Instead, I keep my eyes on Jake's. They harden instantly, his shutters coming down putting an end to whatever kind of moment we were just having.

"Brit's just leaving."

My chin drops in shock.

"What are you even doing? Having breakfast together?" Chelsea asks. Total disbelief for what she's seeing clear in her voice. "Your looks might get you whatever you want in London, but they won't work here."

Chelsea juts her hip out, impatiently waiting for me to move but I ignore her and focus on Jake.

"What the hell are you doing?" I whisper but it's not quiet enough.

"Jesus, you really are a whore, begging for him to want you."

Jake's eyes stay locked on mine but I can't read anything in them. The boy who was here expressing his need to protect me has long gone. Taking three calming breaths, I push myself from the seat, preparing to go nose to nose with the school bitch.

"You're in my seat."

I stand and just like the first time we met in the principal's office, she has to look up at me and I can't help the smirk that twitches at my lips. She must fucking hate it.

"I thought you'd be too good to be spending time in this part of town."

She visibly pales. I might not really have a clue where we are right now, but it was obvious on the journey here that it's not the nicest area. I didn't think too much of it after Jake said he wanted to get away but as I stare into Chelsea's emerald eyes it suddenly dawns on me. He's ashamed. He came here with me so we could hide.

"I'm done with this bullshit. You're more than welcome to him."

"Like he'd ever go anywhere near someone like you. He's always been mine."

My body stills, my need to argue with her threatening to get the better of me. My shoulders tighten and my emotions burning the back of my throat creeps its way up to my eyes. When a guy starts heading my way, I'm forced to move and thankfully it's toward the door. I don't need the kind of drama Chelsea can bring in my life.

I briefly glance back over my shoulder, I find the guy who walked in with his arm around Chelsea. He's vaguely familiar, I wonder briefly who it is seeing as he's obviously older than her but the stare I feel from the booth I just vacated is too strong to ignore.

Our eyes lock, something flickers through his but it's gone too quickly to be able to read.

The tears that were burning my eyes threaten to drop and I run. Racing down the street, I find an alley and slip down it to allow me a little privacy to fall apart.

My back hits the wall and I slide down until my arse hits the dirty ground. A sob erupts from my throat and I drop my head into my hands. How could I have been so stupid to believe he actually wanted to spend time with me. He just wanted to use me as a dirty little secret.

I think back to how sweet he's been, and it only makes me cry harder. I shouldn't like him. I shouldn't care. But there's so much more to Jake Thorn than he allows the world to see. For some reason he's given me a glimpse of the broken boy hiding beneath the surface and I can't help but want more.

Stupid, stupid girl.

Once my tears subside, realisation hits me. I've no idea where I am and no clue how to get home.

Pulling my bag onto my lap, I dig around until I find my phone at the bottom amongst a load of receipts and coins. Thankfully, the battery's not dead, although it is at fifteen percent thanks to the stream of messages, missed calls and voicemails that I've totally missed from Camila and Shane.

Guilt sits heavy in my stomach that they've no idea where I am or if I'm okay or not. Do they even know I left with Jake last night?

Hitting call on Camila's number, I put my phone to my ear and listen to it ring.

When she eventually picks up, it's clear I've woken her. Her voice is deep and rough with sleep but she soon sobers when memories of last night must hit her.

"Amalie? Where the hell are you? Are you okay?"

"Yeah, I'm good. Is there any chance you could do me a favour?"

"Of course."

I explain briefly where I am, listing of a few places I can see from my hiding place. Thankfully, Camila knows and promises to be there in no more than thirty minutes. I can already tell by the tone of her voice that I've got a million questions coming my way.

I want to go and get more coffee but the thought of running into Jake again is enough to make me stay put. Seeing him in school is going to be bad enough after everything that happened between us.

34

AMALIE

I t's only twenty minutes later when I spot Camila's car pull up to the curb. Dragging my exhausted body from the ground, I brush the dirt from my butt and head her way. As instructed, she stays in the car and in seconds, I'm pulling the passenger door open and climbing in.

"What the fuck is going on, Amalie? You get carried out of a party off your fucking face by your worst enemy and now I'm here picking you up. You've got some serious explaining to do."

"Take me somewhere quiet for coffee and I'll explain. Not Aces," I quickly add before she even suggests it.

So for the second time this morning I find myself in another backstreet diner with another waitress pouring me coffee.

"So he marched in all alpha-like and demanded to know where I was?" I ask, my brows drawn together in confusion. "Why?"

"Who the hell knows? But according to Shane he lost his shit with him, dragged you away from him and out of the house."

"He thinks Shane spiked my drink and was going to..." I trail off not needing to say the words out loud.

"Shane? Shane Dunn?"

"I know. I told him that he was crazy and that Shane would never do anything like that. But he found me in his room with his hands on me."

"Shane was just going to put you to bed to sleep it off."

"That's what I said, but Jake's having none of it."

"Okay, so what happened with Jake?"

I'm silent for a few moments as I try to figure out how to answer that question.

"Oh my god, something happened with him, didn't it? OMG did you fuck him?"

"What? No, I didn't fuck him." My cheeks heat knowing that although that's true, I'm not totally innocent. I did kiss him this morning and unbeknown to Camila, it's not our first either.

"But..." she encourages, scooting forward on her seat waiting to get the juicy gossip.

"We kissed."

"Oh my god," she squeals, clapping her hands together in delight. "It's like in the movies. He hates you to cover up the fact he really likes you."

Rolling my eyes at her romantic heart, I sigh. "No, I'm pretty sure he just hates me. I was probably just some stupid bet to him or something to see if I'm pathetic enough to fall for it. Well, ding a ling, I clearly am because look what happened. Ugh... I fucking hate him."

"Really?"

"Yes. No. I don't fucking know. There's just something inside him that calls to me. I wish I couldn't see it and just focus on him being an arsehole, but I can't help feeling like he needs help. He wants me to see it even though he's scared."

"So going back to my earlier comment..."

"You're a nightmare. How's Noah?"

"He's good. I told him when I was a little drunk that his birthday night is the night," she says with a wink.

"Wait. You guys haven't..."

"Nope. I told him I wanted to wait, and he respected that. But I'm bored now. Everyone else is at it so..."

"You can't do it just because everyone else is."

"I know and that's not the reason. We've been together for ages and I feel it's right. It's time to take it to the next level before we start stressing about college and all that."

I'm still not totally buying it. "You love him, right?"

"Of course." Narrowing my eyes, I try to figure out what she's hiding, but it's pointless especially because I'm not sure she knows it herself. I've seen them together plenty of times now. On the outside, they appear to be the perfect couple, but I can't help feeling like something's just not quite right.

"So what's next with Thorn?" she asks, dragging the conversation back to me.

"What's next is that we stop talking about him. I'm done with him."

"Liar. I can't believe he kissed you. Rumor has it that he doesn't kiss anyone. Ever."

Hearing that changes my mind about talking more about him. "Oh come off it. He's the ultimate school player, he must have kissed loads of girls."

"Nope never, apparently."

I think back to Dash night, which feels like a million years ago now, and his reaction to Chelsea putting her lips on him. Maybe what Camila's saying is true. But if it is, why did he kiss me?

———

I'm no less confused about the whole Jake situation when Camila drops me back at Gran's later that morning. She takes one look at me in a boy's t-shirt and raises her eyebrows.

"So not what you're thinking," I mutter, walking past her and heading straight for my room.

"When you're ready to talk, you know where I am."

My stomach twists as I fall back against my bedroom door. I don't want to shut Gran out after everything she's done for me but how am I meant to explain all of this to her. Even running the events of the past few weeks over in my head makes me feel like a crazy person. How the hell will it sound to her?

I take my time showering and washing his smell from me. It seems that no length of attempting to do that will be effective, his unique scent still lingers in my nose.

After pulling on a pair of pajamas and throwing an

oversized jumper over the top, I pile my hair on top of my head and head out, expecting a million and one questions from Gran.

"You hungry?"

"I can make myself something. You stay there." She's sitting on her sofa reading one of the trashy magazines that she loves. I've no idea how she can keep reading them after some of the lies they've published about my parents and their colleagues over the years.

"Don't be silly. Take a seat and I'll make you a grilled cheese. Sound good?"

"Sounds amazing, thank you."

Silence falls around us as she works, and I sip the glass of water she passed over for me.

"Amalie, I know I'm old and you probably think that I couldn't possibly understand but please, I'm begging you. Talk to me. I'm worried about you."

The lies are right on the tip of my tongue, but when I do speak, the exact opposite fall out. "It's a boy."

"I assumed as much. Anyone I might know?"

I ignore that question, nowhere near ready to admit who it is in case she doesn't approve. If she knows who he is and where he lives, which I'm confident she does because nothing gets past my gran, then I've no doubt she wouldn't approve. Why would she? Jake's the school's notorious bad boy who's mostly treated me like shit since the first day I started at Rosewood.

"I shouldn't like him. He hasn't been exactly pleasant since I started." I skirt around the reality of the situation. "But there's more to the guy than he allows the outside world to see. He's hiding but I can see his vulnerability and I wonder if that's why he doesn't like me all that much."

She smiles at me, and a mysterious twinkle in her eye before turning to plate up my sandwich.

"What's the look for?"

"He's scared, Amalie. He knows you can see deeper than anyone else and he's scared of it being used against him."

I consider her theory for a few minutes and although I can't argue because I think she might have nailed it. I'm not sure that's all of the problem.

"There's more than that. He said something cryptic about Mum and Dad's lifestyle and it being the reason he doesn't like me."

"What's his name?" she asks again.

Laughing at her second attempt, I just shake my head at her. "Nice try."

"What?" The innocent look on her face might work on others, but it's not fooling me one bit.

"I'm not telling you because you probably know every single detail about his life and I don't want secondhand gossip."

Gran gasps, placing her hand over her heart like I've wounded her. "I'll have you know, young lady, that my knowledge of our town and its occupants is factual. No gossip passes these lips."

Laughing at her, I pull the plate she passed over toward me. The smell of the melted cheese making my mouth water. "Riiight," I say, humouring her before groaning in delight when I get my first bite.

"You want my advice?"

"Sure."

"If you think there's more to this boy, then you're probably right. If you think it's worth discovering, then keep digging but just be aware that what you could find might be ugly. If he's not worth the pain, then walk away... if you can."

Gran walks from the room, leaving me with that little nugget of advice. That question rolls around my head for the rest of the day. Can I just walk away? It's one hundred percent what I should do after the way he's treated me. But what we should do and what we want to do are often at either end of the spectrum.

Standing in front of my full-length mirror, I brush my hair out before retrying it up and out of my way so I can sleep. The light breeze from my open window causes goosebumps to cover my exposed skin and I quickly dive into bed.

Gran's got air conditioning throughout the entire house, but I can't get used to sleeping in it. The Brit in me much prefers the warm breeze coming from the window at night. I know I should shut it, especially after my late night visitor the other night but I can't bring myself to do it.

Anticipation mixes with Gran's words from earlier and I'm left tossing and turning for hours, hoping that sleep will claim me. But eventually a noise that I was expecting—hoping—for sounds out around the room.

The crunch of feet against the ground outside has my heart jumping into my throat.

He came.

I lie as still as I can, hoping I look like I'm fast

asleep. I missed his visit last time and I'm desperate to know what he's going to do.

The click of the door opening makes me jump even though I'm expecting it. I fight to keep my breathing steady as he slips inside the room.

"Motherfucker," he whispers, sounding frustrated. I can only imagine it's because I didn't lock my door like I was requested to do.

His footsteps slowly get closer, before he kneels down beside me. His scent surrounds me once again. My heart threatens to thunder out of my chest as I wait for what he's going to do next.

"I'm so fucking sorry, Brit. You should wake up and send me away for being such a fucking screw up. I wasn't ashamed to be with you earlier, I just... I fucked up."

His voice cracks with desperation and I can't help my eyes flickering open.

He's left the door curtain open enough that the moon lights him up like he's under a spotlight. His head's hanging between his shoulders, he looks as broken as he sounds. And instead of anger filling my veins like it should, I find my fingers twitching at my sides to reach out to touch him.

"I shouldn't fucking be here. I just needed to know you were safe."

His head lifts and my breath catches as I wait for his eyes to find mine.

His lips part when he realises that I'm not asleep like he was expecting.

"Fuck, I—shit." He stands, his hands going to his

hair and pulling to the point I think it's going to come out. "Fuck, I'm..."

He steps toward the door and I panic.

"Jake, wait." My voice is barely a whisper, but it's enough to stop him.

He stills but doesn't lift his gaze from the floor.

"I shouldn't be here," he admits, sadly.

"But you're here anyway."

Flipping my covers back, I push up onto my elbows and look at him. His shoulders are slumped in defeat, his hands hanging loosely around his hips.

"Jake," I breathe.

Something in my voice makes him turn, his eyes find mine before they drop down over my scantily clad body.

"Fuck."

His feet eat up the space between us and in mere seconds his hand is sliding into the back of my hair and his lips find mine.

I sense the change in him as we connect. Gone is the broken boy who just stood before me instead the man kissing me is lost to his need.

His tongue plunges into my mouth and I hungrily suck it deeper. I shouldn't allow this after what he did today but the second he puts his hands on me, it's like everything aside from the two of us in this moment exists.

Jake climbs onto my bed, his knees pinning my thighs in place as he continues to kiss me like it's our first and he can't get enough.

When we're both desperate for breath, he pulls

back. His eyes are dark and hooded as he stares down at me. My core throbs for more as his fingers tickle over my chest and run along the hem of my tank causing my nipples to pucker behind the fabric.

"Tell me to leave. Tell me that you hate me and that I need to leave."

His fingers ghost lower and brush over my nipples, making me shudder.

"You're right, I hate you but—"

I don't get to tell him that I don't want him to leave right now because he lowers my vest and pulls my nipple into his hot mouth.

"Oh, fuck." My hips buck involuntarily but it doesn't achieve anything as Jake's still pinning me to the bed. His lips twitch in delight at my reaction.

He moves to the other side, exposing that breast as well so he can do as he likes. He licks, nips, and sucks while I moan and writhe beneath him.

I want to scream at him when he moves up my neck and runs his tongue around the shell of my ear.

"I'm going to make you feel so good, Brit."

My response is a moan as he starts crawling down my body. He licks at my breasts once again before lifting my tank and kissing down my stomach.

By the time he curls his fingers around the edge of my sleep shorts, they're soaking, my need for what he's got to give too much to bear.

"Jake, please."

"Fuck. Say that again."

"Jake," I breathe, his lips landing on my hipbone and trailing toward my center. "Please, I need... ohhh..."

Before I know what's happening, my shorts are gone and his breath tickles against my most sensitive part.

"So fucking sweet," he mutters, pushing my thighs wider and licking up the length of me.

"Oh, shit, shit, shit, Jake," I squeal, forgetting where I am and that we could be heard.

His tongue presses down against my clit before he starts circling, building me higher and higher. My hands alternate between fisting the sheet beneath me and sliding into his hair to keep him in place.

I shamelessly buck against his face, needing everything he has to give to wash away the anger and rejection he caused within me earlier. I've no idea if this is an apology of sorts, but right now I really don't care as pleasure like I've never experienced tingles at every single one of my nerve endings.

Lifting his fingers, he circles my entrance while continuing the blissful torture of my clit with his tongue.

"Jake, Jake," I chant as his fingers plunge deeper. My muscles pull tight as the beginnings of an earth shattering release begin to consume my body. "Yes, yes."

He continues for a few more seconds before something inside me snaps and I fall into an all-consuming bliss as he continues to lick at me, dragging out every last drop of pleasure.

My chest heaves, my breaths rushing out past my lips as I try to get my heart under control.

Jake sits up, wipes his mouth with the back of his

hand, a shit-eating grin on his face at what he just achieved.

"Do you need to look so smug?"

"Brit, I—"

"Amalie, are you okay?"

"Fuck." Jake moves faster than I thought possible and flies into position hiding behind the door. His ability to know exactly what to do makes me wonder how many times he's got caught sneaking into a girl's bedroom.

A sick feeling bubbles up in my stomach at the idea of him doing what he just did to me to others but I don't get a chance to linger on it before a light knock sounds out and my bedroom door is pushed open.

I just manage to grab the sheets to cover up before Gran's head pokes around the door.

I'm lying with one eye cracked open just enough to see what she does. She briefly looks around the room but when she thankfully finds nothing suspicious, she silently closes the door once again and her footsteps head back down the hallway.

Breathing a huge sigh of relief, I watch as Jake appears from the shadows and kneels at my side.

He reaches up and cups my cheek in his warm hand. "I should go."

As much as I want to say no, I know it's not the right thing to do. This has already gone too far and we've come too close to getting caught.

I nod and his face drops, his mask has gone and I'm once again allowed to see the real boy hiding beneath.

When he stands, my mouth opens to argue but I

can't. He needs to get out of here before Gran comes back or I do something I'm going to really regret. He's already under my skin, us spending anymore time together right now will only cause me more pain in the long run because it's not like he's going to take my hand at school tomorrow and walk around proudly that I'm his.

The thought alone frustrates me. I don't want to be his, do I?

Silently he backs toward the door. My muscles twitch to reach out for him but I manage to keep them at my sides and allow him to disappear into the darkness, leaving just the taste of his kiss and the fast beating of my heart as evidence he was ever here.

35

AMALIE

"**D**id you sleep well? You look better," Camila says the second I drop down into her car for our daily drive to school.

"Uh...yeah," I lie. In reality, it took hours for me to fall asleep after my nocturnal guest left and when the alarm went off this morning, I was far from ready for it. "You think anyone's forgotten about what happened at the party yet?"

"What, that someone drugged you and you were rescued by none other than Jake Thorn?"

I wince, I really don't need the reminder of how I ended up on Friday night. "Yeah, that's it."

"Shane feels awful, he's been texting me all weekend seeing as you're ignoring him. He really didn't do it."

I shrug, because although I was adamant that it wasn't him at the beginning, I don't really know him. Just look at Jake, I thought he was an arsehole through and through but he keeps proving to me that there is a little nice in there somewhere. Maybe Shane is the opposite.

"I just want to forget it now and not go to another party again for a long time."

"That might be a problem because Homecoming and Noah's birthday is this weekend."

"No one will miss me at homecoming and just tell Noah I'm busy or something."

"Nope. Not happening. Whether you like it or not you're a part of this school now, so Homecoming is non negotiable. You can wear that sexy little silver dress, and as for Noah's party, I'm sure I can convince you."

I mumble my frustration because sadly, she's probably right.

As we both walk toward the school, I feel eyes on me. Only they're not just on me because they flick back and forth between me and Jake where he's sitting in his usual spot surrounded by his posse.

His gaze follows me and burns a trail across my entire body.

"That's weird," Camila comments.

"What is?"

"Jake's not looking at you like he wants to kill you, he's looking at you like he wants to—"

"Enough."

Turning her curious stare on me, her hand lands on my forearm and comes to stand in front of me.

"Did something else happen that you're not telling me about?"

My cheeks heat and I know I've got no chance of hiding the truth.

"Maybe, but it's not a big deal."

"Anything that turns your face that color is most definitely a big deal."

"I'm going to be late for class."

Glancing at the time on her phone, she groans. "I'm only letting this go because you're right."

"Great, see you later," I call, sidestepping her and marching toward the building for my first lesson of the day.

The morning passes without any drama, it's almost how school should be, so naturally I'm on high alert waiting for something to happen.

I'm heading toward my locker before my meeting with the guidance counselor when I feel him. Jake's standing at the other end of the hallway with Chelsea practically hanging off him and Mason and Ethan flanking his sides.

Something crackles between us when our eyes meet, but I refuse to allow anyone else to see it. Dragging my eyes away, I open my locker. A small square of white paper catches my eye. Glancing around me to make sure I'm not being watched, I unfold it.

Same time tonight? J

My breath catches and anger ignites in my belly. Have I just turned into his dirty little secret?

Taking a step back, I go to turn toward where they

were just standing but I don't need to look far to find him because the four of them are right behind me.

"How are you feeling, lightweight?" Chelsea snarls, her fake smile firmly in place.

"I was better before having to look at your face."

Mason snorts in amusement while Jake stands there with tense shoulders and his face set in his usual mask. Only when I look into his eyes, I see more. My broken boy is still in there.

"Give it a rest, Chelsea," Jake demands. My eyes almost pop out of my sockets at him defending me in public.

"Don't tell me you actually like the skank."

"No." That one word kills every little bit of hope that was bubbling up that things might be changing. "I just think it's time we lay off."

Flinging her hair over her shoulder she mutters a, "whatever," before waltzing off.

Jake goes to take a step forward but I refuse to allow him time to try to apologise for that. Slamming my locker, I storm past him, shoulder barging Ethan in the process.

"Brit?" Jake calls. I hate that the sound of his voice has butterflies erupting in my belly, but I refuse to turn around and acknowledge him. I've got a meeting to get to.

I head toward the library but stop a little short at Miss French's office. I've been putting this meeting off since I started because I knew she'd want to discuss my future, but it's become obvious all these weeks on that

I'm no further forward with what I might do when high school comes to an end.

I knock lightly, hopeful she won't hear and I can pretend she wasn't here but I know that's just wishful thinking when she calls out for me to enter.

"Amalie, it's so good to meet you at last. You've been a little elusive to pin down."

"Sorry about that."

"No need to apologize. I understand that thinking about your future after everything you've been through is difficult. I just want to help focus your mind and answer any questions you might have. I know the education system here is different from what you're used to."

"Yeah, I should be at university right now," I say with a sigh, dropping down into the chair in front of her desk.

"I know and I really do understand your frustration at seemingly going backward, but I can assure you that this is the right thing to do."

"I get it, I do. It's just... frustrating."

Miss French flips open my file and quickly scans the information she's got in front of her. "Your grades are looking really good. It seems your teachers are really impressed with your progress."

"I've been working hard, the last thing I need is to be behind before I've really started."

"If only all our transfer students thought that way," she muses. "Anyway. It says in your transfer document that you were going to study photography in college. Is that still your plan?"

I'm silent for a few moments as I consider the answer to the question I knew was coming. "I don't know."

"And why's that?" I'm pretty sure she must know the answer. It seems that she has all my details in that folder so she must know why I'm here.

"I was always inspired by my dad. He was a genius behind the camera and he always said I had it too. I was taking photographs before I could talk apparently, like it was in my blood."

"And now?"

"I haven't picked up my camera since they died," I admit quietly, fighting the lump that's threatening to block my throat.

"Do you think that's what he would want? You to give up something you loved."

"No. never. It's just... hard."

"Amalie, I lost my parents at a young age too, so trust me when I say that I know how you feel. It's the hardest thing you'll ever have to go through, but you can't lose sight of what makes you happy, no matter how much the memories might hurt. Although painful, memories are good. They take you back to happier times and ensure that you'll never forget them. Your dad was a very talented man, I won't lie and say that I didn't look both your parents up. They were both very inspirational people, they achieved so much. I know they'd hate for you to give up because of them."

I wipe at my eyes, trying to clear away the tears that have dropped at her talking about them. One of the things I've mostly managed to avoid since moving here is having people talking about them. Other than the few days with the rumours about why I was here, it's only Gran who brings them up really. It just shows that although I've been feeling like I'm coping better, I fear I might just be hiding it instead of properly dealing with it. We're still waiting for news on the accident and whether it was actually an accident and I think I might be burying how I feel about it all until we get that verdict.

Miss French continues talking, dragging me from my dark thoughts. "If you decide to continue down the photography route then there are so many colleges with great photography programs both in and out of state. Have you thought about if you'd like to move away from here?"

Part of me wants to say yes, to start over somewhere I've chosen to be but another more nagging part knows that my only family is here, so why would I leave to be alone?

"I don't know," I answer honestly. "I can see pros and cons to both."

"I hope you don't mind, but I took the liberty of printing out some of the best programs just to give you something to think about. These ones are spread across the country, and here's a couple in state. Just give them all a read, check out the college websites. See if any of them speak to you. I know it's still early and you've got plenty of time to make a decision but there's no harm in starting to get ideas and having something to work toward."

"Thank you," I say, gathering up all the paperwork

she's just spread across the table. Seeing some of the college names at the top of the printouts makes my heart race a little. I'm not totally naïve on this subject, in fact, studying for my degree in America was something I'd discussed with my parents more than once. They thought it would be good for me, and some of these institutions have incredible courses that could really help kick-start my career, along with my name, of course. But in the end, I decided that I didn't want to go that far away. I looked up some of Dad's suggestions though and I couldn't deny that what some of them could offer was incredible, plus the opportunity to live in stunning cities like New York was very tempting.

I'm walking out into the corridor when raised voices coming from the entrance to this part of the school make their way down to me.

"I'm sorry, but I can't just allow you to march into the building."

"But he's my son. I have every right to see him."

"Yes. Once classes are over, you may do as you wish but I won't have you disrupting my school or my student's education."

"This is infuriating. Do you know who I am?"

I round the corner right as she says those words and my chin drops.

Kate Thorn. Supermodel. Porn star. Drug addict. *Jake's mum.*

Fuck.

How did I not see this coming?

My movement catches her eye, and she drags her

stare from the principal to me. Her eyes narrow as she looks me up and down.

"I know you."

"I'm Amalie Win—"

"Windsor-Marsh. I know who you are." Her lips curl in disgust as if I'm nothing more than a bit of dog shit on her shoe.

Turning away from me, she continues where she left off. "I don't know how long I'm in town for. I need to see my son."

As they stand and continue arguing, it gives me a chance to take her in. She looks completely different from the last time I saw her in person and everything like the images that have been plastered all over the gossip magazines for the past year or so. She used to be one of the industry's most sought after models. She was gorgeous, had the flawless face and the slim figure every designer wanted. Dad had photographed her more than any other model in his career, he was her favourite to work with and she often demanded it was him shooting or it wouldn't happen. But as with so many young success stories, the fame and money got to be a little too much. She was burning the candle at both ends and something had to give. She started drinking, snorting too much cocaine and lost job after job. According to the gossip, she'd snorted and pissed away every penny she earned and after a sex tape leak, she obviously realised there was money to make in sex and turned to that. I've not seen anything, but the screenshots and comments that have graced social media haven't been pleasant.

Her once porcelain skin is now almost grey, her cheeks sunken and her eyes tired and bloodshot. Although she was always very slim, her skin is now hanging from her bones. But it's her blue eyes and blonde hair that stand out to me. Although that blonde is anything from natural. It's peroxide yellow and even from this distance, it looks as brittle as straw.

Everything Jake's ever said to me suddenly makes so much sense. His hatred of where I came from, my parents' industry, even my looks to a point.

His mother is Kate fucking Thorn. I feel like an idiot for not putting two and two together. But why would I? I'm sure there are a million eighteen-year-old kids with Thorn as a surname who could have been the son she abandoned as a young child. The little boy she left behind was regularly mentioned when they were slating her in the press.

It should have been obvious, the voice in my head screams. But as I stand and berate myself, still eavesdropping on their increasingly heated argument, I spot movement over by the benches.

Jake rounds the corner, the shouting in the distance catching his attention and he looks up. Everything happens in slow motion. It takes a second or two for reality to hit him, but when it does, I've never seen a look on his face like it. I thought he'd looked at me with pure hatred but I'm realising that I was let off lightly because as he stares at his mother, he looks murderous. His entire body tenses, his fists clench at his sides like he might just walk up to her and punch her in the face. I step forward, needing to go to him but Kate sees where my focus is and her eyes land on Jake.

"Jake, my boy. Come here."

I drop my bag and books and race toward Jake as his chest swells and his entire body vibrates with fury.

"Come on, baby."

"Don't baby me, you fucking whore." With that, he spins on his heels and runs. I attempt to chase him but he easily outruns me and I'm left panting, bent over with my hands on my knees trying to catch my breath.

"Fuck," I mutter between heaving breaths. Looking back, Kate and the principal are gone.

I should leave him to his own personal hell but now I've got an understanding of why he is the way he is, I know that I won't be able to.

Walking back toward the school, I pick up everything I dropped and try to figure out where he might go.

I don't give school a second thought as I walk off-campus. I catch a bus toward the seafront. My first thought being Aces, although I'm pretty sure he won't want to be around people right now, but it's close to my second guess, the beach. If I'd just had my world turned upside down, I think I'd head straight for the ocean. There's something so relaxing listening to the waves crashing.

I come up short in both places, so with nowhere else to turn, I head toward his trailer. Even if he's not there right now, hopefully he'll reappear at some point.

I get the bus to his house, not wanting to be caught by Gran. I sneak through the driveway and down to the bottom of the garden. I forego the trailer, thinking that he might be in his make-shift gym, but it's empty with no signs he's been here.

Thankfully, his trailer door is unlocked, so I pull it open and step inside.

It looks exactly as it did the other day. It's much tidier than I would have expected knowing an eighteen-year-old lad lives here. I'd expect to find beer cans, clothes, and all sorts lying around but in reality, the only thing out is an ashtray.

Not wanting to pry into his life too much, I take a seat on his sofa and wait.

I must fall asleep because when my eyes flicker open, the sun is beginning to set and I have a very angry pair of eyes staring down at me.

36

JAKE

Dismissing Brit like I did in front of Chelsea was physically painful. Why couldn't I just grow a pair and admit that things had changed? The girl I'd quite happily have never seen again when she first arrived has somehow managed to bury her way under my skin and no matter how hard I try, I can't get her the fuck out.

I'm so used to playing the part of the carefree asshole at school that the act just comes naturally. No one questions the mask I wear, no one, aside from Mason, even knows it exists. They think this douchebag is actually me. They have no idea I use the persona to cover up what's really festering inside me. The anger, the hurt, the betrayal. It's been years, but it doesn't seem to make any difference, that little abandoned boy still lives inside me.

I should be in class but I managed to find out that Brit has a meeting with Miss French and with everyone else busy learning, I decided I'd surprise her and make up for being an asshole. The taste of her coming against my lips last night is the only thing I can taste and, fuck, if I don't need more of that. She has every right to tell me to go fuck myself, which I did multiple times with my hand once I got back to my trailer last night, but my need for her means I make a pathetic excuse to my teacher and march out of her room. I didn't even hang around to find out if she'd given me permission or not. Who gives a fuck. It's not like anyone in their right mind would question me.

When I spot the principal at the end of the hallway, I go to duck into the shadows so I can get to Miss French's office another way. But the figure standing in front of him has me stepping out in the open.

My heart races and an uncomfortable knot forms in my stomach.

It can't be.

Thinking that I must be imagining things, I take a few steps closer, my eyes locked on the woman who I now realize is going batshit at Principal Hartmann.

Fuck.

I've imagined a million times how I would react if I were ever to see her again. A million and one ways I could hurt her after what she did to me. But in that moment, before she sees me, everything inside me freezes.

She looks nothing like I remember, or like the one and only photo I have of the two of us together. She's no longer the stunning supermodel that I picture every time I think of her but some haggard old woman. The fact that life clearly hasn't been easy on her makes me feel a tiny bit better about everything, but it goes nowhere near making any of the anger or hurt go away. She left me without a backward glance for a life of glitz and fame. I will never forgive her for the selfish decision she made when I was a child. Maybe I could possibly consider going easy on her if she had made the decision with my best interests in mind, but it soon became clear that my happiness was not a factor in her decision. She left me with two people who quite obviously didn't want me and who had no time for the disaster child she'd turned me into.

As was inevitable, she turns to look at me. Red hot anger pours through my veins and my fists clench to make her feel just an ounce of the pain she caused me over the years. But as much as I might want to acknowledge her, I won't give her the pleasure.

When she opens her mouth and calls to me, my stomach turns over, threatening to empty itself on the concrete at my feet.

How fucking dare she call me *her boy* after everything? So what, her fancy life didn't go as planned and she's now a coked up, washed-up, old porn star? I'm not here to fall back on when everything's gone to shit and there's nowhere else to go.

My body trembles with the adrenaline racing through it. Fight or flight kicks in and after replying with words I don't even register, I run.

I run as fast and as far as I can. Just like she did to me all those years ago. Sadly, I don't have the kind of money I'd need to skip the country to get away from her. Instead, I find myself at the end of the beach between the dunes just like I did a few nights ago after getting thrown out of the game.

I rest my elbows on my knees as I drag in much needed deep breaths. I clench and unclench my fists, trying to release the urge I have to punch something— or someone—until that bitch can no longer affect me. I should be over this. It's been years, but still she's up in my fucking head, screwing me the fuck up.

Hitting my fist against my temple, I try to force her out. I haven't even laid eyes on her in over ten years, yet she has this power over me. Exactly why I've always refused to date. I don't want another woman to have this power.

Only you have, dipshit. Brit weaseled her way in despite what a douche you've been. Seeing the woman who gave birth to me once again only pointed out the alarming differences between her and Brit that I really should have acknowledged that very first day I saw her, but I was too blinded by her past and the life she came from. In reality, I should have seen her for who she is, not who I made her out to be in my head. She's proven time and time again that she's nothing like the woman I just left behind. No matter how many times I've hurt her, she's come right back like she knew there was something inside me she needed to drag out. With every insult I threw at her, she came right back. It's why I can't stay away. She challenges me like no one I've ever met before and she makes attempting to look indifferent to my advances a full-time job when all it really does is make me push harder to break her.

The thought of Brit has the anger and tension

starting to drain from my body. It's enough to tell me that she's what I need right now.

Jumping up, I set about going to get her. She's probably still at school, and like fuck am I going back there right now, or ever again if she's going to keep turning up. Instead, I head home for a shower to waste some time before she comes home and I can get to her.

I focus on her as I make my way to my trailer. I don't bother catching the bus, the long walk is exactly what I need to attempt to clear her from my head. It's not lost on me that not so long ago I'd have been walking to get Brit out of my head and now I'm restless because I need her.

Fuck. I need her so fucking bad and I'm just about fed up trying to hide it.

My legs burn and sweat runs down my back by the time I walk down the garden toward my trailer.

Reaching behind me, I drag my shirt over my head, ready to go straight to the shower as I pull the door open and climb in.

I step toward the bedroom but something to my left catches my eye.

Fuck. She's here.

How did she know I needed her?

Dropping my shirt to the counter as I pass, I drop down to my haunches as I take in every inch of her beautiful face. How could I ever compare her to that old hag? There's nothing even remotely similar between the two of them. *Her* looks are mostly fake, Brit is a pure, natural beauty.

As if she can sense me, her eyes flutter open. She sees me immediately and her breath catches in fright.

"Jake, shit. I—"

I don't allow her to say anymore. My fingers thread in her hair and my tongue delves into her mouth. All I need right now is her. Her kiss to remind me that not everything in my world is totally fucked up.

She sags in my hold and allows me to take what I need. Little does she know though, it's never going to be enough.

"I need you," I say between heaving breaths when I pull back and rest my forehead against hers. I stare down into her blue eyes and it's the first time I admit to myself that I never want to look into any others again.

"Anything," she breathes. The honesty in her voice throws me for a moment. My fingers twist harder in her hair as I try to accept what she just said.

"Why? After everything, why are you still here and willing to give me anything?"

"I've no idea, I just know it's where I need to be."

"Fuck," I bark, releasing her and taking a huge step back.

"Jake, what—"

"Let's go somewhere."

"Okay, sure. Where do you want to go?"

"I don't mean for dinner or for the evening, I mean let's get out of here. Just me and you. What do you say?"

"I say... are you crazy?"

"Probably. I just... I can't be here right now." It's the truth. If she came to find me at school, I'm sure here will be the next place she visits. Fuck, she might even be up in that fucking house right now. "I need to go. Now."

"Uh... yeah. Okay. Can I go and get some stuff first?"

"You've got ten minutes to get back here or I'm going without you." I have no idea if that's true or not, the way I'm feeling right now, I'd wait forever for her to come back to me.

"Okay." Jumping from the sofa, she slips her feet back into her Chucks and takes a step toward the door. At the last minute, she turns back to me, wraps her fingers around the back of my neck and presses her nose gently against mine.

"I'm nothing like her, I promise," she whispers before placing a sweet kiss to my lips and running from the trailer.

My hands tremble as realization dawns.

She knows.

37

AMALIE

I run through the undergrowth, the thistles scratching my bare arms but I don't care. I need stuff and I need to get back to him before he leaves. He wasn't expecting me to be waiting at his trailer but one look into those tormented eyes and I knew it was exactly what he needed, just like this trip. I know he wants to get away before she finds him which is why I sigh with relief when I find Gran's bungalow empty, allowing me to shove a few things in a bag before running back toward Jake.

When I break through the trees, he just opens his door.

"Ready?"

"Yes."

I loiter for a few seconds while he locks up, then he takes my hand and leads me toward the house's driveway.

"What are you doing?" I whisper-shout in shock when he goes straight for his uncle's old car.

"We're getting the hell out of this place as fast as we can."

I watch in horror as he pulls the driver's door open, throws his bag in the back and jumps in.

"You coming or what?"

"Shit. Yeah. I'm coming."

I follow his lead by throwing my case with his and falling down onto the seat right as he leans forward to jump start the car.

"What is this? Grand Theft Auto?"

"Something like that. You ready for a wild ride?" He glances over at me and winks, making me think that he's not talking about the drive.

"Can't wait. Show me what you've got."

Jake groans as if he's in pain before doing whatever you do to hotwire a car. The engine rumbles to life, and he backs out of the driveway at record speed.

"I'm assuming that wasn't your first time."

"You'd assume right. Anywhere you want to go?"

"Nope. Just drive."

"Done."

I lower the window and sit back, allowing the warm breeze to flow past my face. I might be in a stolen car with Jake Thorn, a guy I would have quite happily thrown under one when I first encountered him, but as we drive along the coastal road with the radio blaring and the windows down, I feel freer than I have in a very long time.

"How did you know?"

"About your mum?"

"Yeah, but please don't call her that."

"I saw her arguing with Hartmann when I came out of my guidance counsellor meeting. I had no idea until then though. I feel a little stupid for not figuring it out."

"How would you have figured it out?"

"Just from some stuff you've said. Seeing her, it all made so much sense."

"I'm sorry."

"Sorry, what was that? You're going to need to repeat that, I didn't quite hear properly."

"I'm sorry, for everything. I was projecting all my hate for her onto you because of your parents and where you came from. It wasn't fair."

"I understand."

"You shouldn't. I was an asshole."

"I can't deny that, Jake, but you had your reasons. I'm glad I know the truth now. You should have told me."

"I don't talk about her, Brit. Ever."

"Will you?"

"Will I what?"

"Talk... about her. About what happened?"

His fingers tighten on the wheel with a white-knuckled grip.

"Everything I know about her is from magazine gossip or snippets I overheard when she was talking to my parents."

"From the bits I've seen, the press didn't get it too far wrong." He falls silent, the muscle in his neck pulsing steadily. I allow him the time he needs to gather his thoughts. "I don't have many good memories of her, she was always pawning me off anywhere she could so she could go out. But I guess, looking back, at least she was there. The day she turned her back, I'll never forget. She dropped me at my aunt's, kissed my forehead and turned away without even a glance back at me.

"I was young, I assumed my aunt was just looking after me, but she never came back. To this day, I have no idea if my aunt knew she was stuck with me from then on or what. She put me in the guest room and her and my uncle mostly just carried on with their lives like I wasn't there. The only difference for them was a little extra washing and another plate to put food on. If *she* was hoping that by leaving me there I'd have a better life, then she was mistaken. She might have been neglectful, but at least she was my mother.

"I used to overhear my aunt and uncle talking about things they'd seen she'd been up to and I used to sneak down to their office and use their old shitty computer to Google her. Even at that age, I was embarrassed. Some of the shit I used to find. I stopped looking the day the sex tape was leaked." A shudder runs through him at the thought.

"She's a fucking waste of space. All she cares about is herself. She never sent me a penny of her hard-earned money or ever came to visit when she was in the country. She just left me with them, not giving a fuck if I was dead or alive. I fucking hate her." The strength of his feelings for his mother comes off him in waves. His arms shake as he tries to control himself.

Needing to do something to help, I reach over and place my hand on his thigh. His muscles bunch before he relaxes slightly.

He glances over at me, the slightest hint of a smile on his lips. "What the fuck did I do to deserve this? You?"

I shrug because I really don't have the answer. "I saw something in you, I guess."

"Oh yeah?" he asks, his usual jack the lad persona slipping back into place.

"Something in your eyes."

"Oh? I thought you were going to say that it was my abs."

"Shut up, you idiot."

He laughs and after the tense conversation we just had, it sounds incredible.

The sun's setting and casting an orange glow over the sea.

"It's beautiful here," I say, totally lost in the view, my hand still firmly in place on Jake's thigh.

"There's a motel up ahead, you want to stop here?"

"Sure. Won't your uncle be mad you stole his car?"

"Probably. I don't really care. They all think I'm a total fuck up. I may as well act the part."

"Wouldn't you rather prove them wrong?"

"Why? They had me nailed as the bad kid they got stuck with from that very first day. Nothing I've ever done has changed their minds."

"That's really sad."

"Maybe, but it's my reality. It's why I'm leaving the second I finish school."

He kills the engine and jumps from the car. I stay seated and watch as he stretches his stiff muscles. It's not until I look at my phone that I realise how long we had been driving for.

Grabbing my handbag from the back seat, I join him at the front of the car.

"Let's go and see if they've got a room," I suggest. I take a step but don't make it any farther. Jake's hand slips into mine and I'm pulled back until I'm flush against his chest.

He stares down at me causing butterflies to start up in my belly. His hand cups my cheek, his thumb brushing gently over my skin.

"Thank you," he whispers. It's by far the most sincere thing he's ever said to me and it immediately brings tears to my eyes. His eyes bounce between mine. "Shit. That wasn't supposed to make you cry."

"It'll take more than that to make me cry, Thorn." His eyes narrow at my use of his nickname. "Come on, let's get that room."

A smile twitches at his lips, his eyes darkening. I can only imagine what he's thinking, and I can only hope it's somewhat in line with what I am.

———

Ten minutes later, Jake is pushing the key into our room for the night. He shoves it open, then steps aside allowing me to enter first.

"That's very gentlemanly of you," I say, looking over my shoulder at him.

"I'm not always an asshole."

"Really? I'll look forward to that. Ahhh," I squeal as his hands land on my waist and I'm thrown onto the double bed in the middle of the room.

I land with a bounce before I flip over to find him looming over me. He crawls onto the bed and pushes my legs apart so he can settle between them. His hands land on either side of my head and he drops down slightly, closing the space between us.

"I meant what I said outside."

"I know." His eyes roam over every inch of my face, the intensity in his eyes making me want to clench my thighs.

"Am I in the way?" he asks, his eyes sparkling with delight.

"That all depends."

"On..."

"What you're intending on doing."

"Oh, I've got plans. There are so many things I want to do."

Heat floods my core as memories of how good his mouth felt on me last night.

"The first thing I want to do." He lowers even more so our lips are brushing. "Is get some food. I'm fucking starving." He jumps from the bed, chuckling with amusement as I groan in frustration. He holds his hand out for me and I pull myself up so I'm sitting. "I saw a pizza place just down the street. Up for it?"

"Oh, don't worry. I'm up for it."

"I change my mind. I'm not hungry now."

"That's a real shame because now you've mentioned it, I'm ravenous. Come on."

I turn back when I get to the door, just in time to see him rearrange himself in his jeans. Fuck, maybe we should just stay in here.

38

JAKE

All I wanted to do was get back between her legs, but I knew she deserved better than that. She didn't have to agree to this little impromptu trip, but she did so without any second thought. Fuck knows what I did to deserve her support right now because I know damn fucking well I don't deserve it.

As much as I want to spend the night doing all the filthy things that are filling my head, I'm more than willing to allow her to take the lead. I don't want to push her into more than she's ready for.

We both sit back in our chairs after polishing off a pizza each. "That's better," I say, grabbing my soda and draining the glass. I almost spit it all over her when she lets out the most unladylike burp.

"Oops," she says, covering her mouth with her hand, her cheeks turning a light shade of red.

"You're ruining all my first impressions of you, you know that, right?"

"Well, seeing as you hated me on sight, I don't think that's a bad thing."

"I... I just saw her. I know it's crazy because really, you're nothing alike but... fuck. I was a dick." Pulling my eyes from hers, I stare across the small diner, regret consumes me.

Brit reaches across the table and laces her fingers with mine. Dragging my gaze back to her, my breath catches in my throat at the hungry look in her eyes.

"Let's go back to our room."

I'm powerless to refuse her suggestion. After throwing a few bills down on the table that definitely covers the check, we stand and hand in hand we walk from the diner.

There's something so freeing about being somewhere where no one knows either of us. While we're in Rosewood, we'll always find someone who'll recognize us. And it's not that I'm ashamed to be seen with her like she thought at the diner. I'm more concerned about her and what people will think when they see her with me. I've got a reputation and I know they'll judge her, make her out to be as bad as one of the cheer sluts. I can already predict what the gossip mongers will spread around.

We're both silent on the short walk back to our room but the tension crackles between us. I know she can feel it too because every minute or two she'll look over at me. Concern creases her brow and I know she wants to help but I'm not sure what she can do right now but be here. I know that I'm going to have to go back and deal with my mother. If she's made it this far to see me, then I can't imagine she's going to get back on a plane and disappear all that willingly. She's done the hard part, she's made her presence known after years of avoiding the place, avoiding me.

Pulling the key from my pocket, I unlock our door and allow Brit to enter before closing and locking the door behind me.

Turning, I take a step forward but stop just short of crashing into her.

She stares at me, her eyes assessing as she chews on her bottom lip. "What are you doing?"

"Trying to figure out the best way to make you get out of your own head. You wanted to escape but you've spent the whole time with your head back in Rosewood worrying about what you left behind."

"I know, I'm sorry but—"

Stepping closer, her body heat burns into my chest. "I wasn't looking for an apology, Jake. I understand. Family shit can be... hard."

"Shit, Brit. I'm so s—"

"No. We're done talking." Her voice comes out harder and I start to panic that I've pissed her off again and that she's about to run. Thankfully when she moves, it's the very opposite.

Her hands rise and link behind my neck, our mouths just a breath apart.

"You think I can take your mind off it?"

Our noses press together, her lips just tickling lightly against mine. My cock stirs in my pants at just the thought of tasting her again.

"I don't know. Do you need me to leave and then sneak back in when you're not expecting it?"

"I'm not really a fan of time-wasting."

"Maybe not, but you can't deny that having someone sneak into your room at night and get you off isn't hot as fuck. You know you owe me, right?"

"No, you most definitely owed me those."

I nod, there's no way I can disagree with that after everything I've put her through.

Our breaths mingle as our chests heave and we continue staring at each other. Her blue eyes darken the longer we stand here. It's almost as if we're daring the other to make the first move. It's hot as fuck but my need for her is at a breaking point. Every muscle in my body is locked up tight and my fingers twitch at her waist itching to explore every inch of her perfect fucking body.

It's almost like someone counts us down because the second I break, so does she. Our lips collide, our teeth clash as we fight to get closer. My hands slip inside her t-shirt, my need to feel her skin against mine too much to deny.

Finding the clasp of her bra, I flick it open and run my hands around the front to get what I really need. Her breasts might be small, but they fill my hands perfectly.

She moans and I swallow it down as I pinch both her nipples between my fingers.

Her hands find their way under my shirt and she lifts until I'm forced to break our kiss so we can pull it over my head. I immediately drop it to the floor, pulling her body back to me, wasting no time.

With one hand under her t-shirt, I wrap the other around her waist and walk her backward until her legs hit the bed.

"Amalie, fuck. I need you."

She stills in my arms and pulls her head back so she can look at me.

My stomach drops. She's just changed her mind. *Fuck.*

"W-what's wrong?" My cock throbs against her, willing her not to put an end to this right now.

"You said my name," she says softly, her cheeks heating when she realizes what she said. "It's just, you've never used it before."

"Using it meant accepting what I really wanted."

She wants to ask, it's right on the tip of her tongue but I'm not ready to express everything I've been keeping buried since she first walked into my life. I've bared enough of myself to her today. So instead of allowing her to say anything, I grip the bottom of her shirt and pull it off her quickly followed by her bra.

"Fuck," I grunt as I'm greeted by her rosy pink stiff nipples. They're as perfect as I remember.

Dropping my head, I suck one and then the other into my mouth ensuring I run my tongue around each one. Her hips thrust toward me as she moans my name and fuck, if it doesn't make my cock leak for her.

"Need more," I demand, dropping to my knees, I kiss down her flat stomach before flicking open the fly of her jeans.

Feeling her stare burning into the top of my head, I look up as I begin to pull the fabric of her jeans and panties down her legs.

She looks so innocent as she bites down on her bottom lip, my balls ache for her as she waits to see what I'm going to do.

With our eyes still connected, I lean forward and place a kiss to her hipbone. Her eyelids flutter but they don't close fully.

I can't fight it any longer and I have to pull my eyes from hers. Sitting back on my haunches, I stare at her body.

She might have the body of a supermodel, but that doesn't mean she doesn't have curves. And fuck me if those curves don't bring me to my knees.

"Sit on the bed."

She follows my order but instead of staying upright, she falls back onto her elbows, giving me an incredible fucking view.

Reaching forward, I wrap my hands around her thighs and pull her so her ass is hanging over the edge, then I lower myself toward her core. Her scent makes my mouth water before I suck her swollen clit into my mouth.

"Jake," she cries, and I feel like a goddamn king.

Fuck ruling the school, the only person I want to be a king for is her.

39

AMALIE

Jake doesn't pull back until he's allowed me to ride out every second of the orgasm he gave me.

He stands from his position on the floor and goes for his waistband. Not wanting to miss anything, I sit myself up on my palms and watch intently as he pushes the fabric of both his jeans and boxers down his thighs.

His cock springs free and my eyes widen. I'm not a virgin, but shit, that's bigger than I've experienced before.

Before he drops the fabric to the floor, he digs into his pocket and pulls out a strip of condoms.

"Wow, someone was optimistic."

"Better that than being caught shor—" His words falter when he looks up and finds me staring at him.

"Jesus, Amalie. Could you be any more beautiful?"

The sound of his deep voice saying my name causes

even more butterflies to erupt in my belly. I never knew hearing my own name could affect me so much.

He takes a step toward me and my heart pounds inside my chest.

"I need you... so fucking badly, but if you don't then—"

"Stop." I place my finger against his lips as he begins to climb over me. If I wasn't sure about this, then I wouldn't have put myself in this position. I'm laying here naked willingly. It might be the stupidest thing I've done to date because all the sweet stuff he's saying to me could be one big fat lie, but after seeing his mum earlier and the effect it had on him, I'm pretty convinced that he's telling the truth. He was too vulnerable to bullshit me when he first found me earlier.

Placing my hands against his rock hard abs, I skirt them up and over his chest and then up into his hair. My nails scratching his head slightly, making him moan.

"Fuck. I don't deserve for this to happen. You should kick my naked ass to the curb and make me walk back to Rosewood."

"You're right. That's exactly what I should do. But I'm not."

"Fuck." Settling between my legs, he drops his lips to mine and kisses me like he'll die without it. His tongue plunges into my mouth and tangles with mine as his hips thrust in an attempt to find the friction he needs.

Scratching my nails down his back, I grab on to his

arse and pull him closer to where he needs to be.

"Condom," he mutters against my lips.

"I'm covered, it's okay."

"No," he says harshly, sitting up straight. "I'm not taking any chances on my life being turned upside down again, not yet anyway."

I can't argue, he's just being sensible.

Ripping one of the squares from the long length he pulled from his pocket, he opens it with his teeth and quickly rolls it down his cock. I watch his every movement, my pussy clenching to feel what it'll be like pressing inside and filling me to the hilt.

Lining himself up with my entrance, I fall back onto the bed and wait.

"How slow do I need to take this?"

I know it's his way of asking if I'm a virgin and I can't help smiling to myself. "However you need. It's not my first rodeo."

"Fuck," he barks, a conflicted expression crossing his face.

"Hey," I say, reaching up and cupping his cheek. His eyes find mine and he seems to come back to himself.

He pushes forward and I wince a little. I might not be a virgin, but it's been a while.

"Holy fuck, you're tight," he groans as he slowly continues to push inside until he's as deep as he'll go.

I expect him to fuck me. To take all his frustrations over everything that's happened today out on me, but that's the exact opposite of what he does. In reality, he drops his face into my neck as he slowly grinds into me.

It's not long before his well-considered movements begin to awaken another release within me.

"Jake, Jake," I chant, my nails scratching down his back as my muscles lock up ready to fall over the edge.

Pulling his head up, he finds my lips as he holds himself up with one elbow while the other caresses my face. It's softer and more emotional than I ever could have imagined with him.

My muscles clamp down on him as my release crashes into me. He sits up and stares down at me. My eyelids are heavy as wave after wave of pleasure races through me, but I can't break my contact with him. Something is happening between us and I don't want to miss a second of it.

"Fuck, Amalie."

Before my orgasm fades, he slides his hands under my arse and lifts me. Then, much like I was expecting, he thrusts hard and fast into me. His head falls back as his muscles pull and ripple before my eyes.

The sight of him taking what he needs is enough to bring on the tingles of another release. One he ensures he drags out of me by pressing his thumb down on my clit.

"Fuck," he roars before I feel his cock twitch. "Amalie," he cries as he empties himself inside me.

Pulling out, he drops the used condom over the side of the bed and then rolls over and pulls me tightly into his body.

Our chests heave with our exertion and my muscles continue to twitch with pleasure. I know I'm not alone in wanting more because I can feel his still semi-hard cock against my arse.

We lie there in silence for the longest time, neither of us ready to give in to sleep quite yet.

"You still awake?" he whispers eventually.

"Yeah. You?"

"Yeah," he chuckles. "Amalie?"

"Yeah?"

"I never said it before because I was an asshole but, I'm really sorry about your parents. That must have been really hard."

The mention of my parents immediately has tears burning my eyes and only reminds me of the conversation I had with Miss French earlier today.

"Thank you. It's—" My voice cracks and he clearly notices.

"Shit."

Turning me so I've no choice but to face him. He kisses the two tears that fall and pulls me tighter to his chest.

"I'm so fucking sorry."

I've no idea if he's apologising for the loss of my parents, which he clearly had nothing to do with, or for the shit he pulled over the past few weeks. It doesn't really matter what it's for specifically because I accept it, nonetheless.

"Do they know how it happened?" he asks after a few more minutes of silence between us.

"They're still looking into whether or not their helicopter had been tampered with. I'd hoped they'd have the answers they need by now. It's taking forever. I just need it to be done so I can attempt to move on."

"If it helps at all. I think you're doing a pretty incredible job already. What you've been through would have broken most people."

"You did a pretty good fucking job."

"Which I'll probably regret for the rest of my life. I was so stuck in my own problems that I didn't even give what you've been through a second thought. I was so fucking pig-headed."

Rolling him onto his back, I throw my leg over his waist and lie on top of him with my chin resting on his chest.

"It's in the past. No point in beating yourself up over something you can't change."

"I need to let go of the past. Seeing her today showed me that. I need to look ahead, figure out what the fuck I want to do with it."

"Have you had a meeting with Miss French?"

"Plenty." I hate to bring up the idea of college again because he shot me down pretty quickly last time but there must be something he can do to get there.

"And what does she say about college and stuff?"

"That I should look into it and stop ruling it out. Don't give me that look," he says when I raise my eyebrow at him in an 'I told you so' way.

"How about we look into things together?"

"Go to college together?"

"Whoa, hold your horses there, Thorn. We just had sex, not got married." His face drops and it makes me wonder if he's more serious about this thing between us than he's letting on. "I meant just do some research, try to figure out the future together."

"I guess we could do that."

"Do you have any idea what you'd like to study?"

"Hmmm... how about your body?" he asks, flipping us both over and sucking one of my nipples into his mouth.

"I'm not sure that's an option." I laugh as he tickles my sides before settling between my legs once again like it's his new home.

"I want to do photography so I could most definitely make use of your body."

"Is that right?" he asks with a wink.

"I learnt a few tricks from my dad, I'd be able to take a few inches off you."

He gasps in mock horror. "See I was right, I knew you were a bitch."

"That might be a little more convincing if you were to say it when your hard cock isn't poking me between the legs."

"You can take photographs of me any day. I'm not shy."

"So I see." My gaze drops to where his fist is stroking his cock slowly.

———

It's safe to say that we leave our stamp on that motel room, and the bathroom, when we decide it's probably time for a shower.

By the time I swing my legs from the bed some time

long after sunrise the next morning, I swear every muscle in my body pulls.

"You okay?" Jake asks, looking over at me with the covers pooling across his waist. It sure is a sight to wake up to. His hair is sticking up in all directions and his lips are still swollen from our hours of kissing. Something inside my chest swells at the sight of him, but I put the feeling to the back of my mind, afraid that if I focus on it too much, it'll only result in heartache.

I smile at him but it's anything but convincing.

I've no idea what's going to happen once we walk out of this motel room, but I know things between us are never going to be like there are in here.

There are too many obstacles that will get between us once again when we get back to Rosewood. Jake's mum is the most obvious issue but I can't forget all the kids at school who are going to be less than impressed if something were to happen between us.

"Why do you look so worried?"

"Because we've got to go back to reality soon."

"So? I should be the one stressing about that. It's my whore of a mother that's waiting for me." I rear back for a number of reasons and I think he realises his mistake because he rushes to apologise. "I'm sorry. I wish I could trade mine for yours."

"It's okay," I say, reaching my hand out and squeezing his. "But..."

"But what?"

"What happens between us when we walk out of here. Last night was—"

"Incredible. Mind-blowing. Earth shattering," he

says, pulling me back down to the bed with him and kissing me on the tip of my nose.

"Yeah but—"

"But nothing, Amalie." Goosebumps prick my skin at the sound of my name, and it makes him smile. "We can walk out of here hand in hand and it can continue for as long as you want it to, if that's what you want."

"It's not that easy though."

"Why isn't it? In case I didn't make it obvious enough last night, I want you, Brit. I'm done with the bullshit and the pretending. I'm yours, if you'll have me."

"But what about everyone else?"

"No one else matters."

"I'm not sure everyone will see it that way."

"Like who?"

"Chelsea for one."

"Fuck Chelsea. She has nothing to do with what's between us."

"No, but she'll have an opinion and she'll make sure others do too."

"Fuck 'em. All of them. If I need to stand on the fucking school roof and announce to the world that you're mine, then I fucking will."

"I'm not sure that's necessary," I mutter, getting embarrassed just thinking about him doing something so ridiculous.

"How about we just take it as it comes. I need to deal with Kate when I get back, no doubt she's waiting for me and we'll just go from there. Maybe you'll let me take you out."

"On a date?"

"Yeah, if you like."

A smile twitches my lips at the thought. "Have you ever been on a date before?"

"No, never. Never dated and never kissed anyone."

"That rumour was true?"

"Until you, baby." My eyes widen in surprise. "I meant it. I'm serious about this, about us."

"Me too," I admit, putting my heart on the line.

"Okay then. Shall we get this show on the road? We've probably got people looking for us at home, well you will have at least." He's right, it's a school day and neither of us are there. I left a very brief note for Gran yesterday saying I was sleeping elsewhere but I'm sure she was still expecting me to turn up to school today, Camila too.

"Fancy a shower first?" I ask, quirking my eyebrow at him.

"Fucking right I do." He's up from the bed faster than I can blink and then I'm in his arms and we're making our way toward the bathroom.

"Argh, that's fucking freezing," I squeal when he turns it on and we're both blasted with ice cold water.

"I'll warm you up, baby."

He's not wrong. Those few words are enough to do just that, but he ensures he finishes the job by backing me up against the wall and surrounding me, inside and out, with his heat.

40

AMALIE

Pulling my phone from my bag, dread sits heavy in my stomach when I find a load of missed calls and texts from both Gran and Camila.

"Fuck," I mutter, putting my phone to my ear as it starts ringing.

"Amalia? Where the hell are you? I've had the school on the phone telling me that you haven't turned up."

"I'm so sorry. I'm just with a friend who needed me." Jake's elbow jabs me in the arm and his eyebrows rise as he mouths 'friend?' to me.

"I trust you, Amalie, which is why I told them that you're ill, but I'd appreciate the head's up in the future."

"I'm really sorry. We just got carried away. We're on our way back. We'll be there in a couple of hours."

"Okay. I'll see you soon. You might want to speak to Camila before she finds you first."

"Will do. See you soon."

"Friend?" Jake asks, looking pissed off with my description of him.

"It just wasn't a conversation to have over the phone. I'll introduce you properly in person when we get back if you like." He swallows nervously at the thought. "What?"

"I've just never done the whole meet the family thing before, plus she'll know who my mother is and—"

"And nothing. Gran's pretty open-minded. She'll be fine."

"If you say so."

Looking at the clock, I know Camila will be in class but not wanting to freak her out more than she probably already is, I ring anyway.

It goes to voicemail but not five minutes later she's returning my call.

"Where the utter fuck are you? And don't tell me, you're with Jake?"

"Um... not sure where we are exactly, but yeah, he's here."

"Jesus fucking Christ, Am. I've been going crazy."

"We're both fine. We got a motel room for the night."

"Okay, so... I expect to hear every detail from that later, but for now, I'm just glad he hasn't killed you and sent your body out to sea."

"I heard that," Jake calls with a laugh.

"Good, I hoped you would. You fucking hurt her, Thorn, and I'm coming after you."

"I'd like to see you try."

"Don't tempt me. She's already too good for you."

"I couldn't agree more."

"Okay as fun as this has been, I am here and listening to this conversation. Come by Gran's after school, yeah?"

"Uh of course. We're going dress shopping remember?"

"Um...no."

"Shit, I might have forgotten to tell you, but I need your help getting something sexy for both homecoming and Noah's birthday because, well... you know."

"Yeah, I know. That's fine. I'll see you later. You can buy me dinner."

"After the stress you've caused me today? I don't think so."

"Whatever. Bye."

"What the hell was that about?"

"Camila's been saving herself."

"Her and Noah haven't..." He trails off. "Wow. I bet Mason doesn't know that."

"What's it got to do with him?"

Jake rolls his eyes like it's so obvious that I shouldn't even need to ask the question. "He's been in love with her forever. He just won't admit it."

"I knew there was something between those two. They both refused to talk about it when I asked."

"They're both as dumb as each other. Pretend they can't stand each other, but in reality, they're exactly what the other needs."

"That's rich," I say with a laugh.

"Hey, at least I got my shit together."

"Yeah, just make sure you keep it that way."

Reaching over, I place my hand on his thigh, but he grabs it and brings it to his lips. "Always." His promise makes my heart flutter, but I fight to keep my head in charge of what's growing between us. He's got the power to break me and we've only been officially whatever we are for a few minutes.

We chat about random shit all the way home but it's nice. I know hardly anything about him, so I soak up mundane things like his favourite food and colour.

It's not until he pulls up to his aunt and uncle's that the reality of the situation makes itself known. There's a twitch at the living room curtains before his uncle comes flying from the house, closely followed by his aunt who waddles with her giant pregnant belly.

"What the fuck were you thinking, boy?"

"I just borrowed it for a few hours. No harm done."

"You didn't borrow it. You stole it. You should be fucking lucky we don't have the cops on your ass right now."

"Like they'd give a fuck. Have you seen the state of that thing?"

"That thing is my '91 Pontiac Sunfire. I'm gonna do her up and she'll be a classic."

Jake scoffs. "A classic piece of shit."

"Just because we allow you to stay on our land doesn't mean you have the right to take our shit whenever you feel the need. What if your aunt went into labour?"

Jake glances at his aunt and then to the other car in

the driveway. "She looks pretty pregnant to me. Come on," he says to me, grabbing my hand and leading me away.

"Fine, walk away, but you haven't heard the end of this, boy."

Jake flips his uncle off over his shoulder.

"Shouldn't you at least apologise? He does kinda have a point about you stealing it. You hotwired it."

"I would if I cared. They're no better than the bitch I ran away from. They've done fuck all to help me. Why should I help them?"

I refrain from pointing out that it works both ways and that if he was a little nicer, then maybe they would be. I have a feeling that too much time has passed for Jake to attempt to fix any relationship he once might have had with his family. It's sad, especially seeing as I'd do anything to have mine back, but it is what it is. I can't hold his irresponsible family against him just because my loving ones died.

"Are you ready to meet my gran?" I ask as we emerge into her garden from the undergrowth. When he doesn't respond, I glance up at him. "Jacob Thorn, are you nervous?"

"What? No. I don't get nervous. Life's too short for that shit."

"Whatever you say."

"Hello," I call when we step in through the open back door.

"Why are you coming in from-ooooh," Gran says, her eyes dropping to our joined hands. "So this is the friend you skipped out on school for?"

"Gran, this is Jake. Jake, this is my gran, Peggy."

"It's nice to meet you."

"You too," Gran manages to get out once she's wiped the shocked look from her face.

"I'm so sorry if we caused you any concern with Amalie's disappearance. It was totally my fault, I needed to clear my head, and she agreed to go with me."

Gran's eyes assess Jake the whole time he's talking, and I can't help wondering what she's thinking.

"Would you both like something to drink? You can tell me about your little trip."

Thankfully Gran turns away to pour us both a lemonade, so she misses the colour that hits my cheeks as I think about what our trip mostly entailed.

Jake stays for almost an hour before he excuses himself. "Walk me out?" he asks, reaching out for my hand. I slide mine into it and he pulls me from my seat and out to the garden.

He comes to a stop just before the trees that hide his trailer from Gran's bungalow. He pulls me to him and rests his arms around my waist.

"I don't think she likes me."

"She hasn't had a chance yet. Give her time we kind of ambushed her."

"She's only seeing my reputation and my surname."

My gossiping Gran is probably well aware of who his mother is and what his life is like.

"Just let her see the real you. The person you show me, not the arsehole the rest of the town see."

"You really think I'm an asshole?"

"Jake," I say with a sigh, lifting my arms over his shoulders and linking my fingers behind his neck. "That is you surviving. I get it. I understand why you wear the mask you do but I think maybe that it's time to start shedding it." I make a rash decision and one I hope doesn't come back to bite me on the arse. "It's Homecoming on Friday. Will you be my date?"

Terror flashes over his face and I immediately regret the question. I'm forcing too much on him too fast.

"It's okay. Forget I said anything. It was stupid."

"No, no. It wasn't stupid. I just didn't see it coming. If you want me to be your date, then that's what I'll be." He lowers his head and brushes his nose against mine. Butterflies flutter in my belly at the thought of him announcing what's between us to the world.

"Are you sure? Everyone will be there."

"More people to be jealous that you're mine then."

My heart tumbles in my chest before he presses his lips to mine in a soft, simple kiss.

"I'll see you later. *Don't* lock the door."

Heat pools between my legs at the prospect of a late night visitor.

"Okay. See you soon."

He drops another kiss to the tip of my nose and disappears into the trees.

————

"You know who his mother is, right?" Gran says the moment I walk back into the house. The second I turn from the direction Jake went, I saw her looking through the window.

"I do now. She turned up at school demanding to see him yesterday."

"She came back?"

"Yep. It knocked him for six."

"Amalie, come and sit down a minute."

I follow her order, although it's with a ball of dread in my stomach.

"I'm not going to tell you what you can and can't do, or who you can and can't see. But that boy, from what I've heard, is bad news."

"Trust me, Gran. I know exactly what Jake is capable of. I know about his reputation and how he's forced to live his life. Our relationship wasn't all flowers and hearts when we first met but for some reason, we keep finding ourselves drawn to each other."

"And that kind of connection shouldn't be fought," Gran says, the old romantic within her bubbling up once again. "I just need you to be aware of who he is. His mother is—"

"A disaster?"

"Yeah, something like that," she chuckles. "I trust you, Amalie. You've got a smart head on your shoulders and if you say he's worth it, then I'll welcome him into this house with open arms."

"Thank you, I really appreciate that."

"So, Homecoming dress shopping with Camila later then, huh?"

"How do you know about that?"

"She wanted to know if you'd be back for it when

she came to pick you up for school this morning. She looked pretty excited about it."

"She is."

"Are you going?"

"It looks that way."

"You should probably be a little more excited about it."

"I know. It's just that parties and I don't seem to mix all that well so I've no reason to think this one will be any different."

"I'm sure it'll be fine. You'll have a strapping young man on your arm this time."

My lips curl up into a smile at the thought. "Yeah, I just hope that won't bring me any more trouble."

I fill Gran in on some of the high school drama that is now my everyday life before going to get ready for Camila to pick me up for dress shopping.

She ends up dragging me into every single clothes shop at the mall. And in true female style, the dress she buys was the very first one she sees.

As promised, she makes me buy her a burger and chips for dinner and nags me for every minute detail of my time with Jake.

"You know all the girls at school are going to want to kill you, right? Not only has Jake Thorn kissed you, but he spent the entire night with you."

"Yeah, I'm aware."

"It'll be fine. If he's as into you as he says, then he'll kick them all into shape. No one will say anything to you if they've got half a brain."

"I bloody hope so."

As I lie in bed later that night waiting for my late night visitor to appear, I run through the events that led up to us skipping town yesterday. I still feel stupid for not putting two and two together, especially after he explained that it was where I came from and my parents' industry that he really hated.

I'm just starting to drift off to sleep when the phone ringing fills the bungalow. I listen as Gran walks down the hallway to get it before her voice filters down to me.

"Amalie, are you awake?"

"Coming."

Pulling a hoodie over my shoulders, I make my way down the dark hallway to where she's standing by the phone with just a lamp on lighting the room.

"It's the detective from London. I thought you'd want to hear first." My stomach drops into my feet.

"Shit." Blowing out a slow breath, I try to prepare for whatever he might have to say to me. I take the phone from her and lift it to my ear. "Hello?"

"Miss Windsor-Marsh, Detective Griffin. I have some news regarding your parents' crash."

"Okay," I say, my voice shaky as my hand trembles at my ear.

"The crash has been deemed as a horrific accident. Our investigators can't find any evidence of anything on the helicopter being tampered with."

"Oh my god," I breathe.

"It's over, Amalie. I know it won't be easy, but I hope that now you have the answer you've been waiting for that you'll be able to move on with your life. You'll need to speak to your solicitor but your parents' possessions and accounts etcetera will now be released. I'd advise setting up a meeting as soon as you can."

"Thank you."

"I know it's late there, but I wanted you to know as soon as I got word to tell you."

"I really appreciate that. Thank you so much."

He says his goodbye, I place the phone back on the unit and fall back against the wall. My knees give out and I crash to the floor.

Tears stream down my cheeks, but I don't sob like I'd expect.

"What did he say?" Gran asks impatiently.

"That it... that it was an accident. No evidence of anything untoward. It's over, Gran. It's done and they're gone." It's those words that make my dam break. Gran drops down beside me and holds me to her as we both cry for everything we've lost.

I've no idea how long we sit there crying on each other's shoulders, but all of a sudden, a thought hits me and no matter what, I can't make it go.

"I need to go back."

"What?"

"I need to go back to London." The thought of being able to pick up some of the things I was forced to leave behind has me on my feet in seconds.

"Let's try to get some sleep and then we'll look for flights in the morning."

"No. I need to go now."

"Don't be crazy, Amalie," she says, but I'm not

listening, I'm already halfway to my room to grab my laptop. In minutes I have the website open and searching for flights.

"There's one for tomorrow." Grabbing my card from my purse, I book it and slam my laptop closed.

"You can't just run to London. What about school?"

"I'll just be a couple of days," I say as I fill a holdall with clothes. "I just need to be there. I need to... I need to say a final goodbye now that we know."

"Hold your horses and I'll come with you."

"I'm sorry, I don't mean to sound harsh, but I need to do this alone. I need to figure out a way to put my old life behind me."

"Okay," Gran says with a nod and a sad smile. "I understand. I'll drive you to the airport. Just promise me something."

"Anything."

"Promise me you're coming back."

41

JAKE

I should have been expecting it, but when the knock comes on my trailer door, I call out for whoever it was to enter, stupidly assuming it's Ethan or Mason. But when I look up, my blood runs cold as I watch my so-called mother step up into my home.

"Jake," she whispers as if I'm a wild fucking animal that's going to bolt at any second. If she wasn't blocking the door waiting for me to run, then I might consider it, but I've spent the last decade planning what I might say to her should she ever reappear and now it's my chance. "I can't believe how big you are, and so handsome."

"Because that's all that matters to you, isn't it? Looks. You couldn't give a fuck about what's in the inside because your heart is black."

"Jacob Thorn," she scolds and it just fires me up more.

"No. You don't get to come storming in all these

years later and attempt to parent me. You gave up that responsibility the day you walked out of my life, leaving me with those two cunts."

"How can you say that about them? They took you in when I couldn't do the job properly. I was ill, Jake."

"Bullshit, *Mother*. You weren't ill, you were just fucking greedy. Someone told you that you had a pretty face, offered you a decent paycheck and off you went like you had no one depending on you. And as for those two." I point up toward the main house. "They were so good at looking after me, they shoved me down here on my own when I was barely old enough to look after myself."

"I'm sure there was more to it than that. From what I heard, you were a bit of a terror."

"So they removed me from their house and left me down here to do as I wished. Are you fucking surprised?"

"I've made mistakes, Jake. I'm only human."

My muscles tense and my chest heaves that she can stand there and make such claims after everything. My fists clench with my need to hurt something, mainly her but I won't give her the privilege of calling the cops on me, because I've no doubt she would, followed by selling the story of her abusive, uncontrollable son to the press.

"No. You've not just made mistakes. You've ruined my fucking life. You had one job the day you gave birth to me. To put me first. To make me your priority. But you failed. You failed every step of the fucking way. So I'm sorry if you expected to walk back into my life and I'd welcome you with open arms but that is never going to happen. If you came back a few weeks, even a month later, I might have considered forgiving you. But now, no fucking chance. Too much time and too much pain has passed." Taking a step toward her, she visibly cowers like I'm about to hit her.

I swing my fist, but it ends up nowhere near her face. Instead, it smashes through the kitchen wall and into the spare bedroom.

"Please, Jake," she cries.

"Your pathetic tears won't work on me."

"Please, I want to make up for everything. I'm not going anywhere this time."

"Well, I am. I've got nothing more to say to you."

Pushing past her, I jump down from the trailer and run.

She has no right getting up in my space and trying to make up for mistakes. No fucking right.

I run until my legs burn with pain and my lungs aren't capable of sucking in air fast enough. What I need is Amalie, but I'm no good to her showing up like this.

Instead, I come to a slow jog as I head up Mason's drive. Other than Amalie now, he and Coach are the only ones who know about my mom. I do my best to keep her a secret for fear of the guys Googling her and watching her fucking porn videos. I'm not stupid enough to think they're all oblivious. When she was riding high, this town loved to ride her fame coat tails. Weird how it all came to a grinding halt when she was caught snorting cocaine off dirty old toilet seats in some backstreet bar.

I bang on the door as I try to get control of my breathing. Thankfully, it's Mason who comes to the door, I'm not sure what anyone else would make of the state of me.

"Glad you're still alive," he says, opening the door wider for me to enter. "Where the fuck you been?"

"Uh..." I follow him down to his kitchen, the sound of kid's TV blasts from the playroom as we pass. "Your mom here?"

"Na, she's... out."

Mason likes talking about his home life and family situation just as much as I do. So I just nod in understanding and continue following him.

He pulls two beers from the fridge and passes one over.

"Kate's back."

The bottle stops halfway to his mouth and his chin drops.

"Please tell me you're joking."

"Be a fucking hilarious joke, right?"

His lips twitch up but seeing as he lived through the whole thing with me, he finds it about as funny as I do.

"She turned up at school yesterday afternoon demanding to see me."

"Shit, man. What did you do?"

"I ran. Seems Brit saw the whole thing and when I got back home, she was waiting for me. We stole my uncle's car and fucked off for the night."

His eyes widen in surprise, but I swear I see a little bit of pride in them too.

"And how was that?"

"Fucking mind-blowing, bro. But I don't kiss and tell."

"Fucking knew you were in love with her."

"In lov—" My words falter as I consider his statement. Am I in love with the girl who I thought I hated? "Fuck."

"Took you long enough to figure out, bro."

"Jesus." I scrub my hand over my chin as a child screams bloody murder.

"Mason, Charlie keeps hitting me with his truck."

"Fucking hell. Let me go deal with them."

Mason walks back down to the playroom and has a stern word with his two younger brothers before coming back looking exasperated.

"Is your mom ever planning on investing in a real sitter so you can get out and live your life?"

"She keeps promising things will change, but I gave up hope of that ever happening a while ago. Just gotta keep going. One day we might win the lottery or some shit. Anyway, my issues aren't the most pressing right now. What the fuck are you gonna do about your mom?"

"Other than hope she fucks off as quick as she did last time? Stay out of her fucking way. I can't be dealing with her bullshit."

"Na, not now that you've got a girlfriend to worry about."

"Fuck. I've got a fucking girlfriend."

"Bro, the chicks at school are gonna lose their shit. They've all been vying for your attention for years and then Amalie walks in and sweeps you right off your feet."

"She didn't sweep—"

His eyebrows almost hit his hairline.

"Fine. Okay, maybe that happened a little bit."

I drain my beer as Mason chuckles.

"Another?"

"Gimme all you got. Gotta drink that bitch out of my system."

I hate that I miss sneaking into Amalie's bedroom when I told her specifically to keep her door unlocked. But getting fucked up with my best friend is exactly what I needed. Even if he did spend the night playing daddy to his kid brothers.

––––––

When I wake the next morning, it's with a banging head but Mason ensures I'm up by ripping the sheets off and threatening me with a bucket of cold water.

"If you don't get your ass off my floor, get dressed, and show up for practice, Coach will have your balls."

"I know, I know," I mutter, trying to get my arms and legs to work enough to get me off his rock hard floor. I already know I'm going to be in his bad books for missing the previous two days of practice.

Coach isn't the reason why I drag my ass off the floor though. It's Amalie that has me stumbling toward Mason's bathroom so I can shower off the scent of last night's alcohol consumption. Day two into our relationship and I'm already going to be groveling after not showing my face last night.

The thought of her waiting in bed for me wearing a tiny pair of panties and a shirt thin enough to see her nipples though makes me wonder what the fuck I was thinking staying here last night.

I avoid our usual spot when I get to school. The last thing I need right now is fucking Chelsea pretending to care where I was yesterday. Instead, I head straight toward Amalie's locker. Only, she's not there.

I have no idea what her schedule looks like, I've spent the past few weeks trying to pretend that I don't care, something which I'm now regretting more than ever because it would help me find her faster.

Knowing who I need to ask, I walk toward Camila and her small group of friends. Sadly, that also involves Shane, someone who never needs to cross me ever again. Everything inside me begs for me to hit him for what he did to my girl at that party, but something tells me she wouldn't be happy if I did. She seems to be under the illusion that he's a good guy and couldn't possibly be the one who drugged her.

Ignoring his death stare, I place my hand on Camila's shoulder and turn her my way.

"Where is she?"

"Wha..." It takes her a few seconds to register it's me. "Amalie?"

"Yeah, Amalie. Who the fuck else would I be asking you about?"

She just shrugs and it pisses me off.

"Where is she?" I spit.

"Don't you know?" She's baiting me, I know she is, but I can't help but let it get to me. I fucking need her.

"Does it look like I fucking know?"

My raised voice is starting to cause a scene, but I don't give a shit.

"She's gone to London."

My head spins as I try to accept what she's just said to me. I spent practically all of the past two days with her and she never once told me she was leaving. My heart starts to race as panic begins to take over. Why wouldn't she tell me she was leaving?

"When's she get back?" My voice is rough as I fight like hell to keep myself in check.

"I don't know. Her gran said she booked a one-way flight."

My chin drops in shock. "One-way?"

"Yeah, probably trying to get the hell away from you," Shane bravely pipes up, giving me the perfect excuse to do exactly what I was craving the second I laid eyes on him.

"Motherfucker."

My fist flies and I hit him square on the jaw. He stumbles where he wasn't expecting the hit but manages to catch himself before he tumbles to the floor.

The next thing I know, a pair of large hands wrap around my upper arms and I'm being pulled back while Shane groans in pain.

The taste of copper fills my mouth telling me that he must have got a few of his own hits in but my body is too pumped up with adrenaline to feel anything right now.

I'm forcefully shoved forward as people start to surround Shane.

Fuck him. I hope it hurts like hell.

"You don't deserve her," he calls out above the commotion.

A smirk curls at my lips. *Ain't that the fucking truth.*

By the time I'm pushed through the door to Coach's office and shoved onto the seat in front of his desk, I'm starting to come down from my high and my face is starting to ache.

"You need to start talking, boy. First fighting during a game, then missing practice two days on the trot and now this. I'm this close to benching your ass, Thorn. This fucking close." When I glance up, he's holding his thumb and forefinger about a centimeter apart. "What's going on? Please don't tell me all of this is over some skirt."

"She's not just some skirt," I seethe.

"So it is a girl. Who is it that's got you all strung up?"

Dropping my eyes to my lap, I keep my mouth shut.

"I can't help you if you don't talk."

"It doesn't fucking matter who she is, okay? She's gone. Fucked off and left me behind like the trash I am."

"Well, this one really has got herself under your skin."

"It's not just her, Coach."

He leans back and crosses his arms over his chest,

waiting for me to spill. I'm surprised he doesn't know. Gossip spreads through the teachers here just as fast as it does around the kids. "Go on."

"Kate showed her face."

He nods, waiting for me to spill, which I do. Coach is the one and only parent figure I've had for most of my life so unlike most of the world around me, he knows all my dark and dirty secrets. He's also bailed me out of the shit more times than I can count.

"You need to get her out of your head or you're going to be useless Friday night. It's our big game against Eastwood, in case you've forgotten. We win this one and we're well on our way to state. But I need you, Thorn. I need you and I need you fully focused. No screwy mother, no girl issues. Get them out of here and focus," he says, tapping my head. "Now get the fuck out of here and go sort out your face. I'll see you on the field after class."

"You're not benching me?"

"Not yet. I need you Friday, you're just going to have to keep your nose clean until then or my hand might be forced. Now fuck off before you get blood on my office floor."

No sooner am I released from Coach's office and I'm hauled into the principal's office and given an ass-kicking for my actions. Much like Coach though, he also knows he's relying on me for Friday night's game, so in the end, he goes easy on me.

————

By Friday night, my bruising is starting to reduce and my cuts on my knuckles healing, shame the ache in my chest is yet to abate. I tried phoning her when I first discovered she'd left, but it didn't even connect. So after fucking up my trailer a little more than it already was after my mother's visit, I sent her a text that I regretted the second I hit send. In reality, I didn't mean any of the harsh words. Her sudden disappearance just hurts so fucking much, her actions are exactly what I accused her of when she first arrived. She's no better than my mother who ran at the first hint of a better life. Was her few hours with me so fucking bad that she had to leave the country?

The last thing I want to do is go to school and get cheered on as we hopefully thrash Eastwood's ass. They're our closest rival and almost every year they fucking beat us, leaving with smug as fuck smiles on their faces.

The entire school body fills the stadium for tonight's game. Homecoming is a big deal, hopes are high after our last couple of wins and all eyes are anxiously on us as we hit the field. The roar of excitement from our fans makes me wince, but it helps to push aside everything I'm feeling and allow me to focus on what I should be doing right now.

Fuck her, if she doesn't think this place is good enough for her then good riddance. This place is mine and right now my people need me.

The game's fucking hard and not helped by the fact that Shane taunts me with overly amused eyes or a shove in the shoulder if he thinks he can get away with it. He's pissed that I had her, even for a short amount of time but he's equally fucked off that I made her leave. I might gloat that I had Amalie to myself, but at least I didn't have to drug her to get her into bed.

Coach notices the tension between us and mouths over to me to calm my shit down. We both know that I shouldn't be on this field right now after I jumped Shane the other day. I'm determined to finish this game and not have him ruining it, like he's attempting to do.

We win, but only just, and the excitement is off the charts as we make our way back into the locker room.

"Fuckin' yes, boys," Ethan hollers. "Now let's shower this shit off and go find the pussy."

Everyone else cheers but I just start stripping my uniform off and it doesn't go unnoticed.

Mason and Ethan appear at my sides.

"You're coming, right?"

"Do I look like I want to go to a fucking dance?"

"Aw, come on, you'll get the crown and then you'll have even more girls hanging off you than usual."

Neither of them so much as flinch when I raise my arm and slam my fist into the locker in front of me.

Pain radiates up my arm, but I welcome the distraction from my heart.

"I don't want other fucking girls," I whisper, not wanting the rest of the team to overhear that I've grown a fucking pussy.

"Fine, well how about you come to celebrate with the team. You don't have to stay all night. We can leave early and get fucked up."

Now that sounds more like an offer I can't refuse.

"Fine, but only because you're offering something to kill the memories of it after."

"That's my man." Ethan slaps my shoulder before heading off to the showers.

"You still haven't heard from her?" Mason asks, sounding more concerned about me than just missing out on tonight.

"She's gone. I hope she's laughing her fucking tits off. She played me at my own game, made me want her and fucked off."

"Na, man. That's not her style. Have you even gone to speak to her gran, find out what's going on?"

My silence clues him in to the fact I've done no such thing. I ain't chasing her and allowing the whole fucking town to see that she's got me on my knees.

I shower and then pull on a white button-down with some black pants and shoes. Dressing up is the last thing I want to do, but I don't want to let my team down more than I already have.

I can plaster on a fake smile for an hour before someone hopefully hands me a bottle of something strong.

42

AMALIE

W alking back into my parents' house is the weirdest feeling. It's exactly the same as when I left. The housekeeper that's still employed has kept it sparkling clean.

My heart ached more than I thought possible as I look at all their belongings, their lives.

I shouldn't have run like I did, but the need to be surrounded by them was too much. I miss them more than words could ever express and hearing the news that no one wanted them dead made me need this final closure.

This place might feel familiar in so many ways, but it's obvious the minute I step inside that it's no longer my home. The two people who made this place feel like a loving family home are gone, leaving it as no more than a house.

I spend my first day wallowing in the loss of my parents and going through all their stuff. As much as I hate to remove pieces of them, I know it needs to happen to help me move on. I select a couple of my favourite items from my mum's wardrobe and jewellery collection and I let go of the rest. It's time to move on.

Once the house is mostly cleared, I feel a little better and like this trip was actually worthwhile and not just a crazy spur of the moment decision that I'm going to regret.

It wasn't until I turned my phone off ready for the flight, I realised that in my haste to pack I didn't pick up the charger.

I told myself that there was a reason I forgot it and when I walked past the shops at arrivals in Heathrow Airport, I didn't stop to get a new one.

Miss French kick-started thoughts about my future, I need this time to figure out what I want to do. It might be selfish to shut myself off from the world, I know Jake won't be happy about it, but I'd hope he'd understand my need for a little time. My life's been crazy, and I just need a minute to take a breath. I need everything to slow down, all the changes to stop just so I can be me.

I organise a meeting with my parents' solicitor to discuss what happens next along with another at the bank as I try to figure out what the hell to do with the money they've left behind. I knew they were well off, but having the reality of the situation on the screen in front of me was a little overwhelming. As their only child, everything, including their business has been left to me. Thankfully they've got very capable people running it which means I don't need to do anything. They were sensible enough to have things set up just in case the worst were to happen. So apparently, I just get to sit back and reap the rewards my parents would have got. If I'm honest, I'd rather just have my parents, but it's a bit late for that now.

The second I step from the bank I know what I need to do. Since the moment I landed, I think I knew that this place wasn't my home and more time here has only proved one thing. I left my heart behind in America. It's firmly in the hands of a hard-headed, sexy and broken guy who I think feels the same way, despite every way he tried to prove otherwise.

Allowing thoughts of Jake in, my heart aches to see him again. To feel the security of his arms around me.

Flagging down a taxi, I rattle off my old address and tell him to hurry the hell up. I've got a flight to book and hopefully catch.

———

The flight back is excruciating. Once I'd made the decision, I wanted to be back there that instant. So sitting for almost an hour even waiting to take off took its toll.

I called Gran the moment I booked my last minute flight, and she agreed to pick me up at the other end.

I purchased a phone charger at the airport and made use of the onboard power supply to charge it.

When I turn it on at the other end, it goes crazy with messages and voicemails. Almost all of them from Jake and Camila.

I ignore every single one. My focus is on one thing, and one thing only.

Gran greets me at arrivals like she hasn't seen me in years, not just a couple of days.

"I missed you too," I say into her hair as she holds me tight.

"I was so scared you wouldn't come back," she admits, making my heart ache.

"I think I needed to go back to realise where I really wanted to be. I love London but this place has become home to me now. There was never a chance I wasn't coming back."

"Thank God for that." When she pulls back, her eyes are swimming with tears. "I love having you here, Amalie. I didn't realise how lonely I was before you came."

Emotion clogs my throat and only confirms something I'd pretty much decided on in London. I'm not leaving her to go to college. Once I've got tonight out of the way, I'm going to get out the paperwork that Miss French gave me for the local colleges and check out their courses. This is where my heart and my family are, so this is where I need to be.

"I really like it here too. I didn't realise quite how much until I left."

"That's so good to hear. Now, let's get out of here, I understand there's a dance tonight and I'm pretty sure there'll be a boy waiting for you."

"I'm not so sure," I mutter, walking out of the terminal beside Gran.

"No?"

"I haven't spoken to him since I left," I admit with a wince. I know it probably wasn't the most sensible thing to do where Jake is concerned but I needed the time.

"Well, even more reason to get dolled up to the nines and sweep him off his feet."

The second I'm through the front door of Gran's house, I run toward my bedroom.

I have the quickest shower of my life before blow drying my hair and throwing a little bit of makeup on. I might be in a rush, but I still need to look like I've made an effort.

Pulling open my wardrobe, my eyes land on one dress. The little silver one that my mum bought me for my end of sixth form night out.

Pulling it out, I allow myself a few seconds to admire it. I've no clue if it's the kind of thing girls wear to Homecoming but right now, I don't really care, it's exactly what I need to give me the confidence to walk into that gym and claim my place in this school.

I forgo the fancy arrival seeing as the dance has already started and allow Gran to drop me in the car park.

After waving her off, I walk up the short path toward the gym. My hands tremble and butterflies flutter so hard in my belly that I think I might take off.

I'm terrified that he's going to turn me away after I left him. It's exactly the kind of behaviour he roasted me for when I first arrived, but I'm determined to make him see that it was a one-off, that I'm back and one of the biggest reasons is him.

Blowing out a long breath, I shake out my arms and lift one to pull the door open.

The sound of the chatter and excitement inside filters down to me, but to my surprise, there's no music.

My curiosity along with my need for Jake has my feet moving. I walk down the short corridor and the reason behind the lack of music soon becomes clear.

"And your Homecoming queen is..." There's a brief silence before whoever is in charge of the microphone announces Chelsea's name. *Of course she fucking is.*

I roll my eyes and inwardly groan before continuing.

The gym is filled with balloons and streamers to make it look less like a sports hall and more like a room to celebrate in, but my eyes don't focus on any of that or the hundreds of kids staring at the stage because it's just one man on the stage who captures my attention.

He's dressed in a white shirt with the collar undone at the neck, sans tie. His black trousers are skinny enough to hug his thighs and make my mouth water, but it's his eyes that I get lost in as he stares into space. They look haunted in a way I remember all too well. They're just like the first day he saw me, and then again when he looked at his mother only a few days ago.

Chelsea flounces up on stage making a right song and dance about receiving her crown and being objectified by everyone.

Jake doesn't so much as glance her way as he stands there like he wants the ground to swallow him up. I'm not surprised he's been crowned king because that's exactly what he is. He rules this place. He knows how much they need him for any potential football success, and he uses it to his advantage.

I'm frozen to the spot watching this little ceremony playing out in front of me when every muscle in my body tenses as Chelsea slides up next to Jake. She has a twinkle in her eye that I don't like as the photographer gets a couple of shots of them. Just as he takes a step to leave, she blocks his path and crashes her lips to his. His body stills, his eyes widen, but it's that moment he finds me standing in the doorway.

It takes about a second too long for him to react. I'm just about on the verge of walking up there myself and pulling the hussy from him when his arms rise, and he forcefully pushes. The entire student body gasps in horror as she loses her footing and falls from the stage.

I've no clue what happens to her because my focus is solely on Jake's angry eyes. As the commotion continues in front of the stage, Jake effortlessly jumps down and sidesteps the crowd that's formed.

My heart pounds with every footstep he takes toward me. I've no idea what he's going to do, but the look in his eyes and the hard lines of his face terrify me.

At no point does he break our contact and I think that's even more unnerving. He wants me nervous.

My entire body is trembling by the time he steps up to me and I prepare for what abuse about my leaving is going to fall from his lips, but nothing happens.

He's inches from me, his eyes locked on mine, his chest heaving almost as mine is. His arm lifts and I flinch, not that I really think he's going to hit me, more that the movement surprises me.

Then he does something I really wasn't expecting.

His hand cups my cheek before his fingers slide into my hair.

"Thank fuck," he mutters, his voice is broken and defeated before his lips land on mine.

I've no clue if it's because I shut off the world around me to focus on his kiss or if the gym really does turn silent as he kisses me in front of the entire school.

His hand tilts my head to the side so he can plunge his tongue into my mouth and totally consume me.

The arms he has around my waist tightens, pressing our bodies together and the unmistakable feeling of his length pressing into my stomach ignites something inside me that I'm not going to be able to ignore.

Pulling back, he rests his forehead against mine, our increased breaths mingling, his eyes softer than they were previously but still full of hunger, just this time he's not hungry for pain or revenge he's just hungry for me, that knowledge only makes my need for him even stronger.

"We need to get out of here."

43

JAKE

I thought I was imagining things when I looked up and saw her standing like a fucking angel in the doorway.

I blinked, expecting for her to be gone when I opened my eyes, but she was still there. Unfortunately, Chelsea took advantage of my moment and not only was Amalie still there, but fucking Chelsea was attached to my lips.

The force I used to get her away with was stronger than necessary, but she's pushed her luck with me one too many times. The only girl I want touching me is currently chewing on her lip, looking unsure of herself in the sexiest dress I think I've ever seen.

I thought I'd be angry seeing her again but all I feel is relief. She's back, and she's here for me. That's all I need to know, that she's mine.

Marching over, the only thing I can think about is having her lips on mine. And the second I get my wish, everything that has been wrong with me this week suddenly rights itself.

"We need to get out of here." With her hand in mine, we walk out of the gym and away from everyone but not before I spot a delighted Poppy smiling at us. I wink and she laughs lightly before giving me a little wave.

It's already dark out, but the sky is full of twinkling stars. I've never paid much attention before, but I swear they're brighter tonight.

"Can you walk in those shoes?" I come to a stop and look down at her feet. I don't want to have to walk home. I want to be the kind of guy who can help her into my car to get her back to my bedroom as fast as possible, but unfortunately, that guy isn't me. The best I've got to offer is a moonlight walk along the beach on our way back to my shitty trailer.

"I'll walk as far as you need me to." My heart races hearing the words I had no idea I was longing for.

Giving her arm a tug, she falls back into step beside me as I head toward the beach. We walk for quite a while in silence, just soaking up each other's presence.

"I'm so sorry for leaving like I did."

"I'm sorry for the message I sent. I didn't mean any of it."

She's silent for a few seconds and I panic. I regretted that message the second I sent it, but it was too late. The vile words were already out in the wild.

"I haven't read any of them. My phone died and when I got back my first priority was getting to you. I realised something while I was away."

"What was that?"

She stops as she slips off her shoes and we step down onto the sand.

"The detective rang to explain that there was nothing suspicious about my parents' crash and my first instinct was that I needed to go home. Only, the moment I stepped foot on English soil, I realised that it was no longer home to me. The place I'd left behind was home now. The people I'd left behind were my home."

I bring her to a stop in my hidden spot between the sand dunes and take her cheeks in my hands.

"Me?" I ask, hating the hesitation in my voice. But seeing her again tonight only solidified the strength of my feelings for her. I'd barely survived a couple of days without her, it's pretty clear that I can't live the rest of my life without her by my side.

"You, Jake. I just need you."

"Fuck." A ball of emotion I'm not all that used to clogs my throat and the backs of my eyes burn as I stare down at her beauty. "I love you, Amalie. I love you so fucking much." I don't give her time to respond, instead I slam my lips down on hers, intent on showing her just how much I mean those words.

When I eventually let up her for air, tears are streaming down her cheeks, but she has the widest smile on her face.

"What?"

She chuckles and I can't help but join her. "I'm pretty sure you're the biggest arsehole I've ever met, Jacob Thorn. But do you know what?"

I shake my head, hoping to fuck she's going to say exactly what I said to her. My heart feels like it's bleeding out not hearing the words.

"I love you, too."

EPILOGUE

Amalie

Telling Jake how I really felt was like a huge weight lifted off my shoulders. The look in his eyes as I said those three little words to him is something I'll never regret. I wanted to sob like a baby when it hit me that there's a very good chance he's never been told them before. Thankfully, he saw the onslaught of fresh tears coming and quickly distracted me.

With his lips on mine, he lowered us both to the sand and right there, under the stars and in the privacy of the dunes, he set about proving just how he felt by making love to me until neither of us could stay awake any longer.

I've no idea what time we eventually stumbled off the beach, both grinning like loons and laughing like we had no cares in the world. It was the most incredible feeling and one I have no doubt Jake will continue to make me feel for a long time to come.

When we got back to his trailer, we both showered the sand off together in his tiny cubicle, it was cozy but neither of us had any intention of separating anytime soon, so it was kind of perfect, before we both fell into his bed.

———

"Are you ready for this?" I ask, standing outside Noah's house where his party is spilling out into the backyard and the music's blaring so loud there is no doubt as to what's going on inside.

"I'm so ready. It's time to show everyone exactly who you belong to."

With his hand firmly holding mine, we walk into Noah's house.

The eyes of our intrigued classmates follow our every move. The girls lock their gaze on our hands before their death stares find me. They all gossip amongst themselves, but I refuse to cower down to their petty jealousy.

I don't react other than my smile growing wider with every step I take. That is until we come across a group of girls sitting around the sofa. When a couple of them part, it becomes obvious why they're all sitting there because in the centre with her newly cast ankle propped up on the coffee table is Chelsea.

"You broke her ankle," I whisper to Jake, trying my best to keep any amusement out of my voice.

"I wouldn't have pushed her if she didn't take advantage of me. My lips are for you and you only. It's time all these assholes know it."

He wraps his arm around my waist and pulls me up against him. He doesn't need to say anything to get the attention of everyone in the room. He's Jake Thorn, he commands everyone's attention just by breathing.

Once he's confident everyone is staring our way, he slams his lips down on mine. He kisses me like it's our first time before bending me backward and really giving our audience a show.

"I love you, Brit," he whispers when he pulls me back upright.

"And I think everyone in the room other than you hates me," I say as a joke, but his eyes harden in anger.

"If any fucker gives you a hard time, you've only got to say the word."

"I'm a big girl, Jake. I can look after myself."

"Don't I know it," he mutters with a laugh.

I open my mouth to respond but a commotion in another room drags everyone's attention from us.

"Mason, no," someone screams, and Jake takes off running. I'm forced to follow seeing as his hand is still holding mine.

The crowd parts for him and it's then we get our first look at Mason throwing punch after punch into Noah's face.

"What the fuck just happened?"

Jake races forward to pull his friend away, when I

look up, I find the horrified eyes of two girls. One belongs to my best friend and the other a girl I barely recognise as another senior and one of Chelsea's crew. Whatever's happening right now, I sense is going to change Camila's life in a way she wasn't expecting.

What to find out what happened between Camila and Mason?

PAINE IS NOW AVAILABLE

ACKNOWLEDGMENTS

Acknowledegments

Well, where do I start? I guess, with my husband. He asked me one simple question on the way to our summer holiday and from the moment the words left his mouth, Jake appeared.

I had a plan for the rest of the year, and I can say without doubt that Jake wasn't a part of it. He had a different opinion. I tried to ignore him, I really really did. I was desperate to finish my Forbidden series without any unplanned distractions but, if you've made it this far then you'll have already learned that Jake doesn't always do as he's told.

So a couple of weeks, some encouragement from Andie M. Long, and a lot of notes in my phone later, I caved and Jake and Amalie were born. It's safe to say that they pretty much consumed me for the two and a half months it's took me to write their story.

I've had many doubts about this book, it's one of the reasons I didn't mention I was writing it until I was done. My alpha, Michelle, who reads all my books as I write them hated Jake, to the point she was threatening to give up. But thankfully, her nosiness got the better of her and she had to continue. It payed off because she fell hook, line and sinker for Jake.

It's different to my usual book, the characters are younger and the angst even more intense and Jake a bigger asshole than I usually write but once I handed it over to be read by my betas they helped shed my fears and pushed me forward. I owe them a huge thank you for taking a chance on a book that's not necesssarily their usual read and falling in love with it anyway. I hope a few more of you trusted me enough to get this far, and also fell hard for Jake.

As always, I started out with the intention of it being a standalone, mostly just to get Jake out of my head, but as soon as Jake started to fade, a couple more popped up so I guess the big question is...what's the deal with Camila and Mason. Well, hopefully soon you'll find out because their story is next on my list!

I have to say a massive thank you to Michelle Lancaster who helped me out when I was in cover hell and found me the most incredible model who just screams Jake. The next two are equally as hot and I can't wait to reveal those as well.

I want to say a huge thank you to everyone who has supported me with Thorn, whether you beta read, ARC read, shared, bookstagrammed or even just picked it up to read. I really wouldn't be here doing this without you.

Until next time,

Tracy xo

ABOUT THE AUTHOR

Tracy Lorraine is a new adult and contemporary romance author. Tracy has recently-ish turned thirty and lives in a cute Cotswold village in England with her husband, baby girl and lovable but slightly crazy dog. Having always been a bookaholic with her head stuck in her Kindle Tracy decided to try her hand at a story idea she dreamt up and hasn't looked back since.

Be the first to find out about new releases and offers. Sign up to my newsletter here.

If you want to know what I'm up to and see teasers and snippets of what I'm working on, then you need to be in my Facebook group Tracy's Angels.

Keep up to date with Tracy's books at
www.tracylorraine.com

ALSO BY TRACY LORRAINE

Rebel Ink Series

Hate You #1

Trick You #2

Defy You #3

Play You #4

Inked (A Rebel Ink/Driven Crossover)

Rosewood High Series

Thorn #1

Paine #2

Savage #3

Fierce #4

Hunter #5

Faze (#6 Prequel)

Fury #6

Legend #7

Maddison Kings University Series

TMYM: Prequel

TRYS #1

TDYW #2

TBYS #3

TVYC #4

TDYD #5

Ruined Series

Ruined Plans #1

Ruined by Lies #2

Ruined Promises #3

Never Forget Series

Never Forget Him #1

Never Forget Us #2

Everywhere & Nowhere #3

Chasing Series

Chasing Logan

The Cocktail Girls

His Manhattan

Her Kensington

PAINE SNEAK PEEK

CHAPTER ONE

Camila

"What the hell are you doing?" I scream, running toward where Mason has Noah pinned to the floor. There's blood streaming from his nose and a split in his lip, but the most striking thing is that he's not trying to fight back. He's just taking it.

"Motherfucker," Mason growls, his voice is so low and menacing that a shiver races down my spine.

What the hell has gotten into him?

Reaching out, I place my hand on his forearm right before he's about to throw another punch into Noah's broken face.

"Stop," I shout. "Mason. Stop, please," I beg, my voice cracking.

My contact is obviously what Mason needs to bring

him out of his trance. He lifts his eyes to find me. The darkness in them makes my breath catch. If I didn't know better, I'd think he wanted Noah dead. But that's not the Mason I know. Well... the Mason I knew. But it seems the boy from the end of the street is long gone these days.

"What the hell are you doing?"

He stares down at Noah a few seconds longer before allowing Jake to pull him up and away.

"I—" He looks up at me and I swear I see pain pouring from his eyes. "He was kissing that skank." His voice is low, so only I can hear as he tips his chin in the direction of Tasha, a member of the cheer squad. Her eyes are wide and she's as white as a sheet, but then so is everyone else as they stare at the scene unfolding in front of them.

"What the fuck is your problem? Not satisfied making me an outcast, now you've got to get involved and ruin my relationship too?"

"No. He was... they were in the bathroom together."

My heart pounds in my chest. He wouldn't, would he? Noah loves me, that I'm sure of. This is a joke. Mason's had too much to drink and has decided to throw his weight around, show me who's boss.

A low moan comes from Noah, and it drags me from my fog. Why am I focusing on Mason right now when my boyfriend is groaning in pain from being on the wrong end of his fists?

"Get him out of here," I bark at Jake, who immediately jumps into action. Amalie looks between the two of us, not knowing which way to go. "It's fine.

Go with him. I'm just going to get Noah cleaned up and put him to bed. Everyone out," I shout, knowing that our entire class is currently watching this play out in front of their eyes.

Dropping to my knees, I place my hand on Noah's warm chest. His eyes flicker open and a small smile twitches at his lips.

Some movement to my left catches my eye, and, when I look up, I find everyone still standing there.

"Get the hell out," I scream. That, along with Alyssa and a couple of other friends starting to usher people from the room, seems to get them moving at last.

My hands tremble as I stare down at my broken and bloodied boyfriend.

"Are you okay?" I whisper.

"Yeah, never been better," he grunts.

"Can you get up? We'll go and get you cleaned up."

"Yeah, I'm good. He didn't hit that hard."

I don't point out that the state of his face right now doesn't confirm his story.

With his arm around my waist, I lead his limp body toward the stairs as the movement of people leaving sound out around us.

No one comes to help, which kind of pisses me off, but I understand that they probably don't want to get in the middle.

"Sit," I instruct when we make it to Noah's bed. "I'll be back in a few minutes. Don't go anywhere."

I walk past his adjoining bathroom, knowing I won't find anything I need, and instead go to the main bathroom.

With a first aid box in hand, I head back toward Noah.

I come to a stop in his doorway and take him in. He's pulled his shirt off and is laid back on his bed. Blood and darkening bruises color his cheeks.

Noah's been my rock. We'd never really had much to do with each other despite being in the same classes for years, but we found each other when I was at my lowest, thanks to my inability to use a computer competently.

We were supposed to be making spreadsheets, but me and numbers aren't a match made in heaven and I was on the verge of throwing the mouse across the room when he offered his help. Grateful didn't even come close to expressing how I felt as he explained how the formulas worked in such a simple way that I couldn't not understand while our teacher focused on Mason and his gang of jocks, ignoring the rest of us.

Anger burned in my belly and I glanced over my shoulder at the special attention they got just because of their position in the school. It was just another reminder of why things turned out the way they were meant to be. Girls like me were never destined to be friends with guys like him. I guess it's just a good thing I discovered that before my heart got in even deeper. We may have been young, but I'm not naïve enough to ignore that fact that I gave part of my heart to Mason Paine long before I even knew it was a thing.

Noah's eyes flutter open like he can feel me standing there. Even with all of the swelling, I can see love in them.

Mason's lying. Noah would never do that to me. Especially not tonight.

"Babe?"

"Sorry," I say, forcing myself from my musings and walking toward him. Perching myself on the edge of his bed, I dip a washcloth into the bowl of warm water and start to clean up his face.

He winces in pain as I gently dab at the corner of his lips.

"I didn't—"

"I know."

I trust Noah with my life. He's been nothing but the perfect boyfriend since he asked me to homecoming a few weeks after that class. Another boy had consumed all my time and thoughts up until that point, and I had no idea that anyone else existed or might have been interested. He totally swept me off my feet, and I haven't had a moment of regret since.

At the beginning, I missed Mason. I was desperate to know what he thought about Noah. I was just so used to talking to him about everything, but Noah soon showed me that I didn't need Mason the way I always thought it did. I had the sweetest new boyfriend and my best friend in Alyssa. I didn't need the boy who turned his back on me when things didn't go his way.

I work in silence, cleaning up Noah's poor face.

"Where do your parents keep the painkillers?"

He tells me where to go, and, after disposing of the bloodied washcloth, I go in search of something that might help him sleep.

When I get downstairs, Alyssa, Lisa, Wyatt, and

Shane are all busy tidying up the mess the rest of our class abandoned on their way out.

"Thank you so much," I say, walking into the kitchen.

"You're welcome. Is he okay?" Alyssa asks, concern shining from her eyes.

"Yeah, he'll be fine."

"What did he do to deserve that? Mason totally flew off the handle. I've never seen him like that, even on the field," Shane says. He knows Mason the best out of any of us these days, seeing as he's on the football team with the douchebags. Fuck knows why, he's nothing like any of them and actually a good guy. Things have been weird for him at school since he was accused of drugging Amalie and having the shit kicked out of him by Jake for it. He's kept his head down and avoided everyone—aside from this party, seeing as Noah's his best friend. I can still see the dark shadows that night left behind in his eyes, but he made the effort tonight. I know he's innocent, Noah too, but that doesn't mean anyone else at school agrees. Jake Thorn pinned him as guilty, so that's what he'll be unless someone's able to prove otherwise.

"Fuck knows. Mason is probably just trying to make my life harder than necessary; it seems to be his thing these days," I mutter.

"What actually happened between you two?"

"Nothing. It's nothing." It's the same excuse I've given ever since shit went down between our families. I have no desire to live through it again, and I can't see things ever going back to how they once were between us.

"You guys can get out of here if you want. I'll finish up."

"Really?" Alyssa asks, looking concerned.

"Yeah. I don't want to give him the satisfaction of ruining everyone's night. Go to Aces or something."

"As long as you're sure."

The three of them finish off what they're doing before saying goodbye and heading out.

Noah's parents wisely booked themselves into a hotel for the night, so I've got plenty of time to get the place back to normal before they get home—not that it's too bad. The party hadn't really had a chance to get going before Mason ruined it. So much for Noah's eighteenth birthday being his best ever.

I throw a few more cups into the trash before grabbing a box of Advil and going back up to Noah.

He's out cold when I walk into his bedroom. Even with just the moonlight illuminating his face, I can see that the swelling has only gotten worse and the bruising darker. He's even got a purple patch emerging on his ribs.

Mason really did a fucking number on him. My fists curl at my sides in anger. How dare he put his hands on Noah? It's like he's intent on ruining everything about my life. I'm surprised he wasn't more onboard with pushing Amalie out of town before Jake realized he was in love with her. Getting rid of someone who's fast become my best friend is just something I can imagine he'd do to piss me off.

Placing the glass of water and painkillers on the dresser, I walk over to pull the curtain.

"Come here," Noah says, barely managing to hold his hand out for me.

"I don't want to hurt you."

"You won't."

After slipping my shoes off, I climb into his bed beside him, fully dressed. This wasn't exactly how I planned on spending his birthday night.

His arm wraps around my waist and he pulls me back against his chest. I don't miss his sharp intake of breath as he does.

"I'm so sorry, Noah."

"Hey, none of this was your fault."

His soft lips press against my shoulder before he drops his head to the pillow and falls back to sleep.

Printed in Great Britain
by Amazon